*Praise for*

## BELOVED WARRIOR

"Pure pleasure . . . proof to what her fans may already know: Potter keeps getting better with every outing."
—*Publishers Weekly* (starred review)

"[A] superb romance . . . It's Potter's unique gift for creating unforgettable characters and delving into the deepest parts of their hearts that endears her to readers. This is another masterpiece from a writer who always delivers what romance readers want: a love story to always remember." —*Romantic Times*

## TEMPTING THE DEVIL

"A finely crafted book, written by someone who, for all her numerous accolades and her many years of experience, is still working hard to master new tricks." —*The Romance Reader*

"The story line is action-packed . . . Fans will appreciate this romantic suspense with the emphasis on the action."
—*Midwest Book Review*

## BELOVED STRANGER

"An absolutely stunning read, rich in historical details, fast-paced and riveting in suspense . . . An emotional tale that will leave you with a lump in your throat and a tear or two in your eyes. Potter brings together a cast of new and fascinating characters as well as old friends from the first book in this wonderful historically set series of the Maclean family."
—*The Best Reviews*

"The action-packed story line moves forward at a fast pace, but it is the lead pairing that drives a fine return to the Maclean clan." —*Midwest Book Review*

*continued . . .*

## TANGLE OF LIES

"Fast-paced . . . a fantastic suspense thriller."
—*Midwest Book Review*

"A chilling, complex tale of revenge, betrayal, and long-kept secrets."
—*Library Journal*

"A tangled web of clues [with] a touch of spice thrown in for good measure."
—*A Romance Review*

"Great characters, a compelling story that's almost impossible to put down, lots of plot twists—*Tangle of Lies* has it all."
—*Romance Reviews Today*

"Exciting mystery [and] hot romance make this a winner."
—*Fresh Fiction*

## BELOVED IMPOSTOR

"Ms. Potter has given us another thrilling drama. Every page proves the reason for her award-winning success . . . *Beloved Impostor* travels at a fast pace with outstanding characters and an expertly developed plot."
—*Rendezvous*

"A wonderful Scottish tale wrought with emotion, tender in its telling and heart-wrenching in its beauty. Ms. Potter captures our hearts and gifts us with another beautiful story."
—*The Best Reviews*

"[A] superb romance . . . It's Potter's unique gift for creating unforgettable characters and delving into the deepest parts of their hearts that endears her to readers. This is another masterpiece from a writer who always delivers what romance readers want: a love story to always remember."
—*Romantic Times*

"Ms. Potter is a very talented storyteller, taking a much-used theme—lovers from warring families—and manipulating it, adding plenty of new ideas and twists, until the end result is the original, highly satisfying *Beloved Impostor*."
—*Romance Reviews Today*

## DANCING WITH A ROGUE

"Once again, Potter . . . proves that she's adept at penning both enthralling historicals and captivating contemporary novels."
— *Booklist* (starred review)

"Gabriel and Merry are a delightful pair . . . Patricia Potter has provided a character-driven story that her audience will enjoy."
— *Midwest Book Review*

"An entirely engrossing novel by this talented and versatile author."
— *Romance Reviews Today*

## THE DIAMOND KING

"From war-torn Scotland to the high seas to the jungles of Brazil, Potter takes the reader on a roller-coaster ride as a rake becomes a hero and a courageous, resourceful woman finds love against all odds."
— *Booklist*

## THE HEART QUEEN

"This is a book that is difficult to put down for any reason. Simply enjoy."
— *Rendezvous*

"Potter is a very talented author . . . if you are craving excitement, danger, and a hero to die for, you won't want to miss this one."
— *All About Romance*

*More praise for Patricia Potter*
*and her bestselling novels*

"Patricia Potter has a special gift for giving an audience a first-class romantic story line."
— *Affaire de Coeur*

"When a historical romance [gets] the Potter treatment, the story line is pure action and excitement, and the characters are wonderful."
— *BookBrowser*

# CATCH A SHADOW

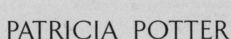

## PATRICIA POTTER

BERKLEY SENSATION, NEW YORK

THE BERKLEY PUBLISHING GROUP
Published by the Penguin Group
Penguin Group (USA) Inc.
375 Hudson Street, New York, New York 10014, USA
Penguin Group (Canada), 90 Eglinton Avenue East, Suite 700, Toronto, Ontario M4P 2Y3, Canada
(a division of Pearson Penguin Canada Inc.)
Penguin Books Ltd., 80 Strand, London WC2R 0RL, England
Penguin Group Ireland, 25 St. Stephen's Green, Dublin 2, Ireland (a division of Penguin Books Ltd.)
Penguin Group (Australia), 250 Camberwell Road, Camberwell, Victoria 3124, Australia
(a division of Pearson Australia Group Pty. Ltd.)
Penguin Books India Pvt. Ltd., 11 Community Centre, Panchsheel Park, New Delhi—110 017, India
Penguin Group (NZ), 67 Apollo Drive, Rosedale, North Shore 0632, New Zealand
(a division of Pearson New Zealand Ltd.)
Penguin Books (South Africa) (Pty.) Ltd., 24 Sturdee Avenue, Rosebank, Johannesburg 2196,
South Africa

Penguin Books Ltd., Registered Offices: 80 Strand, London WC2R 0RL, England

This is a work of fiction. Names, characters, places, and incidents either are the product of the author's imagination or are used fictitiously, and any resemblance to actual persons, living or dead, business establishments, events, or locales is entirely coincidental. The publisher does not have any control over and does not assume any responsibility for author or third-party websites or their content.

CATCH A SHADOW

A Berkley Sensation Book / published by arrangement with the author

PRINTING HISTORY
Berkley Sensation mass-market edition / March 2008

Copyright © 2008 by Patricia Potter.
Cover design by Brad Springer.
Interior text design by Laura K. Corless.

ISBN: 978-0-425-22119-8

BERKLEY® SENSATION
Berkley Sensation Books are published by The Berkley Publishing Group,
a division of Penguin Group (USA) Inc.,
375 Hudson Street, New York, New York 10014.
BERKLEY SENSATION and the "B" design are trademarks belonging to Penguin Group (USA) Inc.

PRINTED IN THE UNITED STATES OF AMERICA

10  9  8  7  6  5  4  3  2  1

# PROLOGUE

SOUTH AMERICA
2000

Pain jabbed like hot pokers. Jabbed, then flowed through him like lava.

Just as agonizing was his thirst. His throat was parched, his lips dry and crusted, his tongue swollen.

He slowly opened his eyes as consciousness filtered through the pain. He tried moving. Thank God, his fingers moved, then his arms. His legs did as well, and he welcomed the new waves of pain that came with motion. He was alive, and every moving part of him seemed to work.

*What in the hell happened?*

He shook his head to clear it, but the pain increased incrementally with the slightest movement, and he stopped for fear he might lapse back into unconsciousness. The others? Where were they? What had happened?

He raised himself up on one arm. Slowly. Every inch took supreme effort. How much blood had he lost? He was weak, weaker than he could ever remember being, and God knew he'd had bad wounds in the past.

"Chet," he tried to call out, but he knew it was only a whisper. A hoarse one.

"Ramos," he tried again. Then "Del," and finally, "Adams."

Only the chattering of a monkey responded. Scolding.

"Chet," he called louder, though the sound—scratchy as he knew it to be—echoed in his head like cannon shots. The silence was ominous. He knew what it meant. He knew he would not be lying here alone if Chet were able to answer.

Which meant Chet must be in a more dire state than he himself. And Adams? Jake had no idea where Adams would be. From the first moment Adams was assigned to his team, he and Adams had fought for control of the small Special Forces unit.

*The diamonds?* Where were the diamonds? He reached out for his pack, knowing instinctively he wouldn't find it.

He also knew he must be badly wounded, or he wouldn't have been left for dead.

Using every last ounce of strength he had, Jake tried to move again. Excruciating pain ripped through him. He forced his hand to explore his body, found the dried, caked blood on his shirt just above his heart. The probing of his fingers brought a new wave of agony. His head throbbed. His fingers felt hair stiff with dried blood. There was stickiness as well. He was still bleeding from a wound.

The effort exhausted him. He lay still for a moment, gathering his strength, trying to recall his last action before the darkness. They'd been driving on the road toward the stronghold of Emilio Camarro. They had encountered a fallen tree, and they had left the jeep to move it.

The joint Special Forces team was posing as terrorists, ready to provide the arms dealer with cash and diamonds for the weapons he'd bragged about possessing. They were charged with discovering whether he actually had the missiles he'd advertised sub rosa. If so, they were to trade a million in cash and four million in uncut diamonds for them. A cheap enough price to keep them out of the hands of less altruistic potential buyers.

They'd been promised safe passage and given the coordinates to a makeshift airport. A guide in a jeep had been waiting for them. Everything seemed to be going according to plan when they encountered a log lying across the path.

That's all he remembered. Camarro must have wanted both the diamonds and the missiles, even risking his reputation as a reliable—if criminal—broker to do it. An ambush? Were the two CIA guys dead? Taken prisoner?

How long ago had it happened?

Then he smelled an odor that was all too familiar: death. He rolled over on his good arm. Chet. Not far from him. The odor didn't lie. He knew from his friend's twisted position he was dead.

He knew not to have friends. It was something he'd learned twelve years earlier when his best friend had been killed on a mission. Since then he'd avoided close relationships. They didn't work for men in his job. Not with the men he served with. Not with marriage. But he and Chet had been part of the same team for five years. He'd liked and trusted him.

Darkness descended on him. It would be all too easy to surrender to it. He wanted to close his eyes again, to return to oblivion.

*Coward.* Three other men were out there. He struggled to his knees, swaying as he fought the pain, the weakness. He crawled over to Chet, turned him over. A bullet in his back. It had gone through his body, paralyzing, then killing him.

Chet's gun was gone. So was the knife he'd always strapped to his leg. Jake knew he'd had the unit's money with him. He checked all the pockets. Nothing. The money was gone as well as the diamonds. All in all, Uncle Sam's five million dollars had disappeared.

He crawled farther, looking for the others. He found one. Ramos had several bullets in him, had probably died immediately.

Why couldn't he remember? Had he been hit first? Where were the other two members of the team?

Dead? Taken prisoner?

Had their mission been leaked? Camarro was known for his hatred of America. If their cover had been betrayed, Camarro wouldn't hesitate to rob and kill them.

*What in the hell had happened?*

# CHAPTER 1

"Hit-and-run, Highland and North Avenue." The dispatcher's voice echoed in the close confines of the ambulance, sending an adrenaline rush through Kirke Palmer.

She hit the Respond button and reported they were two blocks from the location, then signed off.

Her back stiffened, and her pulse pounded. She hated hit-and-runs, but still that rush titillated. It brushed away the weariness from a long, frustrating day as she mentally went over the steps for major trauma. After a year as an emergency medical technician, then three as a paramedic, she'd memorized the protocols, but like a pilot, she went over the checklist on every call.

Hal, her partner, turned on the siren and drove the ambulance like a demon. She usually tried to drive, but she'd been emotionally exhausted by the last call, an abused child they'd barely kept alive on the trip to the hospital. Kirke doubted she would ever forget the boy's eyes. The emptiness in them as if he'd known nothing but cruelty in his young life.

In the years since she'd completed training as an EMT,

she'd tried to build a shield around her emotions to keep her from caring too much. She'd been warned about that. Build defenses or burn out. She was thirty-three and on her second career. She didn't want a third. Not anytime soon. But the kids got to her.

She didn't have to look at the map. Hal knew exactly where to go. She knew the location as well. She'd been there enough, first as a reporter and now as a paramedic. Manuel's Tavern was a landmark in Atlanta, a gathering place for the famous as well as the blue-collar worker.

She glanced at her watch. Four p.m. Three more hours before their long shift ended. Already today, she'd seen too many forms of human mayhem. An arson where two people were badly burned. A bicycle rider struck by a speeding car. Head injury. No helmet. He'd died at the scene. A gunshot wound. Then the toddler with multiple fractures and third-degree burns.

The ambulance screeched to a stop. The street was completely blocked. Kirke jumped out with their two bags and dashed toward the gathering crowd, while Hal backed the truck and tried to maneuver closer to the accident site.

The crowd opened a pathway for her. As she approached the victim on the ground, a man knelt next to him. A Good Samaritan? A doctor? Before she could see his face, he stood and disappeared among the sightseers.

One less problem. Good Samaritans were often more hindrance than help, delaying her as she tried to move onlookers back.

The victim lay bleeding in the street. White male. Probably in his late thirties. She checked vitals. Thready pulse and blood pressure dropping. He was bleeding out from multiple wounds, including a steady stream pouring from a jagged wound on his arm where a bone jutted out. He was conscious, though. Eyes open and focusing. But his color was poor. Body sweating.

First things first. Stop the bleeding.

She took a tourniquet from her bag and started to wrap it around his arm. He knocked it from her hands. "No," he moaned. "No."

"I'm Kirke, a paramedic," she said softly in the most encouraging tone she had, even as she tried again to tie the tourniquet. A small artery was torn. She had to stop the bleeding before anything else. "What's your name?"

He pushed the tourniquet away and reached toward her. Then she noticed a bloodstained envelope clutched in his hand. He tried to thrust it into her hands.

"No," she said. "I can't take it."

He started to thrash wildly. "Envelope. Take it."

The man's agitation was dangerous. Nothing was going to placate him except taking the envelope from him. She took it and shoved the envelope into her pocket. She would turn it in at the hospital.

"Give . . . to Mitch Edwards. Tell him . . . Dallas . . ." He grasped her hand. "Swear."

"I'll give it to the police," she said. "They'll find your friend."

"No. *You!* No police."

Blood trickled from his lips.

Desperate to get him to cooperate, she nodded.

"Swear," he insisted again, then blood rushed down her patient's mouth.

"I swear," she said just as Hal arrived. They both worked to suction the blood before he drowned in it.

She looked at her watch. They were nearing the end of the ten-minute scene time. They were supposed to be on their way by then.

Hal caught her glance and nodded. They immobilized the victim's spine and moved him onto a stretcher, then loaded him into the ambulance. His eyes remained open, and he was silent, though she knew the pain was agonizing. She got in the back with him as Hal drove. As the siren wailed and the ambulance threaded its way through the heavy traffic, she checked his vitals again. His color had worsened, and he was having difficulty breathing. She administered oxygen and started an IV.

He pushed away the oxygen mask. "Envelope," he said again in a choked voice.

*That damned envelope.*

"I have it," she said. "It's safe." What could be so important that it might be his last thought? He said nothing about family. She hadn't even been able to get a name from him.

"What's your name?" she tried again.

He looked at her blankly, the blue of his eyes fading.

"The person—this Mitch Edwards—how do I find him?" she tried again. Perhaps the friend could tell the police and hospital staff whom to contact.

"Mili . . . Virgini . . ." The word died on his lips, and he lapsed into unconsciousness. The monitors showed his heart failing. Kirke started CPR.

The ambulance roared up to the emergency entrance, and they rushed the patient inside. After giving what information she had to the emergency room staff, she started on the paperwork as Hal flirted with one of the nurses. He was a good-natured teddy bear of a man who was both compassionate and gentle. Kirke liked him immensely and felt lucky to have him as a partner. She was also amused by him. Hal was happily married, but harmless flirting was part of his nature.

When she finished the paperwork, she didn't want to leave, not until she knew about her patient's condition. "Why don't you check on our patient while I clean out the ambulance?" she said to Hal. She wanted to know the victim's condition without appearing unduly interested.

He agreed readily enough. As a paramedic, she was senior to his designation as an emergency medical technician, but she always traded the chores: driving, cleaning the ambulance, paperwork. It made for a good working relationship, especially because there was still some prejudice against women in the fire department, even paramedics.

She returned to the ambulance and started to clean out the back. They might well have another call before returning to the station. She started to wash the blood from the floor of the ambulance.

Her eyes caught something on the floor that shouldn't be there. A wallet. It hadn't been there earlier. Either she or Hal always cleaned the interior after a call.

She picked up the wallet and opened it, looking for a name.

A driver's license and one credit card. A lot of cash in big bills. She made a note of the name on the driver's license, then took the wallet inside to the nurse's station. She hesitated for a moment. She should give them the letter as well.

Yet the man was so insistent that it not go to the police.

*You're breaking rules.*

But it was only a letter. And she had to admit that her old reporter's instincts still lingered, despite the fact her outspokenness had cost her a job at the *Atlanta Observer.* She'd always been compelled to solve puzzles.

More important, she'd given her oath, even though it had been partly coerced.

Closing and locking the back doors, she noticed a dark sedan with tinted windows in the drop-off zone. Hadn't she heard someone among the witnesses mention a dark sedan with tinted windows? She couldn't see the front to tell whether there was any damage.

She glanced around for a security officer as she started to approach the sedan to take a better look.

The car sped away. She couldn't make out the license plate, but she didn't see any damage. An overactive imagination, she thought. Someone had probably been dropped off.

Still, a chill ran through her. She'd heard a bystander at the accident scene tell police that it had looked as if someone had deliberately run down the victim.

Hal returned from checking on their patient. He shook his head at the question she knew was in her eyes. "He's not good. They want to try to find family," he added in a matter-of-fact voice that belied the feeling in his eyes. It was one reason she liked him so much. He cared. He hadn't burned out yet.

"I found his wallet in the ambulance. His name is Mark Cable."

"At least he won't die a John Doe," Hal said.

No. Someone would mourn him. Someone named Mitch Edwards. Someone he'd tried so hard to reach.

Her radio sounded. Another call.

She answered.

"Are you clear?" came the dispatcher.

She looked at her watch. Another hour on the shift. "Yep."

"We have an elderly woman down five blocks from you. She's a diabetic."

"We're on our way."

"Let's go," she said to Hal. He was all business now, and he took the wheel. She turned back to her immediate problem. The envelope felt like an anvil in her pocket. Why hadn't she told Hal about it? Or the hospital staff?

But deep inside, she knew why. She hoped with all her heart Mark Cable would survive, and she could return the envelope to him.

He'd been so frantic about it.

She realized then she was emotionally committed. She would protect the letter for him. If he didn't survive, if she hadn't been able to save Mark Cable, she would find Mitch Edwards for him and make good on her promise to him.

# CHAPTER 2

## TWO HOURS EARLIER

Freedom, Jake Kelly knew, was elusive. His was, anyway.

His heart pounded faster as he waited across the street from the tavern he'd been directed to. Every second that passed could send him back to hell.

This was worse than any mission he'd had. He had no intel, no control, no backup. Certainly no expectation of success.

Nearly seven years in Leavenworth bred desperation. Seven years in a high-security prison for a crime he did not commit. Six days out, and he still felt those walls closing in on him, squeezing the very life from him. His world for too long had been a cage large enough only for a hard cot and a toilet.

And he was at risk of going back because of an enigmatic phone call that could well be a trap.

He stepped out of his rental car and into the shadows of a building. He hadn't forgotten how to blend into his environment.

He glanced down at his watch. Five minutes until the meeting time.

He'd been here an hour. Upon arrival, he'd made a quick trip inside the tavern, studied the interior. Then he'd driven around until he found a parking spot where he could watch the front door. Not the back, but the parking lot there stayed full.

So far, no one seemed familiar. No one looked around as if searching for someone.

He thought about walking away, but hope was a mighty force. He recalled every word of the phone call that came five days after his release. His phone had just been installed one day earlier in the modest, furnished apartment he'd rented.

He'd figured, when the phone rang, it was his supervisory officer—one of only two people who had the number.

"Kelly? Jake Kelly?" came a male voice on the phone.

Jake hadn't recognized it. It certainly wasn't the man who now controlled his life.

"Yes. Who is this?"

"Never mind that. I have a message for you," the voice continued. "This is it. My client says he knows what happened in South America. He wants to meet with you at a tavern at 602 North Highland in Atlanta on Tuesday. Four p.m. Back room. Left corner table. Don't be followed."

"Who is your client?" Jake asked, not trying to mask his sudden hope.

The caller hung up.

Jake had checked the caller ID: Unknown Number.

He suspected he wouldn't discover more, even if he had resources to pursue a search. Instead, he jotted down every word. His memory, except for the day that eluded and haunted him, was good, but he wanted the conversation, such as it was, as it had been said.

*"He knows what happened in South America . . ."*

He glanced down at his watch again. Every movement of the minute hand made his freedom more precarious.

He was on supervised parole, required to report in once a week and subject to unannounced checks. He was forbidden to leave the state of Illinois. He was a fool for risking violating his parole, but this might be his only chance to clear his name, to get some justice for Chet and Ramos and the others. And himself. He'd been abandoned—no, condemned—by those he trusted, by the government he'd served to the exclusion of everything else. He'd lost all faith in anyone but himself, and even that was wobbly at best.

He'd tried for the last seven years to discover what had happened in South America. His letters—and those of his attorney—had gone unanswered, queries always blocked by national security walls.

All he knew was that while he was recuperating in a hospital, someone found a half a million dollars in a bank account that led back to him, an offshore account he'd never opened. He'd been charged with stealing both the cash and diamonds his team had carried on that last mission.

He'd also been suspected of murdering his teammates for money. Chet. Ramos. Del. Adams. The army had sought to charge him with that, but they could find no bodies. There was only the offshore account, the missing cash and diamonds, and four missing men. That had been enough for a conviction of theft. His own wounds had been self-inflicted, the JAG prosecutor had charged. Never mind he'd nearly died from them. The army had lost five million dollars, and it needed someone to blame.

The memory of what happened that afternoon had never come back to him. Major head trauma often caused amnesia that wiped away events that immediately preceded the injury. But he was no ordinary person. He was trained to observe anything and everything and catalog it to memory. The failure to remember the events was like a cancer inside him.

The phone call promised to fill that gap, and the bait had been irresistible. But he couldn't dismiss the possibility that it was a trap. Someone had spent great deal of money to see him convicted. They might well be displeased that the government had made a deal to protect some very sensitive information.

His watch, the cheap one he had bought for fifteen dollars, said four o'clock.

He looked around. The bar was obviously frequented by a cross section of people. Men in business suits, students with book bags, laborers in dirty overalls all pushed through the doors.

Why here? Why Atlanta? Why not Chicago? Two reasons came to mind. The person who'd hired his caller was afraid. He didn't feel free to travel. The second was that the individual knew Atlanta and how to get around the city. But Jake didn't, and the location made him wary. Yet the invitation had beckoned like a flame to a moth. He'd been helpless against its lure.

There was a third reason: a trap to lure him back to prison.

He leaned against the wall, but his eyes didn't stop searching the street. Nothing suspicious, but then the tavern might be loaded with bad guys. Or good guys "doing their jobs" which, at the moment, could mean hauling him in.

For a moment, he looked upward. The sky looked brighter without bars dividing it, and the trees—God, it was good seeing trees again.

Then his concentration returned. Since he had not been told to wear anything special, he could only suppose his contact believed he would either recognize him or find him at the designated table.

More importantly, would he—Jake—recognize the other person? A member of the team? One of the two whose bodies he hadn't seen? He'd considered that. Coldly. Unemotionally.

He continued to study every individual who approached the tavern. If any of his team were alive, then they must have been a part of the ambush and theft. It also meant they would have been in hiding with new identities. Probably new facial characteristics, especially if they came back into this country. But it was difficult to disguise the essence of a person: the way you moved, the set of a chin, mannerisms you never recognized in yourself.

Maybe the call didn't come from one of the team but from someone in Special Forces. Someone who'd believed him—maybe even knew something—but couldn't come out in the open. That was the most desirable scenario but not the most likely one.

A figure caught his eye. A man of middle age. He'd parked his car down the street, like others, but something about his movements drew Jake's attention. The man had that singular grace of an athlete or a stealth warrior.

The newcomer hesitated, scanned the street in a way difficult for the untrained eye to detect.

He was slight, both thin and not very tall. His body radiated a tension that no disguise or surgery could hide. The man Jake remembered was even shorter, but perhaps this one wore shoe lifts. His hair had once been dark, and now it was a dirty blond. His facial features had been hidden under a beard when Jake met him, but those quick, nervous movements gave him away. Del Cox had been unique among the other team members who were taught to mingle and mix among a multitude of nationalities. Cox's intensity made him stand out. But he'd been a genius with explosives as well as electronics, and Jake had ignored his misgivings when he'd joined the team.

*Del Cox. Alive!*

According to the government, he was dead. According to a lot of people, at the hand of one Jake Kelly.

Fury boiled in Jake's gut. Cox had apparently left him for dead in the jungle, then let him rot in prison for something he didn't do. Death would have been preferable to the disgrace, the look in his father's eyes when he was charged. Hell, he'd had nothing to defend himself with except his service, and that apparently had meant little.

He swallowed the gall in his throat and waited. Maybe Cox saw him. Maybe not. He wanted Cox to come closer. Didn't want him spooked. Not yet.

Cox started across the street.

Jake caught a movement out of the corner of his eye just as he heard the squeal of tires.

He started to shout a warning. It was too late. A dark sedan careened into Cox, tossing him up in the air. Then it sped away with a screeching of tires, as the driver swerved to miss an oncoming car.

A shout. Screams. People poured out of the bar.

He started for the fallen man, then stopped.

He couldn't be seen here. His presence in Atlanta was a ticket back to prison if anyone discovered who he was.

Still, he moved forward several steps. Cox had contacted him for a reason. Jake had little faith in God these days, but he prayed nonetheless that the man survived. Cox might be his last chance.

Then he stopped. A tall man dressed in slacks and a long shirt that hung loose left the tavern and approached the fallen man. He reached him and started to kneel beside him. Jake's blood ran cold. Another ghost. Gene Adams! He would bet his life on it.

He didn't recognize the face, but he knew the arrogant movements, the muscle flexing in the throat at being thwarted. Most of all, he noticed the clenching of his fist as he straightened when an ambulance screeched to a halt nearby.

Jake started forward as a paramedic—a woman—jumped from the passenger's side and rushed over to the victim. The man quickly moved away.

Jake started after him just as someone appeared from the tavern, showed a badge, and asked everyone to step away.

Jake moved back into the shadows. He didn't think Gene Adams had seen him. He'd been too concerned with Cox. And his own appearance had changed as well. Jake doubted anyone who knew him from that last mission would recognize him today. His hair had been long then and tied back with a thong. He'd had a thick beard for his role as a terrorist. Now he was clean-shaven, his hair short, with gray running through the dark brown. He'd been far leaner then, too. Jake was still in fairly good shape, thanks to endless push-ups, but he had gained pounds. Prison food was fundamentally starch.

He was forty, but he knew he looked fifty. Prison had aged him, and he'd worked to avoid habits that might identify him.

Cox moved slightly, then Jake saw him try to say something as the woman paramedic performed a quick assessment. The woman shook her head, and the victim grabbed her arm, holding it. The woman took something from him and shoved it into her pocket. Jake glanced up to see other eyes following the movement as well, then step back as police cars arrived.

Jake decided to try to follow him. His quarry slipped into the crowd, and Jake was blocked momentarily by police pushing back the onlookers. He couldn't be obvious, couldn't risk a cop stopping him. Still, he moved as quickly as he could. He looked ahead. No one. He took several running steps to the corner and turned just as the man he'd recognized as Adams stepped into the passenger's side of a late-model luxury car, and it went roaring off, blowing through a light.

He had a quick glance at the license plate and memorized the number, then returned to the crowd. Uniformed police arrived and moved among the crowd, asking for witnesses.

He stayed on the fringe, watching as the paramedics— now two of them—loaded Cox into the ambulance. As they neared him, Jake backed away and darted into the bar. He wanted to follow the ambulance, but his rental car was still in front, not far from the crime scene, and he didn't dare go after it. He did not want to be questioned by police.

Everyone at the bar was talking. He found a spare seat at the bar and sat down.

"What will you have?" the bartender asked.

He glanced at the row of taps and chose one, then commented, "Terrible thing, what happened outside."

"Yeah."

"Someone said it looked like he was run down on purpose."

"I didn't see it." the bartender said, "so I couldn't say. But we have some rotten drivers in Atlanta."

The man on his left shrugged. "Accidents out there all the time."

"Anyone know the guy?"

The bartender shrugged. "I called 911, but I couldn't leave the bar. Don't think so, though. Someone would have said something. No one did."

Jake doubted he would get any more information. He paid and left the stool, taking his beer with him as he wandered through the establishment. There were several rooms off the main bar area. He went to the one designated in the note.

While the front areas were packed, this room was empty except for two couples who paid no attention to him. He imagined the room would fill as people left work. He made his way to the table in the left corner and lounged in a chair.

When he was sure no one was watching, he searched the underside of the table.

Nothing. Nor did he see anyone else around. He slowly sipped the beer, waiting for the last of the police to leave as he tried to understand what had happened.

The man he once knew as Del Cox had given the woman paramedic a letter, a letter he suspected was meant for him. Had Gene Adams seen it as well?

Or was his name Gene Adams? Adams and Cox had been CIA, while the other members of the team had been pulled from the Army Special Forces. Jake had previously worked with the other two Special Forces members—all three were Rangers—but not the CIA guys, and all of them, for security reasons, used false identities. He knew his teammates' names but not those of the CIA guys.

He'd liked Cox, but Adams had been a pain in the ass since day one. As a captain in the Rangers, Jake was supposed to be team leader. Adams was along to make the transaction and try to discover who had sold American missiles to Camarro, but Adams kept trying to take charge.

Had the man who knelt next to Cox really been Adams? So many features were different, but not that cold stare that took everything in, nor the compulsive clenching of his fist when agitated.

How could Adams have known of the meeting? He'd obviously been anxious to get to the fallen man before anyone else, and yet he hurried off before questions could be asked. And a car had been waiting for him not far from the accident scene. It didn't take too many coincidences to raise those familiar hackles along Jake's backbone.

*Ghosts.* He'd seen two ghosts tonight. And now he had a lead. No, *leads.*

A license number. A face he would not forget.

And the paramedic who had taken an envelope from Cox.

# CHAPTER 3

Kirke was emotionally and physically exhausted when she returned to her duplex.

The toddler wouldn't leave her thoughts. Neither would the insistent request of the hit-and-run victim.

A sense of failure filled her. Perhaps there had been something more she could have done in both cases.

Sometimes they were just too late.

Usually she could turn those feelings off. Think, instead, of the people they'd saved during the past week. Month. Year.

The fierce demand in Mark Cable's eyes had left its imprint. She took the envelope from her pocket and weighed it with her hand. Light. Probably no more than a page or two.

She placed it on the kitchen table, then took off her blood-splattered uniform shirt and threw it into the washing machine. She headed for the shower.

*Merlin.* She had to get Merlin. But first she wanted to wash away the remnants of the day. She scrubbed every inch of herself, then washed her hair, thankful she now wore it short.

No singing in the shower now. She should have turned the envelope in at the hospital. She still could. She could say she forgot about it.

Do it! *Turn it in and forget about it.*

The water turned cold, freezing her. A dash of reality.

She stepped out and wrapped a towel around herself, then quickly dressed.

Merlin would probably be squawking and driving Sam mad.

She pulled on a pair of jeans and a sweatshirt and went out the front door, across the porch, and knocked at the neighboring unit of the side-by-side duplex.

"Come in, dammit."

She recognized the impatient sound. Merlin was imitating one of his former owners.

Sam appeared at the door, scowling. "You're late. I'm due for rehearsal."

"I know. I'm sorry. We had a call just as before our shift ended."

Sam's scowl disappeared. "Bad day?"

"The worst."

"A beer?"

"You bet," she said, following him inside to the loud cackling of an unhappy Merlin.

Sam had been her neighbor for ten years, ever since she moved to Atlanta to work for the *Observer.* He was a musician who played in a jazz band at a downtown nightclub and sometimes filled in with other bands. He was usually gone all night, and she all day.

She looked after his cat when he was gone at night, and he looked after Merlin, who had a severe separation anxiety problem, during the day.

She went over to Merlin's cage and released him. The parrot flew to her shoulder and pecked her ear. "Merlin lonely."

"I know," she said, soothing his feathers. "Ready to go home?"

Merlin put his head against her cheek in a rare display of affection. It had taken her two years with him before he had displayed any at all.

"I have some pizza in the fridge," Sam said helpfully as he handed her a bottle of beer. "You can take it with you."

Kirke made a face. Cold pizza had never appealed to her, but she remembered she had precious little food in her fridge. She'd meant to go shopping after her shift but . . .

She nodded and swigged down the beer. She seldom did that. She enjoyed a beer with meals and a glass of wine at night, but she was careful when she drank, especially in her current job. Her patients couldn't afford a hungover paramedic.

Sam noticed it, too. "A *really* bad day, huh?"

"Not the half of it."

He waited for her to elaborate. It was one of the things they liked about each other. They never pried into the other's life, but each was there as a sounding board when necessary.

"I broke the rules," she said.

He raised an eyebrow. "You?"

He often kidded her about having a split personality. He complained she had an honesty that went to unhealthy extremes. She would drive twenty miles back if someone handed her the wrong change. Her conscience, he often complained, had been far too tightly wired. But she also had a thing about authority, particularly unjustly administered authority.

He glanced at his watch, then gave her a rueful grin. "You can tell me about it tomorrow." He paused. "Oops. I have an early rehearsal tomorrow."

"Why an early rehearsal?"

"New singer. She's good, really good. You ought to check her out. She has that Piaf sound you like so much."

"No one has that sound."

"No, but she comes closer to it than anyone I've heard. The drinks will be on me."

"Not tomorrow night, but I'm off the next day."

He nodded. "I gotta be on my way. Can't get fired from this gig."

She nodded. "I'll lock up for you."

He grabbed his saxophone case and was out the door. She

took the half pizza from his fridge, slipped the empty beer can in the trash, and put Merlin into his cage.

"Good Sam," Merlin noted in a mimic of her own voice.

She picked up Sam's black cat, named Sam's Spade after his master's passion for the detective, and took him and the pizza to her side of the duplex. Then she returned to Sam's side, fetched Merlin, locked the door, and returned to her sanctuary.

The duplex was side-by-side identical units. She and Sam each had large living rooms, eat-in kitchens immediately behind the living room, then a large bath that she'd modernized, and finally a roomy bedroom at the back. They shared a screened front porch.

It was a remnant of a true neighborhood that had since been redeveloped into luxury apartment buildings. Four houses remained, including her duplex, but growing taxes would soon squeeze her out.

Still, she loved it. She could walk to a neighborhood grocery, an art museum, and symphony hall, or run in the large city park a half block away. She'd bought it ten years earlier, using the insurance policy her grandfather had left. Sam's rent paid the taxes. He'd also become her best friend, though there were no romantic feelings between them.

She put Sam's Spade down on the floor. She'd tried to feed the half-wild kitten when he had appeared on their steps a year ago, but he wouldn't have anything to do with her. Spade wanted Sam. Sam had resisted adopting him. His hours were too odd, and he liked being a free spirit without attachments. He'd finally given up and taken him in, and now he was as silly about the "damn cat" as she was about Merlin. He was going to call him Cat, but she prevailed when she suggested naming him after his favorite fictional detective.

She gave Merlin some dried fruit and seeds and left the door to his cage open so he could fly from room to room with her. Spade followed them.

First the pizza. She nuked it, poured a diet cola, and sat at the kitchen table.

The sealed letter was still there, like the proverbial elephant, on the table. She longed to open it, but it was not meant for her. That darn conscience again.

After finishing the pizza, she went to her computer in the bedroom and Googled Mark Cable. There were a thousand Mark Cables. Same with Mitch Edwards.

*So little to go on.*

"Night," squawked Merlin. She left the computer and went over to where he perched on the back of the small couch. Spade sat next to him. Surprisingly, these two misfits had found companionship with each other.

She rubbed Merlin's head, and he chucked with delight. The parrot had been an unexpected addition to her household. A friend involved with animal rescue had asked her to take care of Merlin for several days. The bird had been found abandoned in a crack house and had pecked away most of his feathers, making him unadoptable.

She'd been just getting over a divorce and had lost her job. She agreed to keep him for two weeks.

Two weeks had turned into three years. Now she couldn't imagine life without the cranky and talkative African Grey parrot, but he required more attention than a cat or dog. Parrots, she'd learned, were sociable birds and did not do well being alone for long periods of time. Sam had turned out to be a great parrot sitter.

Now she found herself talking to the bird. He liked it, and it enabled her to think aloud. "I took a letter today from a patient," she said. "Shouldn't have done it. Shouldn't have made a promise. Might end up jobless again, and then you and I will be on the street."

He tipped his head, listening intently.

"Not so good, heh?"

He flew to her shoulder. He was uncanny at recognizing her moods. "Like Kirke," he said.

"I'm glad," she replied, smoothing his head feathers. "But that doesn't solve my problem."

He cackled.

"I'll give it a day, try to find this guy, and if I can't, well then I'll just say I forgot about it and give it to the hospital."

"Dandy," the parrot said.

She grinned at that. She'd said the word once, and Merlin had picked up on it, just as he did on other words that attracted him. Something about the sound. He would hear a word or sound he liked, then spend days practicing it, driving her to near madness. Sometimes it made sense when he repeated it, and sometimes it didn't.

She liked "Dandy" just now.

"Okay," she said. "I'll try to get more information about Mr. Cable tomorrow. Maybe a relative has already come forward and knows this Mitch Edwards."

Merlin bobbed his head, then said, "G'night?"

"Yes," she said.

He flew through the rooms to his cage and patiently waited for his nightly treat. Then she pulled the cover over his cage.

Exhausted, she climbed into bed. She had another twelve-hour day starting at seven.

Jake stayed at the table in the tavern for an hour. He ordered another beer but just sipped it, wanting nothing to fog his mind.

He knew now no one else was coming, that the man injured in front was indeed the man who had contacted him.

For a while, he'd still had a seed of hope, but that was gone now.

He'd lingered for another reason. He wanted to avoid any contact with a cop.

Now he had decisions to make. Under a different name, he'd flown in late last night and had a reservation to return tonight. Twenty-four hours. He had someone who could cover for him for a few hours but not much longer.

He looked at his watch. A little before six p.m. His flight was at eleven. He had four and a half hours at best to get to the airport. Even then he couldn't be sure he wouldn't be met at his Chicago apartment by the military police.

Jake left the table and went back through the bar area. He hesitated at the door and looked out. Several cops were still there, but their attention was on several investigators taking photos of the blood splatters. Traffic was backed up in both directions.

It seemed ironic that Del Cox might have been fatally injured. He and Cox had shared a few war stories during training. They'd both served in different capacities in Afghanistan and Desert Storm and both spoke Farsi. Their dark coloring and aptitude for languages had made them uniquely qualified to fit into Middle East populations. It had also made them perfect to pose as terrorists to buy weapons.

He'd known Adams hadn't liked the fact that the two of them talked together. Adams and Cox were CIA, and the three Special Forces guys were, in Adams's obvious opinion, mere grunts.

After asking directions to the nearest hospital, Jake returned to his rental car. It took a good a good forty-five minutes before he reached the hospital's emergency entrance. He parked, then went to the reception desk and joined the line.

"I was to meet a friend at a restaurant," he explained when he finally moved to the front of the line, "but when I reached the place, I couldn't find him. Someone said a man of his general description was the victim of a hit-and-run driver and that he was brought here. I'm afraid it was my friend. He's never late, and if something held him up, he would have called."

"I just came on," she said and turned to her computer. "Name of patient."

"John Foster," he said, immediately inventing one. He had no idea what name Del was using now, but it wouldn't have been the one given him by the CIA eight years ago.

She looked back at the computer screen. "No Foster."

"Maybe he isn't in the computer yet. Can you check to see if anyone has been brought in from a hit-and-run?"

She picked up a phone and dialed an extension. "Did you get a hit-and-run in the past few hours?"

She listened for a moment, hung up, then turned back to him. "Yes, we did, but it can't be your friend. We have another name."

"Terrible thing," he persisted. "I go to Manuel's—that's

where we were to meet—a lot. Maybe I know him." The last was more question than statement.

"We can't give out any information except to family," she said, then turned to the person behind him in line.

He turned around. He didn't want to give her any cause to call security. If only he could take a look at the receptionist's computer . . .

He went through doors to a room full of people in various states of flu and injuries, and kept moving. He would have to find another way of reaching Del Cox.

On his way out he saw a TV news truck. Risky, but he was desperate, so he stuck his head inside. "Hey there," he said.

A woman looked up from something she was writing.

He gave her the same story he'd given the receptionist. He was missing a friend. There was a hit-and-run. He wanted to find out if the two were one and the same. Because he wasn't a relative, the hospital wouldn't give out information. Could they get the name?

The two inside—reporter and cameraman—looked at each other and shrugged. "Why not?" she said.

She picked up the phone and called the public relations office. In seconds she had a name: Mark Cable.

"Not my guy," he said. "Thanks."

He disappeared before they could ask any questions.

*Cable. Mark Cable.*

Now, if only he lived.

One down, but now two to go.

Ames Williamson threw the glass of whiskey across the luxurious room and watched as it dripped down the expensive wallpaper.

Dammit, if he'd only had another moment before the ambulance had arrived. He'd been close. So close. He'd even had a hypodermic in his pocket. One second alone, and Cox would be dead. This time for good.

*Damned slippery coward.*

But he had seen the waxy look on his face, saw the heavy flow of blood. It would be a miracle if Cox survived.

He had been tracking him for years. Cox was the only one who knew that Ames Williamson, alias Gene Adams, was still alive, and the man had already cost him more than a million dollars. Ames had been unwise enough to trust the man to finish off Jake Kelly, thinking that Cox realized that his own skin was in as much jeopardy as Williamson's.

Ames had already decided that Del Cox, too, would not survive the mission. Unfortunately, Cox was smarter than he'd thought and had disappeared with the airplane, three hundred thousand dollars, and a million in diamonds. Then, to make things worse, Kelly had turned up in a rustic Mexican town. Alive. A most unpleasant surprise. Jake Kelly would search the ends of the world to avenge his men.

Because Cox hadn't finished Kelly, Adams had been forced to spend half a million to put Kelly on ice. He'd expected a far longer sentence than Kelly received. He'd counted on Kelly's fellow officers being outraged by the betrayal. The CIA certainly would have been. Now he'd had to come out of hiding to make sure Jake Kelly never discovered all the betrayals that had led to his destruction.

Time lost. Money wasted. Risks incurred. All because of lily-livered Del Cox.

Had Cox gotten religion? Or figured he could make a deal? Either way, the moment Ames had discovered that someone had contacted Kelly and asked to meet with him, he knew it must be Cox. He was just gratified that he'd had men follow Kelly upon his release and had his phone tapped. He'd known that Kelly would try to find out what had happened and wouldn't stop until he did. He was a danger.

He hadn't expected the bonus of finding Cox. After learning of the content of the phone conversation, he'd stationed two cars around the tavern, then signaled with his cell phone when he saw the man he believed was Cox.

He'd had to make the decision of killing Cox or trying to get both of them together. But he needed accidents. He couldn't afford anything that would reopen the South American deaths. So he'd chosen Cox as his first victim. He could arrange another kind of accident for Kelly. No one would connect the two, since Cox had been officially missing, believed dead, for seven years.

That left the woman and whatever it was Cox told her when he'd given her something that looked like an envelope. If, that is, he'd managed to say anything at all.

Either way, he had to take care of that problem as well.

# CHAPTER 4

*Coffee.* Coffee first, then a shower.

Maybe then she would feel like a human being again. Maybe. She doubted it.

Kirke hated the hungover feeling from lack of sleep. As well as the guilt that nagged at her.

She'd second-guessed herself all night. Had it been a mistake to keep the envelope? What if she couldn't find this Mitch Edwards? What then? It would be too late to turn it in without laborious explanations. She'd probably lose her job. Yet this letter could be something vitally important to Mitch Edwards. It certainly had been to the hit-and-run victim.

Stubbornness was her worst quality. Once she embarked on a certain path, she rarely retreated. She'd been that way since she was a kid. It was the reason she'd been fired from the newspaper.

She really didn't want to think about that now.

"Where's Sam?" asked Merlin, obviously more concerned about his coparent than her.

"Traitor," she retorted.

"Traitor," he echoed in her voice.

Darn. She knew Merlin wasn't human, but she thought he understood more than people believed, that he didn't just parrot words back to her.

He obviously liked Sam, who did not mind an occasional peck on his neck, but Sam wouldn't be home yet. After his nightly gig, he usually had breakfast with fellow musicians before calling it a night. But he had the key to her duplex, and he would pick up Merlin and Spade.

*Finish the cup of coffee. Then take a cold shower to wake up.*

Maybe then she would feel like a human being again.

She hurried through her shower, then listened to Merlin complain as he watched her pour coffee into a huge thermos. "Poor Merlin," he squawked.

"Poor Kirke," she countered. "She would much rather stay home with you."

Obviously unconvinced, Merlin gave her his evil eye look, one she'd seen many, many times before they had come to an understanding. Now she loved the fractious bird. Since Jon left, she had no one but Merlin and Sam. She'd lost contact with most of her friends who worked at the newspaper, and the paramedics' schedules left little time for socializing.

But then she'd had no one before that, either. Jon had never really been there for her, and she'd realized after the divorce she'd married in haste because she'd wanted a family of her own. Her own family had been limited at best. Her father had left her mother when she was born, and her mother had died of a drug overdose ten years later. Kirke had been shipped off to a strict, widowed grandfather who didn't know how to love.

She had no intention, though, of ever making a marital mistake again. She'd been abandoned three times in her life, the last by her husband. She was never, ever, going to give someone a chance to do that again. She'd learned to be quite content with living her own life the way she wanted to live it. Two years with Jon's exacting standards had made her appreciate freedom.

Jon would have told her to follow the rules, turn over the letter.

That thought reinforced her instinct to do the opposite.

She took a gulp of coffee, then slipped on a fresh uniform. Her other one was still in the washing machine. The envelope was at the computer where she'd conducted the preliminary search on Mitch Edwards.

She recalled the plea in the dying man's eyes, the desperation. There had to be a reason he did not want it to go to someone in authority.

*Wasn't that a reason in itself to give it to them?*

A chill ran through her. What if she was involving herself in something illegal? Or dangerous?

Ridiculous. She would be off tomorrow, and she could make inquiries. She would call her friend Robin and ask her to help.

She stuck the envelope in her pocket and Merlin in his cage. "Have a good day with Sam," she said.

"G'day," he answered in her voice.

He was being easy on her this morning. "Good bird," she acknowledged and gave him a piece of the apple she'd intended for herself. "Sam will be here soon."

"Very good bird," he congratulated himself before taking the chunk of apple.

She left before he charmed her more. He did that sometimes when she was leaving. He seemed to have discovered it was far more effective in delaying her a few more moments than recriminations.

*Smart bird.*

Moments later she was at the fire station that was home base for their unit. The ambulance was there and ready to go. As a rule, trauma and mayhem came later in the day unless it was a morning drive-time accident. The night people had time to clean and restock.

She did a quick check of their equipment and supplies as Hal joined her. He looked as weary as she felt. His brown hair looked uncombed, and one of the buttons on his shirt was unbuttoned.

"Big night?" she asked.

He grinned. "Sarah's birthday. We went out to dinner, then . . ."

"You needn't continue," she said with a smile. "You'd better button your shirt before the captain sees you."

"I hope you have a similar excuse," he said, his gaze settling on her face. "You look tired."

"Yesterday was a bummer."

"Maybe today will be better."

The thought was drowned out by the ringing of the bell, signaling a call. Hal took the info and wrote down the address. "Looks like a domestic abuse," he said.

She had her own radio up to her ear. "Police been called?" she asked the dispatcher. They all hated domestic abuse cases, never knowing what they were walking into.

"The police are already there. They made the call."

She didn't waste any more time but jumped into the passenger seat and buckled her belt as Hal roared out of the station. God, she hated these calls, and she knew them too well. One of her friends had been trapped inside an abusive marriage. Kirke had tried to get Lynn to leave, especially after what she knew was at least a third assault, but Lynn—like herself—was alone and without family. She'd been a foster child, and a true family had been a lifetime dream. She hadn't been ready to give up on the marriage, especially when heartfelt apologies came after a beating.

Then she was murdered by her husband four years into the marriage. She'd finally had enough and told him she wanted a divorce. He shot her the next day.

Those images ran through Kirke's head. She'd held on to her own marriage too long. Although Jon had never struck her, he had been emotionally abusive, belittling everything she did. She'd left after two years. It had been eighteen months late.

They arrived within five minutes. Two police cars blocked the road. All the lights in the house were on.

An officer met them halfway. "He beat the hell out of his wife," he said. "She's barely breathing."

"Where's the husband?"

"In my squad car."

She nodded, grateful. The hardest part of this job was trying to be nonjudgmental. She'd never been very good at keeping her mouth shut in the face of bullies. She hurried up the steps. Another officer was kneeling next to a woman. Blood was everywhere.

She immediately focused on the gash in the woman's head. Bleeding badly. The patient was bent in a fetal position as if trying to protect herself.

She was unconscious, and her breathing was shallow.

"Her name?"

"Susan Whitaker."

"Susan," she said to the injured woman, even as she realized Susan Whitaker was beyond hearing.

She turned back to the officer. "How long since the injury?"

"The husband said several hours ago. He locked her in the garage, thinking she was just sulking."

Kirke wanted to kill the husband.

She checked the woman's pupils. "Unequal," she told Hal. They both knew what that meant: intracranial hemorrhage.

She phoned in the vitals to the hospital and was told to get the patient there as soon as possible. She applied oxygen, then she and Hal loaded the patient on the board, then on the stretcher and wheeled her to the ambulance and lifted her inside. They were minutes away from the hospital.

She started an IV. "Come on, Susan. Stay with me. Don't let him win."

Then they were at the emergency entrance, and they rushed her inside, giving specifics to the triage nurse.

They waited to give any additional information that was needed, then Hal filled out the run report. She went to the information desk. "We brought in a man yesterday. His name was Mark Cable. How is he?"

The receptionist typed in the name on the keyboard and glanced at the screen. "In critical care."

"Do you have anyone listed as next of kin?"

The receptionist looked up at her.

"Sometimes it helps families to know that their loved one

was thinking about them," she said, knowing she was breaking a rule even thinking about contacting a family member.

But rule breaking apparently didn't bother the receptionist, who gave her an understanding nod and turned to the computer. "No name of a responsible party," she said.

"And no one has asked about him?"

"Not while I've been here."

Hal turned from where he had finished the paperwork and raised an eyebrow.

Their pager buzzed. Another call.

She sighed. No more time for questions.

And Hal thankfully didn't ask any. She didn't want to lie to him or make him an accomplice in what she'd done. She was risking her job on what she was beginning to believe was a quixotic quest. She'd gone too far, though, to hesitate now.

◂

Jake waited impatiently at the motel office for the package the forger had promised last night.

He'd decided at the last minute to stay another night. He'd checked his phone messages, and there had been no calls from the supervising officer. Maybe he had several more hours.

But every moment counted now, and when a deliveryman hurried into the office, Jake moved to the desk. After satisfying the clerk that it was indeed his, he moved away and opened it, glancing quickly at the contents. A new driver's license was there, complete with the photo that had been taken for the driver's license he'd carried to Atlanta. The forger had come through.

He'd complained last night when Jake had called and ordered a new identity immediately. He'd said he couldn't do it in time to get overnight delivery.

But he had. At a very expensive price.

Jake tucked the license into his wallet. Now he was David Cable, a resident of New York City with an address that could be confirmed.

Thank God he still had some friends left, men he'd

served with in Special Forces who'd never believed the
charges against him. One had found the forger for him, a
man who did work for the government as well as criminal
enterprises.

Regret ran through Jake. His father died shortly after
Jake, his only child, had been convicted. He'd left an insurance policy and some savings to Jake. Jake had taken that inheritance and some savings of his own and found a good
money manager. During his last year in prison, he'd directed
his money manager to put sums of money in various accounts and safe-deposit boxes. It wasn't illegal, since taxes
had been paid, but he didn't want the feds to be able to trace
funds back to him once he was released. He'd had every intention to start an investigation of his own.

This new identity was biting into that nest egg, but nothing
was more important than finding the truth about that day, especially after seeing the man he believed was Gene Adams.
The puzzle was beginning to come together in his mind.

Adams coldly murdered two of his own men and tried to
murder Jake. Probably murdered a third yesterday. Jake had
always thought the drug dealer had ambushed his team, then
taken the two remaining men to learn who'd sent them, probably torturing and killing them. The money in his account?
He'd believed the South American target had wanted suspicion diverted from himself.

Now he realized. Adams had framed him, plain and simple.

A deep chill settled inside him. If he was right, where had
Adams been these past years? Where had Del Cox been?
Did anyone in the government know they survived the am-
bush? After years in Special Services and dealing with the
CIA, he wouldn't be surprised if someone did.

He stopped at a drugstore where he bought a pair of reading glasses and a package of cotton balls. Then he drove to
the hospital and parked. He stuffed some cotton in his mouth
to broaden his cheeks and change his speech. He added the
glasses. As a disguise it was certainly minimal, but at least it
would slightly obscure his features, if his face was captured
on security cameras.

Yesterday, it hadn't been so important. He hadn't shown identification or associated himself with anyone but as a possible friend. But his actions today might well draw more attention.

He strode inside and went to the information desk.

"I understand my brother was brought in yesterday. Mark Cable," he said, not needing to force urgency into his voice. He just prayed Adams hadn't arrived earlier. "What's his room number?"

The woman turned to the computer. After a few seconds, she turned back to him, a frown on her face. "Can I see some identification?"

He showed her the license. "I gained a little weight," he said to explain his puffy cheeks.

"Haven't we all?" she said and gave him a room number and directions.

He followed the directions, making labyrinthine turns, apprehension mounting by the second. Through the corner of his left eye, he'd seen the woman pick up the phone as soon as he'd turned. Notifying authorities, he knew. It had been a hit-and-run, a crime. Of course there would be official interest.

But at least Cox was still alive.

He reached the critical care unit and went to the desk. The nurse there apparently expected him. A call from downstairs? "You're a brother?"

Jake nodded. "How is he?"

"You'll have to talk to the doctor. He's on the floor now. He'll be here shortly."

"Can you just tell me where he is?"

He was directed to a glassed-in cubicle. The patient was connected to several machines, and tubes ran in and out of the man the hospital knew as Mark Cable. With a dropping heart, Jake realized exactly what they meant. For all practical purposes, the man was dead. He was never going to be able to tell Jake what he'd intended to say.

Just then a doctor appeared and guided him to a corner. "I'm Dr. MacGuire, the attending. I understand you're Mr. Cable's brother?"

"Yes. Someone saw the whole thing happen and called me. I was in New York. I took a plane immediately. Is he . . . ?"

"I'm sorry. We did everything we could, but the internal injuries were too severe. We lost brain activity shortly after he arrived, but we kept him on life support, hoping we could find a relative."

Jake knew exactly what that meant, but he had to be the grieving brother. "There's nothing you can do? We have money. I mean, there must be something?"

Dr. MacGuire shook his head. "I'm sorry. His heart stopped. We got it started again, but he went too long without oxygen."

"I would like to see him."

The doctor hesitated, then asked, "Are you the next of kin?"

Jake nodded. "Yeah. He's divorced and never had kids. Our parents are dead."

The doctor hesitated again. "Have you thought of organ donations?"

Jake closed his eyes for a moment as if in pain. And he was. If he could, he would agree. But he couldn't. Too many papers and forms. It could come back to haunt him.

"No," he said. "I don't think he would want that."

The doctor merely nodded.

Jake went inside and leaned over Del's body. He saw the faint, almost imperceptible lines of plastic surgery on a face that wasn't familiar. For the sake of any onlooker, he leaned over as if to say a prayer, though he'd given up on prayer years earlier. A man who dealt in death had little right to pray.

He then checked the man's arm. A burn scar on the inside of his right arm. There had been a tattoo there once.

Satisfied that Del Cox, or at least the man he'd known as Del Cox, was the near-lifeless figure in the hospital bed, he left. The doctor was gone. He went to the nurse's desk, "Are there any personal effects?" he asked.

"The police have them," the nurse replied. "They're trying to find his family."

"Do you know whether there was a letter?" he said. He hated like hell to ask the question, but he had to know, and if the police had Del Cox's property, he had to find a way to get it. "He called me day before yesterday to tell me he had one for an old friend but couldn't locate him. It seemed important to him."

She shook her head. "Just a wallet and clothes," she said. "I bagged the clothes, and the paramedic responding to the call brought in the wallet."

He nodded. He had what he needed.

Just then, another woman in a white coat appeared. "Mr. Cable?"

News traveled fast. He nodded.

"I'm from the office. We have some questions."

He bet they had. Like insurance.

Sure enough, that was the first question.

"Do you know whether your brother has insurance?"

"No," he said flatly. "We never discussed it." He couldn't quite hide his distaste for the question. He wasn't Cable's brother, but if he had been, he would have had some choice comments.

"Is there a responsible party?"

"I doubt it," he said.

"Did he have a living will?"

"I don't think so."

"Would you have power of attorney for him?"

"No. He never thought he would die before me."

"No one does," she said. "I'm sorry to mention it at this time, but I have documents for you to sign."

He took them from her hand. God help him, there were enough of them. "I'll have to read them," he said. "I . . . have to have time to . . . absorb this."

"I'll wait," she said. Her face was all sympathy, and he felt a twinge of guilt. But he had to disappear now. He had already stayed too long. And he had to take the papers with him. He wanted nothing with his fingerprints left behind.

"Is there a restroom?" he said. "I came right from the airport, and the traffic . . ."

She pointed down the hall. "Take a left, and you'll see the door." She started to reach for the papers, but he turned and was down the hall, the papers clutched in his hand.

He turned left and saw her watching. *Damn it.* He went in the room, washed his hands, then exited. He looked down the hall. She was talking to the nurse at the desk.

He kept going toward the elevators. Just as the door opened, he saw a security officer get off the elevator and start for the nurse's station. He turned his face as he passed and hurried down the hall to the stairs. He was on the third floor. It would be faster to go down them rather than wait for another elevator.

He took the steps down, two at a time, then turned away from the reception area and went down to the main entrance. He noticed video cameras ahead and turned his head away from their view as he hurried through the doors. In minutes, he was in his car turning onto the main thoroughfare.

Jake ran down what he'd learned. Too damned little, though the burn mark on his arm confirmed Del's identity.

He also knew that no one else had come to Cox's side, and the police had been unable to find a relative. The last and most important thing he'd learned was that no letter had turned up among Cox's possessions. Yet Jake had seen him give the paramedic one. Most likely so had Gene Adams.

He had to find her, and quickly.

If he didn't, Gene Adams would. And, as in South America, Adams wouldn't want a witness.

# CHAPTER 5

Kirke and Hal grabbed a quick lunch at the station.

Before they finished the firehouse chili, another call came. Turned out to be the flu.

The next few hours were busy but had little of the drama of the day before. Quirky stuff mostly. A woman hearing voices was transported to the hospital's psychiatric ward. A fender bender with only a few scratches but two irate drivers who had to be calmed.

As they left that scene, she received a call from her captain.

"Kirke, a detective wants to talk to you. Name of Tom Brady. He's investigating the hit-and-run and wants to know if the victim said anything." He gave her a number to call.

Her heart sank. She didn't want to lie to the police. Neither did she want to admit she had taken something from the victim.

Before she could punch in the numbers, though, there was another call. Transport for a cancer treatment.

Mr. Marsh was a repeat customer, and he grinned when she and Hal arrived at the small house where he lived alone.

"I was hoping it would be you," he said with a twinkle in his faded blue eyes.

"I missed you, too," she said. "You're looking better."

"And you, my dear, are a liar, albeit a pretty one."

"And you, Mr. Marsh, are a lovely flatterer."

They waited while Mr. Marsh received his treatment, then there was a call about a child falling from a swing set and breaking an arm. It went that way the rest of the day. No life-saving decisions. No adrenaline rush. Just one call after another.

They ended their shift at the hospital, taking a newborn and her nervous mother to the hospital because of a rash. Kirke made out the run form, then visited the triage area. The reception nurse had changed, and the new one was Sally, with whom Kirke had exchanged more than a few ex-husband tales. Sally looked at her watch and grinned. "Can't stay away?"

"Just wanted to know if there's any word on the woman we brought in this morning. A Susan Whitaker."

Sally glanced at her computer, then shook her head. "We lost her."

"Damn,' " Kirke said. She hesitated, then asked, "And the man we brought in yesterday? Mark Cable? I heard he was in critical care."

"Still is," Sally said. She lowered her voice. "Word is he's on life support."

Kirke felt as if she'd been kicked in the stomach. She'd hoped against hope that he would miraculously return to life and solve the problem of the letter.

"Still no family?"

"That's the strange thing," Sally said. "Ellie said a guy came in and identified himself as the victim's brother. But he left before the police could talk to him. Created a real fuss around here. I've been told to alert security if he shows up again."

"Is he local?"

Sally shook her head. "Don't know. Ellie said he stopped here, showed her identification, then went up to intensive care. But apparently he wouldn't sign any papers and left before admissions got more information. A detective was in here asking about him."

"Do you remember the name of the officer?"

"Detective." Sally corrected as she picked up a card on her desk and handed it to her. "He asked me to call if anyone inquired about Mr. Cable."

Kirke took it, suspecting she already knew the name. Yep, Brady.

Hal interrupted them. "Finished here? We might make it back to the station before there's another call."

She nodded and took just a few steps before another call did come in. Just her luck. They were still on the clock, and it was their responsibility.

"Man down," according to the call. She took down the co-ordinates, and they drove off. Fifteen minutes' arrival time. Near the same street as the hit-and-run yesterday.

Hal uttered an oath under his breath. "Five minutes until quitting time," he groused. "Just our luck."

He drove even faster than usual while she checked her bag. *Man down* could be anything. A drunk. A shooting. She looked at her watch again. A few more minutes, and she would be off for three days. Time tomorrow to start her search. She only wished she could shove away a growing sense of worry. Sally's comments had not helped ease it.

The call apparently was false. When they arrived, no one knew anything about it.

It happened all too often. Sometimes a prank. Sometimes a fall, then the person walks away. She hated those calls because it took the ambulance away from real needs.

"Time to go home," Hal said.

She nodded. She called the dispatcher, telling her they were heading back to the fire station, where another crew would take over the ambulance. Then her cell phone rang.

It was her captain at the fire station. "Have you called Detective Brady yet? I'm getting some heat here. Apparently there's some kind of mystery about your patient."

"We've been busy, but I'll do it right now," she said.

She ended the call.

"What is it?" Hal asked.

"That hit-and-run yesterday. The police want to talk to me."

"Why not me?" he asked.

"I guess because I was first on the scene."

She thought about telling him about the letter, then she remembered Cable's frantic words. *No police.* There had been such desperation in the victim's voice. *Swear it.* The letter was now back at the station, in her purse, in her locker.

It was fish or cut bait time.

It was not her business. *Tell him.*

It wasn't as if she was breaking the law, she told herself. She'd been *given* the envelope, presented with a task—a dying request—that she'd agreed, albeit reluctantly, to fulfill.

She *knew* it was foolish. A stupid heroine syndrome, a Don Quixote quest.

Kirke dialed the number she'd been given. It must have been a direct line, because a male voice answered almost immediately. "Brady," he said gruffly.

"This is Kirke Palmer. My captain said you wanted to talk to me."

"Yep. The hit-and-run victim yesterday. You found his wallet."

"Yes."

"You're sure it's his."

"I found it on the floor of the ambulance. We'd cleaned the interior just before we picked him up. Why?" she couldn't help but ask.

"It's a criminal case, and some witnesses swear the car swerved to hit the victim. We tried to find a relative. No one at the address on the driver's license ever heard of him, and they had lived in the residence fifteen years. We checked the license bureau, and there is no such license. The credit card is billed to a mailbox service. No one there knew him."

He stopped, and the words registered in her mind. *Tell him,* her mind demanded. *Tell him about the letter.*

"We took his fingerprints, and nothing came up. No match. He's not in any files. Not only that, the doctor says he had plastic surgery. This afternoon someone turned up at the hospital and said he was a brother, then disappeared."

"I don't know how I can help you," she said.

"Did he say anything to you?"

"Nothing about who he is," she replied. It was the truth, but certainly not the whole truth. "I asked him his name, but he was too badly injured to make sense."

She knew then that she was committed to fishing.

"If you remember anything, call me," he said. "You have the number."

"Yes," she replied.

The detective hung up, and the words echoed in her head. A fake driver's license. A credit card with a private mailbox address. A relative who appeared and disappeared.

The ambulance arrived at the fire station. It would take them another thirty minutes to clean the vehicle, restock supplies, and finish the paperwork.

She would be off for three days then. If she hadn't found this Mitch Edwards by then, she would surrender the letter and accept whatever punishment she had coming.

━━━

Jake would have liked to stake out the hospital for the ambulance that had appeared at the accident scene. He wasn't lucky enough to find it parked there when he'd left, and after his disappearing act, he didn't think it wise to hang around.

But yesterday he'd noted the number printed on the ambulance. After some difficulty, he found a public phone booth and phone book. Public phones, unfortunately, were a disappearing convenience now that nearly everyone seemed to have cell phones.

He had a cell phone, a prepaid one, but the number would still be available to the answering entity. If the number got in the wrong hands, his movements could be tracked. It was a risk he wasn't willing to take, and a pay phone was cheaper than another disposable cell.

Using a map he'd purchased, he located fire stations in the immediate area. Then he started calling, asking if the ambulance had come from that station. He said he'd found a necklace where an ambulance had been parked and wanted to return it.

He struck out at the first one, but at the second station the person answering the phone hesitated, then said, "It might belong to Kirke. She's out now, but I'll ask her when she comes in. I'll need your number."

"She's on duty today?"

"Yeah."

"When does she get off?"

A pause.

"Look, I just want to get it to whoever owns it. It looks valuable. And I'll be away from the phone all day. I don't mind running over there. I appreciate what you people do."

"Seven," the person said reluctantly.

"Thanks." He hung up before he could ask for a name.

He had until seven. She should be safe enough until then. She had a partner and would be mostly in public. Like the military, fire and police personnel took care of their own.

Jake then went to an Internet café. He had one lead to Adams, and that was the car the former CIA agent had driven off in. He'd jotted down the plate number. He would bet his last dollar that the car involved in the hit-and-run was a stolen vehicle, but the one carrying Adams was a different matter. He wouldn't risk being stopped by police.

If Adams was here for a brief stay, he probably got the car at a rental agency. If so, it was a very upscale rental, and Jake started with limousine services. It was a long shot, and he knew it, but he had little else to go on. He went online for limousine rentals, made a list of five, and returned to the public telephone. He started at the top of the list.

"Someone driving one of your cars hit mine and drove off," he charged in an irate voice. "I got the license number, and I expect you people to pay for it."

He struck out with the first three companies. Then at the fourth, when he gave the license number, he was immediately transferred to someone else with a confident voice. "Have the police been notified?"

"I was late for a meeting. I didn't have time to wait, but I'm calling them next unless I get satisfaction."

"What is the number?"

He read off the license number.

There was a silence, then the man returned. "I'll need your name and number—"

"I want the name of the driver—"

"That is quite impossible, but if you leave—"

Jake hung up.

He wasn't going to get more.

But perhaps he'd directed Gene Adams's attention from the paramedic to himself. The manager no doubt was on the phone to him now.

He looked at his watch. Nearly six o'clock.

*Kirke.* Must be her last name. When he reached the station, he was relieved to find a fast-food restaurant across the street. He went inside, ordered a hamburger and fries, and chose a seat with a view of the station. It was five thirty, and her shift ended at seven p.m.

The cell phone rang, and he tensed.

He answered it.

"Your parole officer has been sniffing around, wanted to know where you were," David Ramsey said.

"What did you tell him?"

"That you'd gone fishing before starting the job. He wants you to call him."

"How long can you stall him?"

"Not long." The caller was the father of a Special Forces friend of his, one who had contacted him in prison to say that he'd heard about the charges and didn't believe them. Jake had rebuffed Cole Ramsey then. He hadn't wanted to taint anyone else with his problems. But release was contingent on a job, and no one wanted to hire a convicted thief. Cole's father, also ex-army, stepped in and offered him a construction job that was to start next week.

Now David Ramsey was risking his own freedom to help Jake. Assisting a felon in evading supervision could well be considered aiding and abetting.

Jake knew he hadn't been fitted with an ankle monitor because the feds thought he would go after the missing diamonds, and they hoped to recover at least some of them.

He'd taken great pains to evade them on this trip without looking as if he was evading them.

But that plan depended on a quick return.

Jake swore under his breath. He'd hoped for another day or so.

This meant he had to head home tonight. It also meant the feds might be looking for him at an airport. He would have to drive a rental back.

Hopefully, he would see the woman in an hour, try to talk her out of whatever Del Cox had given her, and warn her about Adams. Then he could return to Chicago before his parole supervisor knew he'd left.

He thought about this Ms. Kirke. He had, in those few moments at the scene, memorized everything about her. He'd had the impression of energy and efficiency and purpose. She hadn't been a beauty, but her face was pleasant enough.

He took his time eating as the restaurant filled up. He ordered another Coke and a small pie and reached his seat just as an ambulance arrived. He watched as the station door opened, and the vehicle disappeared inside.

He dropped the cup and napkins into the trash and went outside. He got into his car and waited.

When the woman left, he would follow.

➤

Ames Williamson left the library. Using a library computer, he'd discovered the name and address of the paramedic.

What had Cox given to her? Said to her?

Would she reveal what he feared most? Would the CIA learn that he hadn't died seven years ago? And, if so, could they find him? He'd established a new identity in Brazil. Miguel Samara. Seller of U.S. secrets and arms. He'd made many millions these past seven years.

Gene Adams had been buried in a faraway jungle.

Now he needed to stay buried.

He'd seen the number of the ambulance. It hadn't taken him long to hack into the fire department computer system. He'd always been good at computers, had a natural knack, and now his business—and his safety—depended on that knowledge. He transferred funds throughout the world, and he sure as hell didn't trust anyone else to do it for him.

Still, hacking hadn't been nearly as easy as he'd thought. Privacy laws and heightened security had made it more difficult, but he'd anticipated that. He'd used the library's computer. He hadn't wanted to bring attention to his own laptop.

Ames prided himself on not making mistakes, but he'd made a mistake that day in trusting Cox. He hadn't counted on the man liking the team leader. Hell, Cox never liked anybody.

But Cox was on life support now. As good as dead. He'd discovered that early this morning by pretending to be a police officer over the phone. Say you're a cop, and you get anything you want. He knew the language.

"What about personal belongings?" he'd asked the patient's representative. "We're trying to find next of kin."

"His brother showed up but left," she said. "A Detective Brady is trying to find him now."

"That's the department for you," he said. "Left hand doesn't know what the right hand's doing."

"Sounds familiar," she said, responding to the charm he'd put in his voice.

He took a risk. "An onlooker said he thought he saw an envelope at the accident scene, but we couldn't find it. Thought it might have been on him. I'm not sure Brady knows about it."

A pause, then, "There was only a wallet."

"Thanks," he said. "Probably nothing," he said offhandedly. "Just thought I would take a shot at it. Thanks a lot."

He hung up before there were any more questions. For some reason, the paramedic had not handed the letter in.

Cox was no longer a threat, but the paramedic was. And he wanted whatever Cox had given her.

Maybe he would pay a visit to her house, wait for her there.

# CHAPTER 6

Jake watched as a woman driving an elderly blue sedan pulled out of the parking area behind the fire station. He recognized her dark, curly hair.

Jake pulled out behind her. He had to be careful. He couldn't lose her, but he didn't want to scare her off, either. He wished to hell he had a GPS unit somewhere on her car, but that was wishful thinking. He would just have to stay on her tail and hope like hell he didn't lose her.

At least she didn't get on the interstate. He would have had more than a little difficulty keeping up with her then. Instead, she wound through secondary roads. He tried to keep a car between them but finally had to move up directly behind.

He followed her past a large park on his left, then she took a right onto a residential street. He followed, then passed her as she drove into a driveway and parked. He went around the block, then returned to her street. Parking spots were scarce, and he supposed that residents and guests from a corner apartment building usually parked on this street. He finally found a slot six houses from the driveway she'd entered.

He looked up and down the street. Nothing suspicious. Maybe he was a step ahead of Gene Adams.

He looked down at his watch. Eight. The day was fading, and the sun was low, spreading a cascade of brilliant colors across the sky. He'd missed those colors in prison.

No time to think about that. He had to start for the airport within an hour. He had to risk approaching her.

~

As she drove up to the duplex, Kirke couldn't forget the words the detective had uttered.

*We took his fingerprints, and nothing came up. No match. He's not in any files. And the doctor says he had plastic surgery. This afternoon someone turned up at the hospital and said he was a brother, then disappeared.*

Not unusual that there were no prints. If Mark Cable hadn't served in the armed forces or been arrested, his fingerprints wouldn't be on file. But the fact that a relative showed up then disappeared set off an alarm in her head.

Along with that mysterious request. *No police. Swear it.*

After she arrived home she went to Sam's side to pick up Merlin and Spade.

"Late," crowed Merlin. Then "Cops coming . . . cops coming." He imitated the wail of a police siren. It pierced the interior of the duplex. She figured that the drug dealers had taught Merlin that warning. He had excellent hearing and could be shriller than an alarm system.

African Greys—Merlin's breed of parrot—were remarkably intelligent. When she'd adopted Merlin, she'd conducted an Internet study of parrots. Known as the best parrot at mimicry, African Greys actually understood and used the human language. They not only parroted words and phrases and sounds, but they also associated them with events. But often Merlin was simply an alarmist.

"No one's there," she assured Merlin.

He gave her his evil bird look, fastening his little beady eyes on her. "Cops coming," he insisted.

She very much hoped not. She did not want to see or hear from Detective Brady again. She took the envelope from her

purse and slid it between newspaper pages on the bottom of
the cage. "Time to go home. For treats," she added.

"Treats?" he echoed with approval.

"Only for good birds."

"Merlin is a good bird," Merlin asserted, then repeated
the police car siren.

It was remarkably accurate. She'd had visits from neigh-
bors more than once.

Then she heard a sound next door. In her supposedly
empty home. She stilled.

Had Merlin been trying to tell her someone was in her
duplex?

Kirke left Merlin and Spade inside Sam's apartment. She
went outside and crossed over to her own door. She tried the
doorknob. It was still locked, and it didn't look tampered
with.

It was the only way in and out. There was no back door.
One room led to another to another. Since it shared a side
with another unit, the design allowed a minimal number of
windows. There were several in the front room facing the
street, one in the kitchen, and two in the bedroom in back.

The noise had probably been no more than her imagination.

"Help!" Merlin screeched again in a woman's voice from
inside Sam's apartment.

Kirke hadn't heard Merlin repeat that particular word before. She wondered whether he had picked up on the sudden
apprehension that had seized her. She hoped he'd learned it
from the television set and not some victim of his previous
owners.

She ignored him and listened at her door for a moment.
Nothing. Apparently it was just one of Merlin's spontaneous
fancies.

"Ma'am?"

She whirled around. A tall, loose-limbed man rapidly
approached her porch. He had an interesting face. Strong
features. Dark, piercing eyes. The slight cleft in his chin soft-
ened the angular cheekbones. A small scar was visible just

above his right eye. His hair was dark, cut short and tinged with gray.

He reached the porch door and stood there. "I heard a cry for help. I thought it came from here," he added as he looked around.

"A Good Samaritan?" she asked, amused that Merlin's cry had brought such good-looking assistance.

He shrugged with a self-conscious smile. It was stiff, as if the expression didn't come easily.

"Help!" screeched Merlin again. He sounded even more human than before.

"That was Merlin," she said, enjoying the puzzlement on his face.

"Merlin?" he echoed from his side of the screen door.

She left the screen door and went into Sam's apartment, returning with the parrot.

"Help!" Merlin said in a woman's voice, "Cops coming" in another voice, then he broke into a perfect rendition of a siren. He was obviously showing off.

"He's my guard bird," she said, not quite containing a grin. "He also bites."

He shook his head. "I thought I heard a siren but . . ."

"Everything is . . ." She started to say *fine*, but there was still that nagging feeling that she'd heard something in her apartment.

She looked at the stranger. There was a hardness to his features, a wariness to his eyes that reminded her of the cops she knew.

"Everything is . . . ?" He asked when she didn't finish her sentence.

She hesitated. "Who are you?"

"If you're Ms. Kirke, I was coming to see you," he said. "I'm David Cable. I was told you were the paramedic that helped my brother yesterday."

She was stunned. He was the last person she'd expected.

She tried to regain her senses. "I'm Kirke Palmer," she acknowledged.

"I wanted to thank you," he said simply. "And know

whether he said anything to you. The medical people at the hospital said he was unconscious when he arrived there."

"The hospital said Mr. Cable's brother appeared, then disappeared," she replied in a neutral tone. It wasn't her place to judge, but she couldn't help her feelings. One didn't desert family. She'd had too much experience with that human frailty.

Surprise crossed his face.

"I would have thought you would have wanted to stay with him." She couldn't keep the censure for her voice.

"We weren't close," he said, "and I knew he was . . . on life support. I could only do for him what I would have wanted him to do for me. I left to try to contact some of his old friends. Hoped they might know where he'd left some documents. Or whether he'd said anything to you."

*Cable.* He was Mark Cable's brother. She looked at him closer. They both had dark eyes. There were few other similarities.

If he was Mark Cable's brother, then maybe he knew this Mitch Edwards. But something held her back. Everything he said could be true, but it sounded a little facile to her. And there was little emotion in his words.

*We weren't close.*

Her mind was cataloguing everything she knew with what he was telling her. Surely if Mark Cable had trusted him, he would have left the envelope for him.

"Can I see some identification?" she said.

He pulled out a wallet and held a driver's license up to his side of the screen. She noted it was a New York State license, and she memorized the address. Kirke then compared the photo to the man in front of her. His expression in the photo was blank, almost as expressionless as it was now. He said he and his brother hadn't been close, but still she would have expected a little emotion. Of course, some men were like that. Her ex-husband had been. The thought did not endear him to her.

"Why are you here, Mr. Cable?"

"I was hoping you could tell me something about what happened. Was he in any pain? Did he say anything about me? I'm Mark's only living relative. I'm responsible for what happens now, and I have no idea what his wishes might be."

She believed herself a good judge of people, and for the first time she heard some emotion in his voice.

"Just a moment," she said.

She retreated into Sam's apartment and took the cell phone from her purse. She punched a key for Sam's cell phone. She wasn't surprised when he didn't answer, but she left a message that she was with a David Cable and gave him the address on the driver's license.

Then she closed the door to Sam's house, unlocked the screen door to the porch, and went down two steps. If her visitor grabbed her, she could scream. Not that anyone was responding to Merlin's cries for help. She sat down on the step and invited David Cable to sit down with her.

The sky was vivid with color. In a few moments it would be dark. A shiver suddenly ran down her back and she didn't know why. His presence? Or something more ominous? She decided to ignore it. "I'll tell you what I can," she said, "but it isn't much. He was bleeding from an artery, and we were busy trying to stanch that. It looked as if he had internal injuries as well."

"Did he say anything?"

"Nothing about family or wishes . . . I don't think anyone really thinks they are going to die. He didn't even tell me his name. It was in the wallet he dropped in the ambulance."

"He was in pain?"

"Some. But shock is the best painkiller there is. I don't think he suffered much."

"The witnesses said it seemed as if the driver meant to hit him. He didn't say anything about that?"

She shook her head. "He was weak. Could barely breathe."

*Tell him.* But something stopped her just as it had stopped her earlier from telling the detective. What did she really know about him? Maybe he killed his brother for an inheritance, and the proof was in the letter.

She mentally admonished herself. She read way too many murder mysteries.

"He didn't have any other possessions with him? Anything that would help me?" The question was asked quietly, but there was an intensity about it that startled her.

His dark gaze pierced her. He was too close, much too close. He radiated masculinity and, yes, something else that sent tingles of awareness through her. They weren't the kind she'd felt moments before when she thought someone might be in her apartment. It was pure feminine reaction to an attractive male. Inexplicable. Undesired. And new. She couldn't remember when she'd reacted so quickly to a man.

Empathy for someone who'd just lost a brother? Or touched by the hint of quiet intensity that he tried to cover?

Didn't he deserve the letter? It was by rights his. Everything Mark Cable owned probably belonged to him.

Or did it?

She couldn't forget the way he'd disappeared from the hospital. But that was not her call to make. Still, she felt a disappointment in him and an odd feeling that not everything was right with his reactions.

She would check him out before conveying the letter. Now she had a name and address. Then if he was who he said he was, she would give it to him.

"Where are you staying?" she asked.

He hesitated. "I have to return to New York tonight."

"You're not going to stay to . . . I mean . . ."

It was none of her business, she knew. But she knew from her grandfather's death the number of details that needed tending, not to mention, in Mark Cable's case, his suspicious circumstance. Would he not want to know what happened?

"I have business I can't postpone," he said. "But I'll be back."

She nodded, but disappointment cascaded through her. Even if he wasn't close to his brother, shouldn't he be more concerned? Shouldn't he have spent a few more hours with him?

She stood. "I have to go inside."

"Go inside," approved Merlin from the other side of the door.

She'd almost forgotten about Merlin and Spade.

"You don't approve," he said as he rose as well.

"It's not up to me to approve or not approve. I don't know you. I didn't know Mark Cable."

"But you have a connection to him."

She stared at him. "Why do you say that?"

"Your disapproval just then because I have to leave."

She shrugged. "I care about all my patients."

"Thank you. For caring. I didn't think many people did."

"Did that include you?" she asked softly.

He looked startled, as if he hadn't meant to say what he did.

"We had differences. But yes, I care that he . . . is dying."

She did hear some emotion then, and it made her feel better. But she was exhausted, Merlin and Sam were hungry, and it was time to go in. She had some research to do.

"I have to go inside," she said. "I'm sorry, but I really can't tell you any more than I have."

He nodded, opened the door for her. "Thank you for your time, Ms. Palmer," he said with a formal courtesy that appealed to her. Too much.

She stepped inside, aware that he was still on the steps. It was nearly dark, and she turned on the light switch for the porch light. It didn't go on.

"That's strange," she said.

"What?"

"I just put a bulb in."

Without an invitation, he stepped inside the porch and checked the bulb. She had to stand on a chair to replace the bulb, as did Sam, but he was tall enough to reach it. "It's loose."

She would have sworn she had made sure she'd screwed it in tight. She and Sam liked to sit out on the porch, sometimes with light, sometimes without.

Then she remembered the noise she'd heard. She'd almost convinced herself it had been her imagination.

How far did she trust her companion? She had to make an instant decision. "I thought I heard a noise in my apartment before you came. But then I sort of dismissed it."

It was like watching a panther wake from a nap and go into full hunting mode. David Cable's body tensed, and she

knew she didn't want to be on the other end of the hard gaze
of his eyes. She also realized that he had nothing to do with
any noise she might have heard from next door.

"This isn't your apartment?" he said, looking toward the
door of Sam's side.

"No. I own the building and live on the right side. Sam,
my tenant, lives on the left. He takes care of Merlin when
I'm working, and I came by to pick him up."

"Do you have your key?" he said.

She hesitated. Then, inexplicably, she handed it to him,
all the time questioning her sanity.

He went in like a cop, though he didn't have a gun in
hand. But she'd seen enough cops in action to know what
was real. His moves were cautious. Experienced. Defensive.

In seconds he was back at the door.

"It's empty," he said.

He stood by while she picked up Merlin's cage and went
inside. The parrot was unusually quiet. She put the cage
down and opened the door. Merlin flew out and sat where he
could regard David Cable.

Her visitor didn't look like a David. David sounded warm
and friendly and open. She didn't know much about David
Cable, but he didn't appear to have any of those qualities.
Still . . . inexplicably she did not want him to leave.

His lips thinned, and a muscle moved in his cheek. "You
should see if anything's missing," he said.

She nodded. "Thanks for checking."

He simply nodded.

"You can go," she said. "You said you planned to leave
Atlanta tonight."

"I'll wait while you check and make sure everything's
okay."

She studied him for a moment, then decided she felt safer
with him than without him. For some reason she trusted him.
She didn't do that readily, not after her bad judgment with
her ex.

But she still wasn't going to hand over the letter. Not
without obtaining more information. Perhaps because she
saw secrets in his eyes. Secrets, but not the cold vacantness

she associated with a bad guy. It wouldn't make sense to anyone else, but there it was.

Nothing seemed disturbed in the living room nor the kitchen. But when she reached the back, the computer was running. She never left it on. She'd lost one once during a storm and was always careful now to turn it off when she was gone. Summer storms were frequent in Atlanta.

Then she saw a crack in the window that faced the back-yard. That was something else she always kept closed because of Spade.

"Someone was here," she said. "He must have gone out the back."

"He?"

She gave him a weak smile. "Aren't all bad guys men?"

"You've had experience with that many bad guys?" he asked. No smile. Not even a hint of one.

Humorless. He was completely humorless. She didn't like humorless men.

Yet every time she looked at him, she felt the oddest connection. Her body warmed when she'd brushed by him. She wasn't sure why. He wasn't typically attractive. His features were too severe, his manner too brusque and emotionless.

"A few," she replied.

His gaze bored into her again, and she felt as if her soul was being stripped bare.

"What might be on the computer that would interest someone?" he suddenly asked, shattering that hold.

She shook her head in puzzlement. "Nothing. E-mails to friends. A couple of blogs I like." She decided not to mention that she had been trying to find a Mitch Edwards.

She went over to the computer and checked recent searches. It was the same ones as she had made, but with a later date. An hour ago, in fact.

What if she had walked into her own duplex before going to Sam's?

"Call the police," David Cable said. "You should have this on record."

"What should I say? Someone looked at my computer? Nothing is missing."

"Isn't it?" he asked. "Have you really looked that well?"

There was something in his voice that ignited those alarm bells again. It brought back her other doubts.

"I'll do that," she said.

"Do you want me to stay?"

"You said you had a plane to catch, and I have the parrot alarm."

"You need more than that," he said. "I noticed you have an alarm system. Turn it on."

He'd noticed the alarm system. Just, she thought, as he'd noticed everything else in the apartment. His gaze never stopped moving. It had taken in the volumes on her bookshelves and the CDs piled up next to her player. And the pile of clothes on the floor from last night.

"Yes sir," she said with a jauntiness that was all bravado.

He stared at her with those dark eyes. She felt properly chastised.

"And nail down that window," he added.

She noticed he didn't offer to do that for her.

She liked that.

She worked hard to be independent. She never asked Sam to help her put together all those things that came with some assembly required, and she knew how to change a tire, refill oil in her car, and hit the hell out of someone who tried to abuse her.

He headed through the door to the screen porch, then turned. Their eyes met, and something flashed between them. Testosterone and pheromones meeting and finding something they liked. There wasn't a darn thing she could do about it.

And then he was gone, and the home she'd always loved felt empty. And lonely.

# CHAPTER 7

Halfway out of the city, Jake slammed his fist against the steering wheel, then took the next exit off the expressway and headed back.

*Dammit, but the woman is in over her head.*

Adams undoubtedly had seen Del Cox hand an envelope to her. Jake had little doubt that her intruder had been Gene Adams or someone working for him. Either way, she was in one hell of a lot of trouble.

She hadn't seemed to miss anything, so she must still have the letter. Was it on her? Or in the apartment of her friend?

If he didn't return to Chicago now, he would be on the run. He would be violating the terms of his release. Hell, he'd already violated them, but he certainly was worsening the situation. It was the devil's own choice, but his life wasn't worth a shit if he didn't learn the truth.

He *wanted* that letter. And he wanted to protect that damned woman. Correction. He didn't *want* to protect her. He *had* to protect her. He needed her.

He wondered whether she'd called the police about the

break-in. Probably not. She had the attitude of a woman who thought she could take care of herself.

Even if she called the police, no department had the manpower to protect the victim of a burglary, especially one when nothing was missing. Neither they nor she could possibly comprehend the stakes involved in the murder of Mark Cable, alias Del Cox.

No one knew Gene Adams as he did, and Jake knew him even better now. He'd betrayed his country, his employers, and his comrades. And that put a huge target on his back if his continued existence was known.

Jake knew he didn't have enough proof at the moment to go to anyone. He'd just be slapped back in prison, and Ms. Palmer would probably die.

The late hour made traffic less hassle. He stopped at an all-night market. Now that he knew her full name and address, he quickly found her phone number and used the pay phone to call her. As before, he hesitated to use his cell phone. Adams might well have tapped her phone and thus could get his cell number.

"It's David Cable," he said when she answered. "Just wanted to know if you're okay."

"I am," she said in a suddenly wary voice.

"Help!" came her voice but in the background.

"Pay no attention to Merlin," she said. "He thinks he's a hero and won't stop yelling for help."

He liked the fond amusement in her voice. Truth was, he'd liked most everything about her. The tousled hair. The direct, hazel eyes. The lack of pretension. She was no beauty, but she was attractive in a girl-next-door way, and her warmth and personality were appealing. To be truthful, more than appealing.

He'd been too damned long without a woman.

"Did you call the police?" he asked.

"No," she said. "Nothing was taken. And I might have left the computer on."

But not at the times indicated by the computer. He knew it. She obviously knew it. Had she not called the police because she had something or had done something she didn't want revealed?

"The alarm is on?"

"Yes, including the avian one. He's mumbling about my ingratitude at the moment." She paused, then added, "I also nailed the back window."

"Okay," he said and hung up.

She'd had a long day. He knew from the information he'd collected that paramedics here worked twelve-hour shifts four days a week. He knew what a strain that was, particularly with a job as stressful as hers.

He went inside the market and bought a large cup of coffee along with a package of donuts. Then he drove to her street and parked among others lining the street.

From his position, he could see the porch light as well as a light in her front room window. He couldn't see more. He hoped watching the front door was enough. She shared a common wall with the other side of the duplex and had no back door. The back window was now nailed shut, and the other window he'd noticed, the one in the kitchen, was small. And visible.

At least he knew her name now. Kirke Palmer.

He liked the sound of it on his lips. It had a uniqueness that suited her.

*Down, Jake.*

He took a sip of coffee. It was going to be a long night.

He thought of the conversation. She'd held something back. He would bet on it. She hadn't trusted him—not completely, maybe not at all—though she'd allowed him inside her house. It had been a matter of the worse evil, him or a possible burglar. He'd won that battle, but she'd sensed something in his story that didn't ring true. He had to do something to change that.

He had to grin as he remembered the parrot, Merlin. He was a magical bird indeed if he'd frightened off Gene Ames. Jake would like to be there when Gene discovered who, and what, had spoiled this particular ambush.

After David Cable had left, Kirke made herself a cup of coffee and tried to wipe away the exhaustion she felt.

She microwaved the last of the turkey and wild rice soup she'd made and frozen a month earlier. It was thick and rich and just enough. She cut some pineapple slices for Merlin. He signaled his approval by singing a few notes from "Non, Je Ne Regrette Rien," a song on her favorite Edith Piaf CD. Somehow he managed to catch the late French singer's throaty, sultry sound. It was one of the few sounds he'd picked up from her. The others obviously came from the drug dealers. Expletives were, unfortunately, not uncommon.

She needed a bath, a long, hot, scented one. She ran the water, turned on her Piaf CD, poured a glass of wine, and sank gratefully into the tub full of bubbles. Merlin flew into the bathroom and perched on the sink, regarding her with interest. Spade nested in her robe beside the tub.

The bathtub was her thinking place.

The fear was gone. The intruder had been a burglar, plain and simple, and Merlin had frightened him away. As for the computer, maybe the burglar was trying to obtain financial information. She would watch her accounts for the next few days.

She had a good security system. She would just have to ask Sam to make sure it was always on. He was often careless about it. To be truthful, she'd grown complacent as well. But she'd nailed down the back window as soon as David Cable left.

She felt safer.

Her thoughts turned to David Cable. It had been a long time since she'd had such an immediate and visceral reaction to a man. Especially when it wasn't wise. She'd never seen such guarded eyes.

Military. Or law enforcement. He was one of the two. She worked with police and knew the breed. She liked them, admired them, but she would never marry one and had turned down dates from several. They held so much inside that they often found it difficult to communicate with anyone other than another cop. She'd heard of too many divorces for that reason.

Why hadn't she asked him if he knew someone named Mitch Edwards? Why hadn't she mentioned the letter?

Too many mysteries, she answered herself. He was too cautious with his words, too cool with responses. Then there was the fact that Mark Cable hadn't asked her to give it to his brother. If he wanted David to have it, wouldn't he have asked her to give it to him?

She got out of the tub, pulled on a robe, and went to her landline phone. She punched in 411 for information in New York and asked for the number of a David Cable, giving the address she'd seen on the driver's license. No such number was listed.

She hung up, then went to her computer and brought up a site she'd used as a reporter, one that provided background checks of people for a price. She used the free service first, typing in David Cable/New York. Fifty David Cables appeared. The service listed their ages but no addresses.

She eliminated those who were outside his age range. That included anyone over fifty and younger than thirty-five. The list narrowed to ten names. She decided to take those ten to the second level, which meant a fee. None of the subsequent addresses and phone numbers matched her David Cable.

Okay. Instead of pursuing the name, she would try the address he'd given her. She Googled the address. It belonged to a corporation.

Possible. Some people did business from a home held by a corporation for tax reasons. A further search revealed it was headquartered in Delaware. Then a dead end. She could find nothing on the listed officers. Probably attorneys who would claim privilege.

The phone rang, and she immediately recognized the voice of the subject of her search.

She'd been too startled to react immediately, other than to assure him she had taken the precautions he'd suggested. The deep, concerned voice, though, warmed her. In truth, it sent sparks through her.

Before she could say anything more, he'd hung up and left her staring at her telephone.

He was just as much as a mystery as before.

Back to the computer. She decided to try Mark Cable. The detective said the address she'd discovered in his wallet didn't exist. Or at least the police couldn't find it. She remembered it was a Virginia driver's license.

She ran a search for Mark Cable, narrowing the search to Virginia. Nothing likely, so she went to the counties near Washington. Maybe he'd been with the government. Again she aimed for men in the right age range. She came up with nineteen this time. She paid again for the more detailed information.

She looked at the clock. Nearly midnight, and it had been a very long day. Time to end her quest. For tonight, anyway. Dammit. She'd found exactly nothing.

She shut off the computer.

"G'night?" Merlin asked.

"Good night," she agreed.

She went to the fridge, found several more pieces of pineapple, and mixed it with the bird food. Merlin perched on her shoulder, his eyes following the pineapple pieces as a miser eyed his gold. She took the food to his cage, and Merlin flew in and started eating his treats. He'd earned them today. More than earned them.

When she'd first acquired him, she'd kept the cage in her bedroom, but soon she discovered as long as a light was on, he would chat. Incessantly. She'd moved his cage to the living room, and they'd come to a much better accommodation. At night, she would cover the cage, and as long as he didn't hear any noises, he was silent until she she got up.

When he finished his treats, she cleaned out the bottom of the cage, taking out the soiled newspaper pages and replacing them with fresh ones. She located the envelope still tucked among several pages, unsullied by Merlin's necessities.

Could the burglar have been after the letter?

An overly vivid imagination, she told herself. This had been a simple burglary.

Still, she tucked the envelope inside the fresh pages. Safest place for it. If anyone did try to look, Merlin would most certainly bite, and he had a nasty one. She covered his cage, and Merlin fell silent. Spade followed her into the bedroom and jumped up on the bed, making a circle before collapsing in a fuzzy ball.

Sleep didn't come as easily as it usually did after a busy day. She kept seeing those dark, intense eyes and rerunning in her head everything the detective said about Mark Cable. Plastic surgery. An address that didn't exist.

After her admittedly superficial research, there were even more questions. Most people had a background littered with records. Deeds, employment, taxes. David Cable apparently had none. Neither did Mark Cable. But then she'd done little more than a cursory search. Maybe Robin Taylor could help her. An investigative reporter for the *Atlanta Observer* and an old friend, Robin was superb at digging out information.

She ached to open the envelope. But it wasn't hers. It had been given to her in trust by a dying man.

She promised herself that she would call Robin in the morning. If they made no more progress in her hunt for Mitch Edwards, then she would reconsider looking inside the envelope.

# CHAPTER 8

Kirke woke, glanced at the clock, and rolled out of bed. Six a.m.

Even when she'd been up as late as she had been last night, she automatically woke when the sun rose. It was a curse.

No time to loiter, though. She was off today, and she had a mission. She'd remained awake much of the night thinking about the next steps she should take. Her thoughts kept returning to Robin.

Problem was they hadn't seen each other in many months, and her friend Robin had a curiosity that equaled hers. Making things more difficult, Robin's husband was an FBI agent.

*He* was the police Mark Cable had warned her against.

Was a branch of law enforcement involved in some conspiracy? Would that include the FBI?

Or was it something simpler? And possibly illegal?

She went outside. She didn't see Sam's car, which meant he hadn't arrived home yet. She wanted to tell him what happened yesterday and warn him about the alarm system. Maybe he would overrule her decision not to go to the police.

Coffee. That's what she needed. She reached for the can and looked inside. Empty. She needed other things as well. Mainly food. Always happened during those days she worked twelve to fourteen hours. She was often too tired at the end of the day to go shopping. When she got home, all she usually wanted was a hot bath.

Yet she had to admit she was an adrenaline junkie. She had been that at the newspaper and was even more so now. A good story couldn't compare with saving a person's life. Still, some calls were haunting. She'd been told in training that a paramedic couldn't dwell on those. But some memories persisted. She expected that included the battered woman yesterday, as well as Mark Cable, who was so desperate to reach a man named Edwards.

She had gone over the incident a dozen times in her mind, and she was convinced Mark Cable knew he was dying. Some great wrong to be righted?

Which made his urgency so much more imperative to her.

She looked at the clock. Six thirty.

There was a café she often patronized three blocks away, and it was a walk she enjoyed. She dressed in jeans and her old Save the Whales T-shirt. The walk would give her time to think.

Merlin protested as she reached for her purse.

"I'll be back soon," she said. She rubbed his head and tempted him back into the cage. She didn't like to leave him free while she was gone.

"Bye-bye," he said sadly.

Guilt trip. That was better than some of the words she'd heard him repeat. She swung her purse over her shoulder and opened the door. The sky was a deep blue. It would be another scorcher today, but now there was the slightest breeze. The fresh air felt good. She would go for a run in the park tomorrow morning. It cleared her head, but now she had too much to do.

She checked the street in front of her. No one lurking outside. Not even David Cable, and she was surprised at how sorry she was that he wasn't. She'd felt safe with him. Safe and . . . awakened.

She reached the café, bought a paper in the stand outside, and went inside. It was nearly full this morning, and she recognized many of the regulars. She took a small corner table and spread out the paper in front of her. Maybe there would be some news about Mark Cable. Or anything else that might give her a clue.

The waitress brought her a pot of coffee, and Kirke ordered two eggs over light, hash brown potatoes, bacon, and toast. A leisurely breakfast cooked by someone else. Heaven.

She turned to the paper and flipped through it. Nothing about the mysterious patient nor about any leads in apprehending the driver. In fact, the accident wasn't mentioned at all. Yesterday's news. When she got home she would call Robin and suggest she investigate the hit-and-run, tell her that she was worried it would fall through the law enforcement cracks.

That way she wouldn't have to mention the envelope but would be privy to any information Robin gathered.

Satisfied that she had a strategy, she relished every bite of her breakfast as she finished reading the paper. It was eight thirty when she finished. She left a hefty tip since she'd taken the table for so long.

The street was busy when she left. Nothing looked odd, though. She would get back, call Robin, and then do errands. Groceries. Laundry. Gas for the car. Bills. She always tried to get those out of the way her first day off.

Would David Cable show up again? She certainly hadn't expected him to call last night. Nor had she expected the frisson of pure desire that had shot through her.

She walked swiftly, something she'd learned at the newspaper when she had to walk a fast mile from the office to the statehouse.

Kirke turned the corner, when seemingly out of nowhere a man dressed in jeans and a loose jacket brushed against her, whisking her purse from her arm. She forgot everything that she'd been told about just letting it go, and, yelling like a banshee, she grabbed the strap and held on.

He turned so unexpectedly that she wasn't prepared when his hand slammed against her face. She stumbled and went tumbling into the street. A car narrowly avoided her, then another bore down on her before she could scramble to her feet.

Arms swept around her, and she was thrown onto the sidewalk. A body landed next to her. The fall knocked the wind from her. Her right eye hurt like the furies, as did her cheek. She looked down and saw blood running from several cuts.

But she was alive!

She was aware of a crowd gathering, of pain beginning in several distinct sites in her body. She looked at the man who was sitting up next to her. The man who most probably had saved her life.

*David Cable.* The shock was almost as stunning as the blow to her face.

So he hadn't left Atlanta last night. And how had he been so handy?

It didn't matter. She was alive because of him.

A car had screeched to a stop not far from her and a woman ran over to them. "I'm sorry . . . I'm so sorry. I didn't see you until it was too late. Just suddenly . . ." She burst into tears.

"It's okay," Kirke said to the woman. "Someone pushed me . . ." Her voice trembled. She hated that.

"I called the police and an ambulance," a bystander said.

"I saw it all," another said. "I can describe the attacker."

But Kirke's gaze returned to David Cable and the blood running down his shirt, the same one he'd worn yesterday. "You . . . you've been hurt," she said.

He moved closer, knelt beside her. "Never mind me," he said. "What about you?" His hands ran over her with an expertise that told her he'd had medical training. His fingers barely brushed her injured cheek with a gentleness she hadn't expected.

Her heart pounded harder, and she felt a funny jolt deep inside her stomach. Pain seeped away for the moment.

She struggled to keep that knowledge to herself. "I'm battered but alive, thanks to you."

"Next time don't hold on to the purse," he said curtly.

"I've had self-defense training," she protested.

"And what's the first thing they teach you? I think it's sur-rendering whatever an assailant wants?"

She knew that, but everything happened so quickly, she'd just reacted. She decided to change the subject. "Are you re-ally okay?"

"Yeah," he said.

She heard the sound of a siren.

He obviously did, too. He touched her check again and wiped away blood with his fingers. There was an odd tender-ness about it, especially after his curt comment about her purse. Then he stood.

He glanced at his watch. "I have to go. I missed the plane last night . . . can't miss another."

She tried to stand, but she was too dizzy. Her head hurt. "You should wait—"

"I'm okay. Just a superficial cut, but you've had a blow to your head. Stay where you are. Wait for the ambulance."

And then he was gone.

She wanted to go after him, but when she tried to stand, her legs buckled under her, and her head felt as if someone was beating it with a stick.

"Maybe you shouldn't try to get up," one of the by-standers said. It was the person who'd called 911.

He was right—she shouldn't. Kirke knew that better than anyone. You didn't play around with a head injury. Anger filled her . . . anger and humiliation. Sitting there bleeding with a number of people gathered around, she better under-stood now how some of her patients must feel. The public display of helplessness, of being a victim, was mortifying.

"You're going to have one heck of a shiner," another per-son said helpfully.

She touched her face and felt the cut. Probably a ring from her assailant's finger.

Then a man pushed aside the others and handed her a purse. "I followed the guy," he said simply. "He threw it down. Probably didn't want to be caught with it."

"Thanks," Kirke said.

"Better check it," he persisted.

She did as he suggested. Cell phone gone. Wallet gone. Lipstick and other stuff still there. Her driver's license, thank God, was still in a special zip pocket in the front. After losing a wallet prior to taking the self-defense course, she now kept her license separate in her purse.

She didn't worry about the money, but the cell phone was her constant companion.

"My cell . . ."

She stopped. Better her cell phone than her life. She'd come so close . . .

Before she could say anything else, she heard the familiar wail of an ambulance and turned toward the street as it pulled up in front of her.

She recognized the paramedic who jumped out and ran to her. A police car roared up seconds later.

"It's nothing, Tommy," she said to the paramedic, echoing the words of David Cable moments earlier.

Tommy sighed. Paramedics were notoriously bad patients. "You know the drill, Kirke. I have to take vitals and put patches on those cuts."

Kirke waited impatiently until he finished.

"Everything looks all right 'cept for that shiner and those cuts. You'll probably need some stitches and probably should have a doctor look at that head injury.

"Stitches?"

"Shouldn't leave a scar," he assured her.

"I really should talk to the police first."

"At the hospital," he said.

"They're here now."

"Make it short," Tom grumbled.

She talked to the two officers. She knew one of them. Pat Harris. She described the purse snatcher, adding her description to that of the witnesses who remained.

"And this guy who rescued you?" Pat asked.

She hesitated. He hadn't wanted to stay, and she didn't think it was because of a plane. He obviously didn't want to be there when the police arrived. He'd just saved her life. She owed him the benefit of the doubt.

She shrugged. "I can't tell you anything. He left almost immediately."

"If you hear from him, call us. He might have seen something."

"I don't suppose I can expect an arrest anytime soon," she said dryly.

"Now that's cynical," Patrolman Pat Harris said with a grin. "But probably accurate. We don't have that much to go on. Brown hair, brown eyes, medium height, Nikes. Fits half the population of Atlanta."

"Sorry," she said, "it was so fast that I just got a brief glimpse."

"We'll drive around for a while, see if we can't spot someone matching the description. Think you would recognize him?"

"Probably."

The patrolman turned to the paramedic. "She's all yours."

She hesitated, tempted to refuse and try to make it home on her own, then realized how foolish that would be.

The headache was worsening. So was the pain in her cheek. Her clothes were stained with blood from the several cuts. She didn't have a car with her, and she wasn't sure she wanted to walk home. She also knew that she could have a slight concussion.

"Going to East Memorial?" she said.

He nodded.

If there weren't really serious cases, they would work her in. "Okay," she said. She would ask Sam to drive her home. She started to look for her phone in her purse when she remembered it was gone. She borrowed Tom's cell instead.

Sam answered immediately.

"Hi, home yet?" she asked.

"Just got here. Saw your message. What happened yesterday?" His voice was full of worry.

"Burglar, but Merlin scared him away with his siren imitation."

"Where are you now?"

"In front of our favorite restaurant. Someone snatched my purse and knocked me down. I have to go to the hospital for stitches. Can you meet me there and bring me home?"

"You know you need merely to ask, landlady."

"I'll call you when I get through. I don't think it will be very late."

She hung up and stepped into the ambulance. Tom came with her. He'd already taken her vitals, but now he put a bandage on her cheek. "Is it deep?" she asked.

"No. Just a stitch or two, but you'll have the black eye for a week."

Just what she needed.

After they reached the hospital, Kirke waited an hour before a nurse practitioner cleaned the several wounds inflicted when she hit the pavement. Finally, a doctor looked at her. "Doesn't look like a concussion," he told her after asking several questions, "but take it easy today. Put something cold on that eye. Contact your doctor if you feel any dizziness." He quickly wrote out two prescriptions, one for an antibiotic and the other for pain.

She called Sam, then tested her legs. They worked. She probably had twenty minutes before Sam arrived. She went up to intensive care and talked to the nurse on duty about her former patient. "I brought him in," she explained. "Just wondering if there's any change."

The nurse shook her head. "No. We're still hoping his brother will change his mind and donate Mr. Cable's organs."

"He said no?" she asked, surprised.

The nurse shook her head. "He refused, and we haven't seen him since."

That seemed very strange to Kirke. David Cable had flown down but wasn't at his brother's bedside, had apparently refused to take any responsibility for him. Nor had he offered to help others by agreeing to organ donations. Yet he hadn't hesitated to risk his life for hers.

Almost as strange as the gentleness of his fingers when he'd explored her injuries. Nearly as baffling as the shafts of electricity that coursed through her when he was near. She'd never felt that kind of physical awareness of a man before, not even with her ex. It was maddening that she felt it now for an elusive stranger who appeared in and out of her life like a shadow.

"And no one else has been here?" Kirke asked after a moment's pause.

"There's been some queries, but we're not allowed to give out information. Probably shouldn't even be talking to you about it, but we're all frustrated."

Sam was at the emergency room door by the time she collected her paperwork and prescriptions.

"You look like hell," he said as they got into his car.

"Thank you very much."

"You know what I mean. You have one hell of a shiner."

She could have done without hearing that again. She hadn't had the heart to look in the mirror. She would see soon enough.

She always thought she would be ready for an attack. She knew the rules. Keep purse close, but let go if someone snatched it. It had just been so fast . . .

"Did you turn on the alarm at the house?" she asked.

The startled look on his face told her he had not.

"I'm sorry, Kirke. I was asleep when you called and just ran out. I locked both doors, though."

She wasn't going to argue with him about it. They were both creatures of habit. But she did tell him all the details, including about the mysterious David Cable.

"There's something else," she said. "I don't think it has anything to do with the burglary, but maybe you should know about it."

"That sounds serious."

"I broke some rules."

He glanced quickly at her. "You?"

"I've been known to," she said defensively.

He shook his head. "You suffer the agonies of hell if you're one day late on a bill."

"You don't want the utilities turned off," she objected.

"And you vote in every election."

"Everyone should."

"And you would never ever go to the fifteen-item-limit checkout counter if you have sixteen items."

"That's only courteous."

"And you would never, ever fudge even one cent on your taxes—"

"Enough," she said. "You make me sound like—"

"A good citizen," he interrupted with a mock shiver.

She had to admit a certain amount of guilt. She could be a rebel on behalf of a good cause, but the rest of the time, well, yes, she did have a tendency to toe the line. Sam was a free spirit who often forgot to pay bills, turn off lights, was late for or forgot appointments.

He was conscientious about two things: paying his rent and playing his music.

"Back to those rules," he said. "Exactly which rule did you break?"

She could tell him. He was her best friend, more like a brother, and she trusted him. She needed to tell someone. The one thing he wouldn't do was judge her.

"One of my patients, a hit-and-run victim, gave me a letter. He asked me to give it to someone named Mitch Edwards and not tell the police."

He slammed on the brakes as a light turned red. From his face, she suspected he would have done it even without a light.

"He didn't say why?"

"He didn't have time. He lost consciousness. He's on life support now."

"When did you take the letter?"

"Two days ago."

"You haven't found this Edwards?"

"No. I haven't had much chance to look, but there's some mystery about the guy who gave me the letter. He doesn't seem to have much of a past. And then his brother showed up, and he doesn't seem to have one, either."

"Are you playing Sherlock?"

"No, I just wanted to do what he requested. He was dying. It gave him comfort."

"Why not give it to the police now?"

Why indeed?

Her stubborn streak? "It will mean a lot of messy explanations," she said. "I could lose my job. All I have to do is find Mitch Edwards."

"Want my advice?" he said. "Of course not," he answered himself. "But I think you should open it. See if it's anything important before sweating it."

"It was obviously meant for only one person. That would be invasion of privacy." It was what she had been telling herself over and over again, and she heard the lack of conviction in it.

"Do you think it had anything to do with the burglary?" he asked. "Or this purse snatching?"

"No," she said honestly. "There have been several burglaries in the neighborhood. Since one of us is usually home, we've just been careless about the alarm system." She paused. "And the cops said there's been a number of purse snatchings."

"I'll be careful from now on," he promised. "I'll write myself a note and paste it on the inside of the door."

"You'll still forget," she accused him.

He suddenly turned serious. "No, I won't."

He swung by a drive-through pharmacy, then stopped by a grocery and purchased a small frozen steak. "Better than a cold rag," he said. "I know."

She smiled at that. Sam was slight, but he was tough, having grown up in a rough neighborhood. Music had saved him then, and he often said Kirke had provided him with balance, a home he'd never had before. They were an odd couple, she knew, though there had never been a spark of romance, merely a satisfying need for uncomplicated companionship.

Her cheek was throbbing, and her eye hurt. A little while ago, she'd planned to continue her amateur investigation this afternoon, but she didn't think she could focus on it now.

Sam looked at her. "You'll do the right thing. You always do."

Not always. He didn't know the times she'd done exactly

the wrong thing. She hoped the letter would not be one of those times.

They arrived at her house, and he parked the car in front. Hers was in the small garage in back.

With new awareness, she looked around as she got out of the car.

Nothing suspicious.

She went inside Sam's half of the house and prepared for a scolding for her long absence. Instead, Merlin uttered a calm "Hello" from within his cage. "Merlin's a good bird."

Sam followed her. "After what you told me about Merlin scaring off a burglar, I think he deserves an extra treat."

"He's had several," she said, "but I promise to spoil him."

"You do that anyway," Sam retorted as he carried Merlin's cage into her house.

"Go and get some sleep," she said, knowing he had to be at the nightclub in a few hours.

He hesitated. "I can stay here, if you like."

"I'm fine, really I am. I'm going to take a hot, soaking bath and forget this morning. After," she added with emphasis, "turning on the alarm system and canceling my credit card and cell phone service."

"I'm leaving my cell phone with you," he said. "The club number is one. I'm programming 911 as two. I don't like you being without one."

The supreme sacrifice. He hated being without his phone.

"I have the land phones," she protested.

"I know, but with the burglary and now the purse snatching, I would feel better if you had a phone with you room to room."

He was not going to take no for an answer. She nodded, and he handed his phone to her, then left.

She sank in a chair. She wished she knew how to reach David Cable to thank him. She also wanted to ask him why he'd not returned to the hospital to see his brother and answer questions. Why he'd hurried off after saving her life.

The questions nagged at her.

There was definitely a call she *was* going to make. She was going to call a self-defense academy and take more lessons. Maybe even judo. No one was going to hit her again. Not without suffering some serious pain of their own.

# CHAPTER 9

Jake walked quickly to his car after he'd left her. He was stiff. His knee hurt where he'd landed on the sidewalk. He'd suffered superficial cuts, but, as he had told her, none were serious.

Walking away was a hard thing to do. He wanted to stay and wait with her. He wanted to make sure she was all right.

He shouldn't feel this sense of responsibility. She had accepted something from Cox. She had exchanged words with him. She had chosen, apparently, not to go to the police with them.

Yet his conscience wouldn't still. He should tell her what she'd stumbled into. She would probably run to the police, and he would go back to prison. If he were honorable, he would do that. He'd stopped being honorable when his rank and life had been stripped from him.

She'd been lucky this morning, and probably yesterday as well. He had little doubt that Adams had been in her house yesterday and was behind today's attack. Adams hadn't found anything in her house, thus he tried her purse.

If he hadn't followed her, she might well be dead.

The upside was she might trust him now.

Or not. His hurried departure from the scene must have aroused suspicion on her part.

*Tell her about Adams.* His moribund conscience told him that.

But if he did, she might dig into the whole story. And who would she believe? A convicted felon or the government? Damned few people believed him eight years ago, despite his eighteen years in the military, thirteen of them as an officer in Special Forces. He could count on the fingers of one hand those who had supported him. He'd become poison.

He'd thought hard last night about Gene Adams. He must have had help setting up the South American mission. Carrying five million in diamonds and cash didn't happen often. Jake had, in fact, opposed it. Too much could happen. His superiors had said the CIA was insistent. He suspected the agency had pushed his court-martial. It took the heat off them.

He wouldn't be surprised at one or more rogue agents in league with Adams. The question was how deep it reached.

How many men did Adams have helping here? So far he knew of two or three. Someone driving the murder car. Someone else waiting to pick up Adams after the hit-and-run. Then the purse snatcher today.

He drove to a minimarket, purchased some antiseptic and a roll of gauze and tape, then, ignoring the clerk's curious gaze, headed for the restroom. He took off his shirt and looked at the injury. Skin had been scraped away, but it wasn't deep. He used a paper towel to apply the antiseptic, then bandaged it to stanch the continued slow bleeding.

He looked at his face in the mirror. Damn but he needed a shave. His beard was dark and grew entirely too fast. It was one reason he was always selected for South American or Mideast missions. With his dark hair and dark eyes, he blended in with the population far better than, say, a blue-eyed blond of Celtic descent.

Yeah, he looked more like a bandit than a lawful citizen. And unfortunately, the government would confirm the former. *Traitor. Killer. Thief.*

Jake filled a large cup of coffee and ordered four ham and cheese biscuits to go. He pulled a fresh shirt from his duffel as well as an electric razor. Once in the car, he gobbled down the biscuits, then drove back to the parking space he'd vacated earlier. Thank God the street was lined with vehicles of all descriptions. He sure as hell didn't want to be obvious. It was a fine line to walk, trying to keep her safe without being labeled a stalker.

He intended to be here when she returned home.

Even now, he felt a warmth in his groin as he thought of that energy in the way she carried herself, the grin on her face as she explained the parrot's alarm system, hell, the way her jeans and T-shirt hugged a body not too thin to have very nice curves.

He even liked her house. Small but infinitely liveable with furniture bought for comfort, not show, and bookcases lined with obviously well-read novels, histories, and biographies. He'd glanced at her CD collection while she'd checked her computer. It had been an eclectic collection of jazz, classical, and Celtic music. On top were several Edith Piaf discs, one of his favorites as well.

He'd studied her house in the few moments he'd been there, wanting to know as much as he could about one Kirke Palmer. There had been no family photos, and he wondered about that.

Those observations would help him strategize on how best to earn her trust.

This morning may have helped. After spending the previous night in his car, he'd followed her at a distance. When he saw her go into a restaurant, he'd loitered with a newspaper across the street as if waiting for a bus. He'd noticed someone else loitering across the street nearer the restaurant. When the woman came out the door, the loiterer made his move, and Jake darted across the street. His heart nearly stopped when the thief pushed her into the busy street.

Did she have someone to bring her home? The Sam she'd mentioned yesterday? That thought raised an unexpected spark of jealousy in him.

He was nuts. Completely. She would run as fast as she

could from the likes of him. A convict. A convicted thief and possible traitor. God knew what else they would say about him if she made queries about Jake Kelly.

At the moment, he couldn't do anything but wait for her, then try to convince her she should just disappear for a while. After giving him the letter.

Or had the letter been in her purse? Had that been the purse snatcher's objective?

Three hours later, he saw a car turn into her driveway and stop. A lean man in his thirties stepped out and accompanied Ms. Palmer into her side of the duplex. He stayed a while, then went to the other side of the duplex.

Jake waited and watched for an hour. No more movement.

Finally he couldn't wait any longer. Reluctantly, he broke his own rule about the cell phone and called her. If he got inside, he could search for a bug and get another cell if necessary.

She mumbled when she answered, and he knew she'd already gone to sleep.

"I'm sorry," he said. "I hope I didn't wake you. This is David Cable. I just wanted to check on you."

"David Cable?" Surprise edged her words. "I thought you'd left Atlanta. Twice." She paused, and the silence was pregnant. Then she said, "When I was at the hospital, I asked about Mark Cable. They're really anxious to talk to you."

"I need to talk to you about that."

She hesitated.

"I won't stay long," he promised.

Another silence, then, "Okay. Where are you?"

"Not far."

Another silence.

"I was worried about you," he persisted.

"Like this morning? You were following me."

"Yes," he said simply.

"Why? How did you know I would be attacked?" Her voice was suspicious now.

He couldn't afford any more lies. "I didn't know. I just wanted to make sure you were safe."

He waited, not wanting to push her.

"Come on over." She hung up.

He left his car where it was and walked to her house. She was in an overlarge shirt and pair of shorts when she met him at the porch, unlatched the door, and let him inside. The shorts, he noticed immediately, revealed a pair of very nice, long legs.

She didn't turn toward her own front door but waited for him to speak. She had a cell phone in her hand.

She also had her neighbor next door.

She was no one's fool, but she lacked experience. She thought she was taking precautions, but one quick sweep of his arm, and the phone would go bouncing across the floor.

She was still too trusting.

He hated to disabuse her of that quality. It was appealing. It aroused something protective in him. He tried to push it away. It was an emotion he couldn't afford.

A white bandage covered part of her cheek. The area around her right eye was dark and bruised. Several bandages dotted her arms. Another emotion surfaced in him. Anger. White-hot anger at the man who hit her.

"Ouch," she said.

He raised an eyebrow.

"You didn't say I looked like hell—as Sam did—but your look said it all . . ."

"Looks are deceiving."

"Now, that's very true." She crossed her arms in front of her. "You're very much a puzzle, Mr. Cable."

"Can we go inside?" he said.

"Why?" Her body was tense as if ready for battle.

Unaccountably, he reached over and started to touch her. She shied away.

"I'm sorry," he said softly as he dropped his hand.

"Why?" she said, her hazel eyes searching his. "You didn't do anything. Just the opposite, I would say." She paused, then added quietly, "Or am I wrong about that?"

He met her gaze but didn't reply.

"You expected something to happen, didn't you?" she charged directly.

"I thought it could," he admitted.

"Why?"

He noticed her fingers clutched the cell. He thought about what he wanted to say. He hadn't expected such a direct approach.

"You were following me," she persisted. "You said you were leaving and . . ."

"I meant to leave. I'd planned to leave. I had a plane ticket. Then . . ."

"Then?" she prompted.

"I started worrying about you. I didn't think you took the burglary seriously enough. Whoever did it was careful not to disturb anything. He didn't want anyone to know he'd been there."

"Maybe he didn't have time."

"Maybe." He turned and looked down the street. He'd driven down it several times, looking for anyone, anything out of place. That he hadn't noticed anything didn't mean someone wasn't there, waiting for another chance.

"Who are you?" she asked suddenly. "Not David Cable, I think." Her right eye was nearly closed. She looked embattled, but there was a determined glint in her eyes.

"I do think we should go inside," he said again. He didn't like the fact that both of them were visible to the street, but there was a new wariness about her. As well there should be.

He saw emotions flicker across her face.

"Why?" she asked again.

"Talking in plain sight could be dangerous. For both of us."

She looked rebellious, then sighed. "I guess if you meant harm to me, you wouldn't have risked your life to save mine."

"No," he agreed softly.

She hesitated, then opened the door and went inside. One hand continued to clutch the cell phone as he followed.

"G'day," Merlin said with good cheer.

"Not a good day," Kirke muttered.

Well, she had a right to a certain surliness.

She turned back on Jake. "You lied to me," she charged. "I did some research last night. I'm not sure David Cable exists. Or Mark Cable, for that matter."

"They don't," he said quietly. "They never did."

He saw shock cross her face. Despite her statement, she hadn't really believed it. Then she asked, very quietly, "What do you want from me?"

Something caught in his chest. He might be an ax murderer for all she knew, and yet she stood her ground. There was a certain gallantry about her. She made her living saving lives and had probably encountered horrific situations, but now she was alone.

He had no choice now but to present his case and hope to hell she believed him. "I think you have something meant for me."

"I'm not sure what you mean," she said, but something flickered in her eyes, and he knew that she understood exactly what he meant.

"I was at the accident scene," he admitted. "I was to meet the man you know as Mark Cable. He arranged the meeting. I saw him give you something, talk to you."

"The man I know as Mark Cable?" she asked. "That's not his name?"

"That might be one of his names. I knew him as a CIA agent named Del Cox. But that was an alias as well."

She stared at him, her gaze steady but insistent.

"You're not his brother?"

"No."

"Then why . . ."

"I was to meet him at Manuel's. I saw him get hit by the car, and I saw him give something to you."

"And you didn't come forward to help him."

"No," he admitted.

"Why? Why didn't you talk to the police then? Or this morning?"

He hesitated. *Hell, in for a penny, in for a pound.* If he didn't get that letter, he might well be in prison for many more years, anyway.

"I'm not supposed to be here," he said quietly. "If the authorities found out, I could—would—be sent back to prison."

She looked startled then. Her hand clutched the cell phone even harder. "I think you should explain that."

"It's better you don't know."

"The hell with that," she retorted with outrage. "That's crap. I've never agreed with that dumb statement in books, and I don't now. Someone almost killed me this morning, so I don't know why it would be better that I don't know who or why." She lifted her hand with the cell phone. "If you don't tell me who you are now, I'll call the police. I don't care if you did save my life," she added defiantly. "In fact, maybe you planned the whole thing this morning."

He was making a mess of the situation, and it was obvious she was beginning to realize she might be in something far deeper than she'd previously thought.

"My name is Jake Kelly," he said. It was a hell of a risk, but other than torturing her to tell him the whereabouts of the letter, truth seemed the only option. "I was a captain in the army. More specifically in Special Services." He paused, then added, "I was convicted by a court-martial of stealing government property," he said.

"And you're innocent?" Her voice was noncommittal.

"Would you believe me if I said yes?"

"I would be more likely to believe you if you'd told me earlier."

"I thought you would go to the police."

"And why shouldn't I now?"

"You probably should," he admitted. "You shouldn't trust anyone."

Her eyes searched his. She wanted to trust him. He saw it in her eyes.

"Why?" she asked.

So many whys. She wouldn't stop until she knew the whole story, or as much as he knew. This was his one and only chance to regain her trust. "I don't know everything," he said. "All I can do is guess at some things."

She waited intently. "Then guess," she demanded.

God, he wanted to reach over and touch her. That earnest look on her face as she tried to understand the inexplicable touched him to the core.

"I'll tell you what I can. Seven years ago I led a five-man mission into South America that went bad. We were ambushed, and I was injured. I thought the others were dead. I know two were. The other two were missing, presumed dead. Also missing was a great deal of government property, and I was accused of stealing it. I didn't. Now people I thought dead have come back to life. I don't know how, but I'm sure as hell going to find out."

"Mark Cable was one of the two?"

He nodded.

"If he was Del Cox then, who were you?" she asked suddenly.

He hesitated, then said, "Mitch Edwards."

# CHAPTER 10

*Mitch Edwards.*

Kirke didn't know what she expected, but that wasn't it.

Mitch Edwards, the man she'd been asked to find.

But the man in front of her had lied to her before, and she didn't trust him now.

She tried not to show that the name meant anything, but she'd never been a good liar. Nor had she wanted to be. She wondered now how wise she'd been to invite him inside. All she'd considered was the fact that he'd saved her life earlier.

Now she knew there was much more involved. He had been at the hit-and-run scene. He had not stepped forward. He had pretended to be the brother of a man near death.

She knew she should tell him to leave, not that he had to obey her. He was bigger than she was. Much bigger. And she'd allowed him into her house. She should punch that 911 key on Sam's cell. She could yell for Sam, but Jake Kelly might well be dangerous to him, as well as to herself.

Something in those dark eyes stopped her from doing either of those things. A plea. Desperation. He was *willing* her to believe.

*No police. Swear.* A dead man's words. And now this man, this stranger who had saved her life, was talking CIA and secret missions and people returning to life. Dammit, *what* was she involved in?

If even a little of what he said was true, she *should* be heading for the nearest police station. Someone had been murdered on an Atlanta street. Her apartment had been searched. She'd been thrown into a street to die.

It staggered her that she was not halfway to the station, that she was standing here, listening.

Mitch Edwards. The name had been like an explosion in her head.

She wanted a drink. Something stronger than the one glass of wine that was usually the limit of her alcohol intake.

*Not a good idea,* she told herself as he tore his gaze away from her. She watched as he moved away and started pacing the room like a caged panther. He was giving her time to digest what had been said. Would a murderer do that?

*Tell him to leave,* she warned herself. *Scream if he doesn't.* All she had to do was punch one button.

Yet something about him kept her finger from pushing down on it. Maybe the electricity that flashed between them yesterday and lingered today. Now it flared again as she studied him from the advantage of new information. Had he gotten that scar on his forehead in the jungle? Had the lines in his face come from years in a cell? Were the guarded eyes the result of years in Special Forces? Or prison?

She only knew there was a physical awareness between them, one that rocked her to her core. The bad boy attraction? She prayed not.

Whatever it was, she felt it in the heat that pooled in her stomach, in the way she'd wanted him to touch her cheek before she'd shied away minutes earlier.

But she hated lies. She hated them more than anything in the world. Her ex had lied to her. Her mother had lied to her, repeatedly returning to drugs before disappearing forever.

She realized now how much she'd been caught in the mystery of the hit-and-run victim. It had woven a sticky web around her that now made escape impossible. She'd withheld information that she'd known the police wanted and needed, and if this man was a fugitive, she was probably guilty of obstruction of justice.

She realized he'd stopped pacing and was looking directly at her. He had given her a few moments to think, and now his eyes were asking questions.

Dear God, those eyes were piercing. They held her as much a captive as bars could. She should run like hell. Instead, she lingered here, listening to a convicted thief and possible murderer.

Were her instincts corrupted by the almost hypnotic attraction she felt so strongly, the odd sense of safety and protection she'd felt yesterday and again this morning when he'd used his body to shield hers?

The awareness between them grew as the silence deepened. He was forcing himself to look relaxed, but his muscles were knotted in his forearms, and she saw a muscle in his cheek move.

*He* was Mitch Edwards.

*Maybe.*

~

The name Mitch Edwards meant something to her.

He saw it in her eyes. They flickered for a second, then she turned as if to hide a reaction.

"You've heard the name," he said.

She didn't answer that question. Instead, she asked one of her own. "How many names do you have? Now I count three. How many more?"

"Not so many," he said.

"How did you get identification for David Cable?"

"It's not that difficult."

"That's not an answer."

"No," he agreed and didn't elaborate.

"Does . . . does the man in the hospital have family?"

"Not that I know of," he replied.

"How well did you know him?"

She should have been a detective.

"Not very well. We were on one assignment together. We

trained a month for that mission. Never saw him before then."

"And he was a friend?"

"No. We were army. He was civilian. There was some friction."

Her eyes narrowed again. "You said he was CIA?"

"Yes."

"If you weren't friends, then why . . . ?" She stopped herself, and he knew then Del had said something important to her.

But she did not trust him enough to tell him.

With good reason. But he wanted her to, and for more reasons than one. God, but he liked her spirit. She'd just been bashed in the face and was questioning him as thoroughly as any military CID investigator. She hadn't flinched—much—when he'd admitted to being in prison.

Unfortunately, she might be a little too gutsy. She was taking everything far too calmly. Or was she?

Damn, but he felt a persistent urge to lean down and kiss her. And an even stronger one to hold her, to keep her from harm, but also to bury himself in the warmth he sensed was there.

But she'd backed away slightly. "You say you're Mitch Edwards, but you don't have any identification. If you had it, I wouldn't know whether it was another fake or not."

He felt a smile tug at his lips. It had been a long time since he'd last smiled, but she had a way of getting to the heart of things. "I'm not Mitch Edwards," he said. "Not any longer."

"You said you watched last night because you were worried about me?" she persisted. "Why?"

"Cox said something to you. And gave you something. I saw it, and I think someone else saw it, too. That someone might think you know something you shouldn't."

"Who was the someone else?"

He shrugged. "One of those people I thought dead. There's been plastic surgery, but I'm almost sure. There are certain mannerisms you can't always lose . . ."

Her face gave nothing away.

"He's dangerous, Ms. Palmer."

She regarded him steadily. She didn't scare easily, and that scared him.

"You haven't really told me anything except there was some mysterious mission and you've been in prison. That doesn't exactly instill trust."

"Would it help if I told you I wasn't guilty?"

"Doesn't every person in prison say he or she isn't guilty?"

"I can attest to that," he said with a touch of black humor.

A spark of appreciation flickered in her eyes, but she didn't smile.

He hesitated. "What did Del Cox tell you?"

"He was too badly injured to tell me anything."

"He handed something to you."

Her eyes met his directly. She didn't flinch. "I think it's time for you to tell me more. What kind of mission was this?"

"It's classified."

She raised a disbelieving eyebrow.

"I've been convicted of one crime. I sure as hell don't want to be convicted of another."

"If you were tried, it must be public record."

"Try to get it."

"I'll do that."

She'd moved a few inches toward him, and he smelled the antiseptic lingering on her. Her eyes shot sparks at him. She was angry. She had every right to be, but there was something else in her eyes.

He touched the right side of her face. To his surprise, she didn't flinch this time. Despite what she'd said about trust, she *wanted* to trust him. Or else she would be shouting for help at this very moment. She wouldn't linger with someone she thought was a murderer.

But neither was she ready to give him whatever Cox had given her. He wouldn't have either, after hearing that half story. He'd left too much unsaid.

"Whatever he had," he said suddenly, "may clear me. I can't think why else he wanted to meet me."

She stepped back from his touch as if burned.

Just then a knock came at the door.

She looked outside. Opened the door.

The wiry man who'd brought her home stepped inside. Curious eyes looked him over, then he stuck out his hand. "I'm Sam Pierce, Kirke's neighbor and friend." He emphasized the last word.

"Jake Kelly," Jake said.

"*And* David Cable," Kirke added. "He's the man who saved my life this morning."

The newcomer's eyes went from Kirke back to Jake.

"Sam should know," she said simply. "He lives here, too."

"Is he bothering you?" Sam Pierce said, drawing up his thin form. The top of his head came to Jake's chin, but there was no lack of determination in him. Although Sam was obviously no match for Jake, he was ready to do battle for his neighbor.

"No," Kirke said. "We were just . . . exchanging information."

Sam's eyes went to the cell phone still clutched in her hands.

"He was just leaving," Kirke continued. She turned back to Jake. "I'll call you if you leave me a number."

He jotted down his cell number and gave it to her. Now three people had it. "I have to leave soon," he said, trying to keep his disappointment from showing.

She nodded. "You don't need to sit outside tonight," she said. "We have a good security system, and now I'll turn it on. And we have Merlin, of course."

He had no choice then but to leave. Staying would only push her, maybe, to call the police.

She needed time to think. He had to give her that time, though he suspected she would immediately check what he'd told her and thereby could possibly lead marshals to him.

He could only hope she would decide to give him whatever Del had given her before the government found him. Or Adams reached her.

Sam followed him out to the porch. Jake was aware his gaze stayed with him until he reached his car and drove off.

◄━

Sam returned to Kirke's apartment. "You should be in bed," he said.

She looked at the clock. Ten. "You should be at work."

"I'm not on until ten thirty."

Affection flooded her. He'd been ready to be pulverized for her sake. And she had no doubt that would have been the result of any contest between the two.

"I don't think you should be alone here."

"I have Merlin."

"I don't think Merlin would be all that effective against determined bad guys."

"I don't think he's a bad guy."

"Neither did the Boston Strangler's victims think he was a bad guy."

"It's time to see what's in the envelope," she said, ignoring his observation.

"Past time," Sam said.

She went back inside her house and straight to Merlin's cage. She'd already released him, and he perched on top of the cage. "Merlin wants a cracker."

"Merlin always wants a cracker. Merlin will have to wait a moment."

She lifted the newspaper sheets in his cage until she found the envelope. She held it a moment. It had no name on it. But it did belong to someone else. She tried to inch the flap open. It was well glued shut.

"Should I steam it?"

"Just open it, Kirke," Sam said.

She did. The anticipation had been building since it was first placed in her hands. She didn't know what to expect.

Definitely not what was there.

# CHAPTER 11

One sheet of paper. No words on it. Only numbers. Seven numbers: 4481999.

Nothing more. No spaces. No hyphens.

She silently handed it to Sam.

He grabbed it, then a puzzled look settled on his face. "What in the hell . . . ?"

"A phone number?" she ventured.

"No area code."

"Maybe a secret bank account?"

"Beats me," he said. "I have enough trouble keeping a few dollars in my ordinary one."

Disappointment rose in her. She'd thought—hoped—the letter would solve some of the mysteries around the man who'd carried it and the one who wanted it.

She turned it over. The back of the page was blank. Her heart sank. The heaviness in her chest felt like a millstone. She'd truly thought she might solve the problem of what to do with it when she opened the envelope.

"I can't believe I worried so much," she said. "I doubt it

would have helped the police much." She stared at it again. "The last part is 1999. The year maybe?"

"And the rest of it?" Sam asked.

She searched her mind for an answer. "Safe-deposit box? Post office box? Foreign bank account number?"

Sam shrugged. "I sure as hell wouldn't know about foreign bank accounts. Do they have seven numbers?"

"I don't know any more than you. But I rather think it's something else. A locker, maybe."

She turned back to Sam. "I told you the guy who was just here called himself both David Cable and Jake Kelly. He also said he's Mitch Edwards." She didn't add that he'd said he'd been in prison, because Sam would pressure her to go to the police if he didn't do it himself. She wasn't quite ready for that.

Sam's brows drew together. "So that's why you didn't give him the envelope."

She shrugged. "I don't know what to think. I'm dizzy from the number of names he has, or says he has. Normal people have one. And he lied to me the first time we met. He's lied several times, in fact."

"But you're thinking about giving it to him."

She glanced down at the paper again. "I couldn't give it to him without knowing what was inside. Maybe it was evidence of a crime. Now . . . I don't know. The numbers are probably important to only one person, and that's the person it was meant for, but I'm going to do a little checking first."

"Maybe you should make a call to one of your cop friends."

"He said he was risking his freedom being here."

"Then maybe he shouldn't be here," he retorted. "In the meantime you should get some rest, and I'm going to get you that steak in my fridge."

"Does it really work?" she asked.

"I've had a few black eyes in my life, and yes, it really does help." He paused, then said, "I have to go, but I'll be back right after we finish tonight. If you feel safe enough."

She nodded. "I'll make sure the alarm system is on, and I have your cell."

"I'll leave my gun with you."

She flinched. She knew he had a permit and carried a gun because he worked so late. He'd been robbed one time after a gig. He'd also insisted that she take lessons. She had, but she hadn't liked it, and she'd never gotten a permit. She saw too much evidence of what a gun could do to flesh and bone.

"Either that or I stay," he said.

"Okay."

"And use the steak on your eye."

"Okay. Now go. You shouldn't be late."

Before he could leave, though, her phone rang.

She answered, and it was her captain. Her heart sank.

"Can you fill in for Larry Greene tomorrow morning?" he asked. "His baby's back in the hospital."

She hurt. Her eye ached, and so did several other parts of her. But she would feel just as bad if she stayed home tomorrow. "Of course," she said, not mentioning her injuries. They all were concerned about Larry and his wife. The baby was born prematurely and had repeated lung problems.

"It may be only half a day," the captain said.

"Okay."

Sam's eyes questioned her.

"They need me to work tomorrow. Larry Greene's baby is back in the hospital."

"You're the world's biggest softy," Sam said. "You should have told him about the mugging."

"I'm just a little sore. Larry would do it for me."

Sam knew Larry. Kirke had several parties at her house for her fellow paramedics and their families. "I still think you need some rest," he groused.

She grinned at him. "I'll get some right now."

"Is that a hint?"

"Yes."

"Okay," he said reluctantly and headed for the door. "Keep that cell phone next to you."

She nodded. After he left, she turned on the alarm, then tucked the page with the numbers back in Merlin's cage. Though she'd memorized them, the message was proof.

What did they mean?

And should she hand them over to the man of many names?

Satisfied that she'd found a safe place for the letter, she sat down in her big overstuffed reading chair and held the steak to her eye.

She wanted to be alone. She wanted to puzzle out those unwanted feelings she'd experienced when David Cable, or Jake Kelly, or Mitch Edwards, or whoever he was, sat close to her. She wanted to think about that calm demeanor that implied everything was normal when, in reality, everything was upside down.

She had no idea what she was dealing with. Ordinary people didn't run around with multiple names. Nor did they exude barely contained anger. There was a tautness about him, an aura of danger that both repelled and attracted her. The strangest thing, though, was the lack of fear she felt in his presence. She wondered whether it was same calm felt by victims just before a cobra struck.

And now he claimed there was someone else out there. Someone who had seen the exchange between Mark Cable and herself. Someone dangerous. More dangerous than him?

Or had it been a ploy to get her to turn the envelope over to him?

She'd never thought she could be attracted to evil. But she'd always been drawn to the underdog.

Villain or victim? She wished she knew.

She simply had no idea what she was dealing with. She only wished she hadn't felt that strong empathy with the stranger. Empathize, hell. *Be honest.* She'd wanted to move closer to him, to feel his lips. Even now she wondered what it would be like to feel his body against hers.

She'd never felt that way before. Not so quickly. Not even with her ex. And certainly she hadn't felt that kind of desire since the divorce. She'd thought herself cured forever.

She curbed her impatience several more moments, then took the steak away from her eye and went to her computer. She Googled Jake Kelly. She'd hit a dead end with Mitch Edwards. Maybe she would have more luck with Jake Kelly.

She typed in military. Then Special Forces. Army. Finally court-martial. Nothing. Not one likely hit.

From working on a newspaper, she knew military records were private. It was like pulling teeth to obtain any information about a soldier unless the army wanted to say nice things about him or her.

But surely a legal action, a court-martial would be public record. Doubts started to nag her. She turned to prisons. She came up with exactly nothing but a headache. After her shift tomorrow, she would call public information at Special Services headquarters. She knew how to ask questions. Maybe she would get something. Or find someone who knew Jake Kelly.

"Be on a plane this afternoon," Ames told the purse snatcher. "Ditch the car and take the next plane home," he said. "I have enough men on the way to do what's needed."

The purse snatcher nodded.

Ames hoped he was a step ahead of Jake. That thought died when the man who'd taken Kirke's purse gave a very thorough description of the person who'd saved the bitch.

Kelly had been able to get to her when he had not. Dammit, he'd missed his chance two nights earlier when he'd barely escaped from her house when he heard a police siren. He'd gotten through the window and hadn't risked hanging around.

Ames had taken a real chance by going into her house alone, but then she was only a woman. And although he paid his employees very well, he wouldn't trust them with whatever was in the envelope he'd seen passed. He'd not been far away during the purse snatch, close enough to monitor the snatcher and see that he followed instructions. Look for a letter. Leave a tiny GPS device in the purse lining.

His mercenaries knew little about him, only that he was a very wealthy Argentinean of European descent. He spoke flawless Spanish and German, and Argentina had no extradition treaty with the United States. But despite plastic surgery and lift shoes, he was taking a terrible chance even being here.

Of course, whatever the woman had been told—or given—could be nothing at all. Or it could provide proof that Gene Adams—his cover name on the mission—was still alive.

Ames still had a friend in the CIA. Well, not a friend. But someone who had taken enough money from him to live in fear. If Ames was ever caught, he would go down as well.

Ames had always been very good at spotting weak points in people. Unfortunately, Jake Kelly's only weak spot had been honor. Within ten seconds of meeting the tight-assed Special Services captain, Ames knew Kelly wouldn't go along with the scheme that Ames had plotted for years.

Kelly was a dangerous adversary. When the mission was formed, he'd tried to have Jake Kelly removed from the team, but Kelly had supporters in the Special Forces, and the mission belonged to them.

He could have taken out Kelly several times in the past few days, but a violent death might lead someone to reopen the investigation. Even an accident might lead to some troublesome questions.

Then he had a thought. If Kelly was accused of murder, then no one would believe a word he said. He was already thought by many to have killed four men. He would be considered armed and dangerous.

And Kirke Palmer was the perfect victim.

# CHAPTER 12

Kirke felt hungover when she arrived at the station. She'd had only a few hours' sleep, and her head ached. The cut also hurt when she smiled or frowned.

And she faced the teasing of the firefighting gang.

"Okay, who did it?" clamored one.

"The infamous door?" asked the other.

"I was mugged," she admitted sheepishly.

"I thought we taught you better than that."

"You did," she said. "It was just . . . so sudden."

The captain took a look at her face. "Why didn't you tell me?"

She shrugged. "I wouldn't feel any better at home."

"I could have gotten someone else," he said.

"It just aches a little."

"Did the scumbag get anything?"

"A credit card and cell phone. My driver's license was in a different pocket, and the guy missed that."

"You sure you can go out?" her captain asked.

She nodded.

"You'll ride with a rookie," he warned, "but Tom said he would try to get back before noon."

Her new partner looked as if he had just graduated from junior high. "I'm Ben Wright," he said.

She resisted the impulse to ask him why he wasn't in school today. "Kirke Palmer," she said curtly. Darn if she didn't already feel a hundred years old.

She'd wanted to call Robin last night, but too much had happened, then it was too late. She intended to do it today. There were just too many questions.

She'd been a fool to get involved. But now she was committed to seeing it through. She'd waited too long to suddenly say to the captain, to the police, "Oops, I forgot something."

She was checking the supplies when her captain called her to his office.

There she saw a man in a dark business suit, white shirt, and dark blue tie. He was of medium height, and his face was unremarkable.

He pulled out a leather case. "Special Agent John Davis, FBI," he said.

She looked at it closely. She'd seen her share of badges. It looked legit.

"What can I do for you?"

"I understand you tended to a hit-and-run driver two days ago," he said.

Her worst nightmare. She nodded. "I did."

"Did he say anything?"

Lying to an FBI agent was a crime.

*No police.* Mark Cable's words—she still thought of him as Mark Cable—echoed in her head. Just as those of Jake Kelly last night. He could go back to prison.

He'd saved her life at the risk of his own.

"Nothing that made any sense," she said.

"Could you be more specific?"

She studied him. Light brown hair. Brown eyes. Middle height. Relaxed. Maybe too relaxed. Why didn't he have a partner? In the movies, they always had partners.

"He said something about military," she said. "He was in

a great deal of pain, and I couldn't make out some of the words."

"Nothing else?" he persisted.

"Are you from the Atlanta office?" she asked suddenly.

He looked startled.

"I know some of the guys there," she continued. "Maybe we know some of the same agents."

"If you can answer—"

"Why is the FBI interested?"

"We suspect he was one of two men who stole over five million dollars, some of it in diamonds," he said. "They've never been found. The other one was just released from prison. He's dangerous, and he'll do anything to get to the diamonds."

"Then why was he released?" she asked.

Just then her partner came into the room. "We have a call."

"If there's nothing else, I have to go," she said. "Tell John Coleman I said hello." She gauged his reaction, then left before he could stop her.

The fact that he didn't even try struck her as suspicious. John Coleman was the agent in charge. She'd met him at Robin's wedding. This man should have recognized the name, had some reaction. Or maybe he was just an emotionless fed.

She followed Ben Wright out to the truck. "What's the call?"

"A nursing home. Sounds like cardiac arrest."

As senior on the ambulance, she decided she would drive. The junior high school kid shouldn't even have a driver's license.

When they arrived, a nurse met them. "He was eating dinner and started having pain in his chest. We gave him aspirin, but his heart stopped. We've been giving him CPR." She led them to where another nurse was administering CPR.

Ben Wright looked at her.

She nodded for him to take over, and he did so, smoothly and competently. A heartbeat, then another.

She got the oxygen out and put a mask over the man's face. Probably in his nineties. His skin was ashen.

She got the personal information, since Ben was occupied. In four minutes, they were wheeling him out.

She did the paperwork at the hospital, then told him he'd done a great job.

He turned red and gave her a huge grin. "It's my fourth week," he admitted.

"I wouldn't have known," she assured him. "You acted like a veteran."

Another man down call. Located in a gang-infested area she didn't like. It was also an area with a lot of bars and homeless people.

"You drive," she said.

The kid nodded. "I passed, huh?"

She smiled back. He would do.

She called the dispatcher and asked for more information.

"Anonymous call," the dispatcher said. "A report that a man is lying in an alleyway off Battle and Line Street.

"Probably nothing," Kirke said to Ben as they sped toward the address and arrived within a few moments.

She grabbed her bag as he parked. No one was in sight. No crowd gathered around a fallen man.

She headed for an alley that ran between two buildings, then stumbled on a piece of loose pavement. As she tried to regain her balance, she felt a rush of flame on her left arm. She didn't stop moving. She caught her balance and dashed into the protection of the alley just as a piece of brick separated from the wall.

She dived behind a Dumpster. Her partner was right behind her. "Get down," she yelled as he joined her next to the wall and flung his body beside her.

Another object—hell, not an object, a bullet—hit the side of the Dumpster. Sniper. Must have a silencer, since she hadn't heard a noise other than the impact of a bullet against the wall, then the Dumpster.

She crouched against the wall and told her partner to do the same. She used her radio to call the dispatcher. "We're under fire. Sniper. We need police." She gave them the location and kept the line open.

Her partner leaned over and gently pulled her uniform shirt from her. She winced as he touched her. The kid didn't look as scared as she felt. She decided he would very much do.

"It's just a graze. Going to hurt like the devil but no real damage," he said as he placed gauze on both the entry and exit wounds. He wrapped a roll of bandage around her shoulder and chest, all the time keeping low.

It might have missed the bone, but it was beginning to burn. She knew from training and experience that shock was a temporary anesthesia, and now she was learning how temporary.

At least there were no more shots. She moved slightly to look across the street where the shooter must be. It looked like an abandoned three-story hotel.

She ducked immediately, as something hit the wall across from her.

Ben slumped to the pavement. Had to be a ricochet. She leaned over him. He looked surprised. Blood oozed from his mouth, and she saw the wound in his chest.

*Where are the police?*

"It'll be okay, Ben," she said, leaning over him. Ignoring the burning pain in her arm, she unbuttoned his shirt and pulled up a T-shirt that had turned red. She saw immediately there was a hole in the thoracic wall. She packed it and sealed it off, then wrapped the chest. Then she called the dispatcher again and asked for another ambulance.

She heard one siren, then two. Squad cars screamed up to the ambulance she and Ben had left. An officer got out of one and yelled to her. She pointed up at the building across from them as she shrugged her shirt back on and managed to fasten one button.

Three other officers sprinted out of their cars and took up positions behind their cars, as the first darted over to her. "Ma'am," he acknowledged as he knelt next to Ben. "How bad?"

"Chest wound. We need to get him to the hospital, fast. I've called for an ambulance. I can't drive mine and care for him at the same time."

"We'll check out the building across the street. Whoever it was probably ran when he heard the sirens." He hesitated, then said, "I can drive the ambulance, and you can ride in back with him. My partner can stay with the other guys and look around." Then he saw the bandage around her arm. "You okay?"

"Just superficial. I tripped just at the right moment. Being clumsy has its advantages. My partner wasn't so lucky. This is his fourth week on the job," she said senselessly.

"He looks young."

"He's good."

The kid opened his eyes then. "Real . . . good," he said.

"Darn straight," she agreed.

She knelt next to him and looked in his billfold for an address.

"My wife . . . Dena . . . expecting a baby."

"I'll call her, tell her you're going to be fine."

When she looked up for the cop, he was talking to someone at the car. Then a third car appeared, and a fourth.

The cop and another officer unloaded the stretcher from Kirke's ambulance and moved over to her. She helped them transfer Ben. Then she followed them to the ambulance.

She sat next to him and started an IV. He'd lost a lot of blood.

She knew she'd been the target. She didn't doubt that a moment. Ben had been hit trying to help her.

She no longer wondered about coincidences. There was no *random* burglary. No *random* purse snatching.

Someone wanted what she had.

And now others were being hurt because of it.

Anger and fear balled up inside her, numbing the burning in her shoulder.

Jake Kelly, if that was his real name, was the man who'd always appeared immediately after any incident. He'd told her a little, but not nearly enough.

And her young partner was a casualty of that reticence.

Jake Kelly would tell her what she wanted to know.

Or, career loss or not, she was going to the police.

—◆—

The gun was a piece of junk.

Jake looked at it and shook his head. "No deal."

The street dealer looked at him with new respect. "Hey, man, I got this other one, too." He motioned to a kid down the street.

The kid came running, a paper bag in his hand.

Jake opened it. A .38 Smith & Wesson. Lighter than he liked. He took it out. Good balance. Clean. He noticed the serial number had been filed away.

"Is it hot?" Stupid question, he realized even as he uttered it. Of course it was hot, or it wouldn't be sold on a corner.

"Find one that ain't," the dealer said. "Wanna clean one, go to the store."

But Jake couldn't do that, and the dealer knew it. Why else would he have found this street corner in one of the most dangerous neighborhoods in Atlanta?

It hadn't taken Jake long to find it. He hadn't shaved this morning, and he had located a too-tight shirt, old jeans, and some good but worn boots at a thrift shop. He looked like a man desperate for a gun. A few bars in run-down areas, a few conversations, a lot of money. It took him less than an hour to locate a seller.

The gun fitted his hand well. "How much?"

The dealer's eyes had a new wariness as he'd watched him check out the gun.

"Four hundred," he said.

"Two fifty," Jake countered. "With ammo."

"What do ya think I am? A Wal-Mart?" His eyes narrowed. "You a cop? You got a wire?"

"Hell no. Just got out of the joint." He held out his arms. "Check if you want."

The dealer studied him for a moment, then shrugged. "Never mind. Don't look like no cop. Last offer, three hundred. You get the ammo on your own. Otherwise I split, man."

It was highway robbery but less than he expected. The man was spooked.

Jake took out his wallet and counted out three hundred dollars. He made sure the man saw he just had a few dollars more. He didn't want to be mugged on his way back to the car.

Next stop would be for ammunition. Far easier since he didn't need a permit for that.

He had another stop as well. An electronics shop. Then some fresh clothes. Nothing fancy. Just some clean jeans and a few shirts.

He had plenty of time to get back to the fire station before Kirke's quitting time. Until then, he was counting on the police, firemen, and paramedics to look after their own.

He hadn't wanted to push any more than he had last night. He feared he'd done as much as he could without sending her into the arms of the police.

Jake found what he was looking for in a upscale electronics store. He purchased a miniaturized GPS unit, along with a listening device. No questions asked. He paid for it with one of the prepaid credit cards he'd purchased before leaving Chicago. Not knowing what to expect, he'd taken five thousand in cash with him, and another fifteen thousand in prepaid credit cards that couldn't be traced to him. Getting his hands on more would be difficult.

One more stop, and he would head for the fire station. Hopefully, he could place the GPS unit on her car without anyone noticing.

Stuck in traffic, he turned on the radio, searching for news.

He found only music and decided to turn it off. He must be getting old. He didn't understand what passed for music these days. But just as he reached to turn it off, the music dissolved into a "breaking news" bulletin.

"Two paramedics have been shot by a sniper in East Atlanta. Police say the two—a man and woman—have been transported to East Memorial Hospital."

Jake froze for a moment, waiting to hear more. Nothing. Only more ear-splitting music. He frantically turned the dial. Again nothing.

He took small comfort in the fact that the radio reported they were both transported to a hospital. That meant they were—or had been—alive. His gut told him one of the paramedics was Kirke Palmer. God, she'd already been hurt enough just for trying to do something for a dying man. Good deeds were a rarity in his life and profession. He was more used to mendacity than generosity.

Icy fingers ran down his spine. What if she died because of him? If he'd not appealed to her, maybe she would have gone to the police.

He honked at the car ahead. The light had turned green, and the idiot just sat there.

If someone in the government, men who'd once been his friends, realized Del Cox had been alive all these years, they would start searching into where he'd been these years. There would be a money trail. No one had looked until now because he was presumed dead, killed by one Jake Kelly.

So far he still didn't have proof. Not without fingerprints, which, apparently, someone removed from the files. Otherwise, the authorities would know by now the hit-and-run victim was not a man named Mark Cable. He needed Gene Adams.

He couldn't go into the hospital. He'd made that impossible. The moment he showed his face, police would probably be called, and security officials would swarm him.

Jake stopped when he saw a gas station with a public phone. He needed a phone book. He didn't know Atlanta well enough to know the media. And he was still reluctant to use his cell phone unless it was absolutely necessary.

He started with the first television station listed in the book and went to others. No one knew more than the brief announcement. Then he looked up Sam's number and called.

"H'lo," Sam said sleepily.

"This is Jake." He paused and added, "From yesterday."

"I remember," Sam said in a cool monotone. It was obvious he didn't approve.

"You haven't heard?"

"Heard what?"

"Two paramedics were shot earlier today. I suspect one of them was Kirke."

"Say what?" All the sleepiness was gone from his voice. These words were snapped out.

"I don't know for sure, but the radio just issued a bulletin about two paramedics shot in the area she works. They've gone to Memorial East Hospital. I can't make queries on my own, but you can."

"I'm on it," Sam said.

"Will you call me?"

A hesitation.

"I care about her," Jake said, knowing as he said the words that he did, and not just because he wanted what she had. He gave Sam the cell number.

"I'm not making any promises," came the curt reply.

He wanted more. A lot more. He didn't know what to say to gain the musician's confidence. Warning him probably wouldn't help but he had to do it.

"She could be in even more danger," he said before Sam hung up.

"Because of you?" The words were antagonistic, and Jake suddenly wondered whether the relationship between Kirke and Sam was platonic or went deeper.

"Maybe," he said honestly.

There was a pause. "I'll be in touch." Sam hung up.

# CHAPTER 13

Jake headed for the hospital. He couldn't go in, but he could look around outside. He could try to find out something from reporters who would be covering the story.

Gene Adams might be there as well.

Jake touched the gun in the bag beside him. He resisted the impulse to speed. Not with a gun in the car. *Let her be all right. Damn it all, don't let someone else die because of me.* Two of his men had died under his leadership. Two men who were owed some justice.

It took him ten minutes to find a parking place at the hospital, then he hurried to the emergency entrance. As he figured, there was a gaggle of print and electronic press outside. The sniper attempt on paramedics was big news. It was an attack on everyone who needed help, reminiscent of a war zone, not an American city.

He didn't see Sam. He went up to one of the reporters. "What's the word?"

The reporter was concentrating on the door, apparently waiting for a hospital spokesman to come out.

"A paramedic said one's critical, one's not." The newsman took a look at his clothes and raised an eyebrow. Then turned away from him.

*One's critical. One's not.*

He took a deep breath as a hard fist of fear tightened in his stomach. He'd hadn't realized how important she had become to him, not only because of what she could do for him but for that intriguing, defiant spirit of hers.

He saw Sam hurrying through the door.

Several minutes later, a spokesman, apparently from the hospital, came out along with someone from the fire department.

"We have two patients from the sniper attack," the spokesman said. "EMT Ben Wright sustained a gunshot wound to the chest and is in critical condition. Paramedic Kirke Palmer has been treated and is being released."

The fire department official then stepped up to the microphones. "At 1:45 p.m. today, we received a call of a man down at Battle and Line Streets. When Paramedic Palmer and EMT Wright arrived, they were fired upon. Paramedic Palmer was struck in the arm. EMT Wright was hit in the chest and is undergoing surgery. That's all we have right now."

Reporters started firing questions.

"Do you think the sniper was aiming at a specific person or just at the fire department?"

"I can't answer that," the official said.

"How long have they been with the fire department?"

"Paramedic Kirke Palmer has been with us four years. EMT Ben Wright has been with us a month."

"Has anything like this happened before?"

"Not to my knowledge."

The questions went on, and the answers were short and mostly unhelpful.

Jake breathed again. She was being released. That meant there was nothing seriously wrong.

If she had any sense now, she would tell the police everything. About the envelope, the dying words, about one Jake Kelly.

Somehow he didn't think she would. Not yet. His gut was telling him that, but then his gut had been wrong before.

He backed away. She wouldn't come through here. She would avoid the news media.

He left the covey of newspeople, went to the public parking lot where he had parked, and searched for Sam's car. It was easily recognized because of its color and sheets of music lying beside the driver's seat.

The musician had left the windows open slightly, apparently because of the heat. In less than ten seconds, Jake had it open, and he sat inside. He would wait for Kirke's friend. First, though, he checked every inch of the car. Nothing there that shouldn't be there.

An hour went by, then another. He looked at his watch impatiently. The spokesman said she was being released. *Where was she?*

A third hour passed. It was near five. He was about to leave and look for them when he saw Sam approach.

Kirke's neighbor glowered at him as he opened the door. "I locked it," Sam said.

"You did, but you left a window open. Not much but enough. I wouldn't do that in the future."

"You can get out now."

"Not until you tell me how Kirke is."

"Not good since she met you."

Jake had no reply to that.

Sam glared at him. "It was a graze on her arm. And no, she hasn't told the police about you. I wanted her to, but she won't. Not until she talks to you."

Both relief and guilt filled him. "Did she say what happened?"

"Just that there was a call. When she and her partner arrived, someone shot her just as she tripped. She thinks that fall saved her life."

"And the other medic?"

"Chest wound, but he should be all right. Kirke wanted to stay until he came out of surgery."

*Thank God.* "I don't think you should go back to the house," Jake said.

"Why?"

"Someone's getting increasingly desperate."

"I have to. There's Merlin and my cat. My sax. My clothes. Kirke's."

"Look," Jake said as patiently as he could. "This guy doesn't miss. Either something happened that made him miss, and he'll try again, or it was a diversion to get both of you out of your house at the same time. Either way, you shouldn't go back there."

"You seem to know him pretty well," Sam said truculently.

"Not as well as I thought," Jake replied. "I'll get the animals and the stuff you need. You find a motel somewhere. I'll meet you there."

Sam was about to say hell no. Jake saw it in his face.

"I wouldn't suggest it if it wasn't necessary," Jake said, not trying to hide his urgency. "I can tail you out of here, make sure you're not followed. Then I'll head for your house and pick up Merlin, your cat, and some of your things. Make a list of what you need."

"Maybe you're just trying to frighten us," Sam said. "Where were you this afternoon?"

"I was shopping," Jake replied. The questions didn't bother him. In fact, he was pleased, if a bit envious, that Kirke had such a good friend.

"What if someone's waiting for you at the house?"

"I know how to protect myself, and I know how to lose a tail. You don't."

You're a self-serving bastard," Sam muttered. "Be honest. You want what he gave Kirke."

Jake looked at him with new respect. Of course he was a bastard, and he most definitely wanted what Kirke had. But he also knew Kirke wouldn't be safe until Gene Adams was behind bars or, preferably, dead.

The police were an option. But not for him. If she took what she knew to the police, he might never find Gene Adams. He would disappear, and Jake could never prove his existence.

"I won't deny that I want to know what was in the envelope

she took," he said. "Two good men are dead. They had families. They were killed by men they trusted. They deserve some justice."

"Not my problem." Sam glanced at his watch. "I have to be at work in six hours. I was late last night. If I don't show tonight, I might lose the gig."

"We'll figure out a way to get you there."

"Just figure out how to go away."

"I wish I could."

"Maybe whoever is doing this would leave if you did."

"You're not listening," Jake replied, trying to keep his impatience in check. "This man does not leave loose ends. Mark Cable was a loose end. Now Kirke is."

"And your solution?" Sam said sarcastically.

"I get him before he gets Kirke. You two stay out of sight until I do."

"And my gig? I'm a sax player. There are dozens ready to step into my spot."

Jake didn't have an answer for that. He didn't have the right to make decisions for others, decisions that could affect their lives. But he felt in his gut that whatever Kirke—and now probably Sam—did, they would continue to be targets.

So he ignored Sam's question. "Play tonight, then disappear for a few days," he said. Then he asked, "Do you have a friend who will switch cars with you? For a few days?"

"Damn you," Sam said bitterly.

"Find a motel," Jake said again, "and call me." He jotted down his number on a piece of paper and pushed it into Sam's hand. "In case you lost it."

He sprinted off before Sam could protest again.

Would she agree? Or would Sam talk Kirke into going to the police?

The musician wanted her to. That much was obvious.

He hadn't believed Jake, but then who would? Boulders by the names of Adams and Kelly had just tumbled over two ordinary people and seemed to be sweeping them down a cliff.

Jake followed Sam to the main entrance. He kept another car between them as Kirke rose from a wheelchair and opened the door of the passenger's side of the car.

She looked tired. Her arm was bandaged, and he could see from here her uniform shirt was stained.

Gene Adams was around somewhere. Jake could feel him. He would be disappointed to have failed. In fact, if the shooter had been Adams, Kirke was damned lucky to be alive. Jake had never known Adams to miss.

*Unless he meant to.*

Nothing made sense, but then Gene Adams didn't make sense. Jake hadn't known the man's real name, and while he hadn't liked the man, he never would have expected him to kill three of his team in cold blood.

Jake had tried to come to terms with that in the past few days. He had been leader. He should have sensed something was off about the mission. He'd known something was wrong with Gene Adams, that he liked killing a little too much.

He had to stop him. He might have to use Kirke to do it.

He didn't want to, but it might be the only way to bring Adams out in the open.

◆

Kirke was beginning to feel like voodoo doll, one with a lot of pins stuck into it.

One more place to hurt.

She was beginning to get angry. She didn't get angry easily, but when she did, she was a force to be reckoned with.

After being attended herself, she had waited at the hospital until Ben Wright's wife appeared, then sat with her until the doctor appeared, a smile on his face. "He came through surgery just fine. He should make it."

She'd waited another hour until Ben had been wheeled into a room and his pregnant wife joined him. Guilt filled her. Had she been irresponsible by just coming to work? This may well not have happened otherwise.

She didn't feel any better now as Sam started in on her about telling the police about Jake Kelly.

"Kirke, dammit, it's dangerous. He's dangerous. You don't

know anything about him except he keeps popping up when something happens."

"He popped up again?"

"Hell yes. He was here just a few moments ago."

"What did he want?"

Sam sighed. "He wanted to know how you were. He also said it might be dangerous to return to the house. He suggested we go to a motel for now."

"Merlin . . ."

"And Spade," he said in a tone totally foreign to her. "He said he would bring them." He hesitated a moment, then asked, "Did you tell the police anything?"

"Just about what happened today."

"No more?"

"No," she said in a small voice.

"I take it those officers were not the same involved in the purse snatching. Or there would have been a few more questions. Don't you think it's time to tell them about your mysterious Mr. Kelly?"

She had little defense. She should have told them. And they would connect it all before long. But she'd wanted to give herself, and Jake Kelly, a little more time. It was illogical and dangerous and probably even very, very dumb, but there she was.

"You're the one who always calls me unrealistic," Sam snapped uncharacteristically.

"I know," she admitted, the guilt swelling in her. She wasn't just disrupting her own life, she was messing up Sam's as well. But she couldn't forget the desperation in the eyes of a man she sensed was rarely desperate. Nor a dying man's plea. There was her job, as well, but she was honest enough to know that was only an excuse.

"Let's hear him out," she said. "If he doesn't tell us everything, then I'll go to the police."

"Where do you want to go now? A hotel? Or home?"

She hesitated. She wanted to go home. But in the last few hours she'd recognized that she really was a target. And she had made her partner one as well. He'd almost died. She didn't want the same to happen to Sam.

She usually considered herself a rational person. Maybe not always. She didn't know when to quit when she believed in something or someone. It had cost her much in the past. She'd clung to her marriage far too long, and she had been fired when she'd protested a principle a little too vehemently.

"I want to talk to him," Kirke said and used Sam's cell phone to call. It was a near miracle she hadn't left it at the scene of the attack.

He answered almost immediately.

"Mr. Kelly?" she said, not quite sure what to call him and settling instantaneously on that.

He didn't bother with courtesies. "Did your neighbor tell you to go to a motel tonight?

"He did. Neither of us agree."

Momentary silence.

"I can't make you, but I don't want either of you dead."

"You're scaring me," she said.

"I sincerely hope so. I was afraid nothing scared you."

She ignored that. "How would you get into the house?" she asked.

"I can get in," he said simply. "It would be easier if you gave me the code to the alarm system."

She hesitated, then gave it to him. "What about the door?" she asked.

"I can get in," he repeated.

She didn't know whether she should be comforted or horrified by his statement. Were homes really that easy to enter? Even with security systems? "It will be easier if you get the spare key," she said, ignoring Sam's continuing glower. "There's one in a small metal case in back of the rosebush in the front yard."

He didn't reply to that, but she sensed his disapproval over the distance. He lived in a different world than she did.

"What do you need for a couple of days?" he asked.

He was taking charge of her life. And Sam's.

She should resent it, but all she wanted now was to go home, get in bed, and forget the last week.

Still, she heard the words come out. "Merlin and Spade.

Their food and supplies. Cage and cat carrier. Two sets of clothes. Shirts and jeans. Several large T-shirts from the bureau. The usual from the bathroom."

How could she put her life in a few words?

And yet something about his manner, even over the phone, told her *he* was worried. She didn't think he was a man to worry over much.

That scared the devil out of her.

She handed the cell to Sam. To her surprise he also listed what he needed. Unhappily. But he did it.

Sam stopped at the first motel he found and went inside. She stayed in the car, knowing her bloodstained shirt, bandaged arm, and colorful black eye would probably raise eyebrows.

He came back. "No pets." He took a long look at her. "Probably not battered wives, either." He paused, then added, "They gave me the name of one that might and called ahead. We have two rooms."

"Did you tell them about Merlin's siren?"

"Hell, no," Sam said.

That damn guilt wrapped around her, smothering her. What was she doing to Sam? Was she betraying that friendship by insisting on going ahead on what was probably a quixotic mission of her own?

She called her captain.

"Are you all right, Kirke?" he asked the without preamble. "Do you need anything? We've been worried sick about you since you disappeared from the hospital."

"I just needed to get away," she said. "Can I take a couple of sick days?"

"With what you've been through these past two days, take a week. You have several due. If you need more, call me. Keep me posted. And Kirke?" he added.

"Captain?"

"You did a good job with Ben Wright."

Wrong! If not for her, maybe Ben Wright may never have been injured at all. Yet it was even more reason for her to find out what was really going on.

Now she would insist on hearing everything from the

enigmatic Jake Kelly. After hearing him out, she would decide whether to give him the information he so badly wanted.

Or go to the police.

~

Jake had not been followed. He was sure of that, but it probably didn't matter. Adams undoubtedly had someone watching her house.

He let himself into her unit with the key and punched in the code to the alarm system.

He heard the siren next door and grinned.

Merlin was on duty.

He started a search through her house. Within fifteen minutes, he'd found two listening devices. One was in the phone in the living room and the other in the bedroom. Adams had not lost his touch with locks or security systems.

He continued to look, even as he located a suitcase and gathered up the items she'd requested. He then went next door. He didn't have a key for Sam's side, but he did have a small tool he'd picked up at the electronics store. In seconds he had the door open and punched in the same code as he had on her house.

Merlin eyed him suspiciously as he entered.

"Good Merlin," Jake said, repeating the words he'd heard Kirke say.

Merlin cocked his head for a moment, then ruffled his feathers. "Goddamned bird," he responded in a male voice, then whistled a tune Jake hadn't heard in a long time.

Jake picked up Sam's litter box, carrier, and food, along with a ratty-looking stuffed mouse. He put them together with a suitcase full of clothes for Sam and another for Kirke. Because of the heat, he wanted to leave Merlin and Spade for his last trip.

Merlin repeated the whistle, and Jake stopped.

Adams had been in here as well. He used to drive other members of the team nuts with that tune. No one knew what it was, and Adams hadn't enlightened them.

Were there listening devices here as well? He started another search. He found one in the living room.

On impulse, he looked under the sink. There were a number of liquor bottles there, some nearly empty, two half full. Scotch. Bourbon. Vodka. Gin. A little of everything and not much of anything. The kind of collection you had if you had people over for parties.

Something caught his eye in the back. Maybe because of the pattern of the bottles. It was neat compared to the rest of the house where clothes were thrown over furniture, and magazines and CDs were scattered all over.

Jake found a flashlight in one of the cabinet drawers, then lowered himself to the floor and peered toward the back. He took the bottles out, then saw the small package connected to a detonator.

His breath caught in his throat.

He reached out and felt the substance.

*Plastique.*

# CHAPTER 14

Adams had been almost as good with explosives as Del Cox.

Jake made sure the plastique wasn't connected to anything under the sink, then slowly pulled it toward him. He studied the detonation device. No timer. Designed to be set off from a distance by a remote.

He very carefully separated the detonation device from what looked like a lump of clay.

When was Adams planning to use it? When he got what he wanted from Kirke? Or did he have another use for it?

Was the shooting today merely a diversion to pull Jake to the house? Or was it something else? Jake glanced around the room. His fingerprints would be all over both sides of the duplex. He might well have been seen coming and going. Like Adams, he was an expert shot as well as adept with explosives. He'd been pegged for Kirke's murder, except she foiled it by tripping. If Adams had been successful, he, Jake, would be a candidate for the death penalty. No questions asked.

Explosives were apparently plan B.

Adams had framed Jake once. Apparently, he thought he could do it again. Any accusations Jake made—if he wasn't dead—would be seen as a desperate attempt to deflect charges from himself.

His stomach clenched. *Run. Run!* But the image of Kirke's battered face surfaced in his mind.

He detached the detonator and took the plastique to the bathroom. He crumbled the whole into small pieces, then searched the drawers until he found a box of matches. He lit each small piece, feeling the heat as the flame flared and consumed the chemical. The acrid smell permeated the small room.

When he was through, he washed the residue down the drain, even as the odor lingered.

Then he went back to Kirke's side of the duplex. He started in the kitchen. Her cabinets were much neater than Sam's. Nothing. He did a quick search of the rest of the house. Still nothing.

That didn't matter, though. There had been enough plastique in what he'd found to blow up the entire house. Apparently whoever planted it thought they had found a safe location. Then it could be detonated at any time.

Jake gathered up Sam's and Kirke's suitcases and placed them in the trunk of his car along with food for the cat and Merlin.

Before loading the animals, he checked the bottom of the car and the ignition. He also checked the trunk and engine. He didn't see anything, but that didn't mean some device wasn't there. He was dealing with professionals.

He wished he knew how many.

He loaded the animals and drove out onto the street, then turned on Peachtree. A few more turns put him on the expressway, where he darted in and out of traffic. He kept an eye on the rearview mirror. He thought someone was following for a while, but he was sure he lost them when at the last second possible he managed to swerve across two lanes of traffic to an exit lane. He heard a squealing of brakes behind him. He accelerated the car, turning right, speeding down a main street, then entering the expressway again. No one was behind him.

He was as sure as he could be in a situation like this.

He looked at his watch. He called Sam Pierce's cell phone, and Kirke answered.

"Where do I go?" he asked.

She gave him directions. He would rather have had found a new vehicle, but he didn't have time. They would move soon again in any event. It wouldn't take long for Adams and his mercenaries to find them at a local motel.

———

"Goddamn bird," Merlin said over and over again as Jake brought him into the motel room. "Goddamn bird."

Kirke fastened her gaze on Jake Kelly's face. His jaw was set, and he had a five-o'clock shadow that made him look even more dangerous than before. His eyes were even darker and colder than she remembered.

He radiated tension, and yet Merlin had hopped onto his shoulder when she opened the cage. He never did that with strangers. Never.

"Traitor," she said to the bird.

Unfazed, Merlin started whistling an odd melody.

Sam apparently had heard Jake's entrance and emerged from the connecting room where he'd been sleeping. He inspected his sax as if Jake Kelly had put a hex on it. He looked at the clothes Jake had bought, then nodded.

"I don't think I should play tonight," he said. "I don't want you alone here," Sam protested.

"I'm not alone," she said. "And I'm in a motel room with lots of other people around, and you know exactly where I am and who I'm with."

Sam still looked uncertain. "I still don't know why we couldn't go home."

Jake Kelly dug in his pocket and brought out in his hand several small pieces of metal. "Listening devices," he said. "They were in both sides." He dumped them on a table, then produced a small clump of something that looked like dough. He'd saved a small piece to show them.

"There was a hunk of this in the back of the cabinet under Sam's sink."

Sam stepped forward. "You searched my house . . . ?"

"Only for stuff that shouldn't be there," Jake Kelly replied.

Kirke stared down at the substance in his hand. "What is that?"

"Plastic explosive," he said.

Somehow Kirke knew what the answer would be before he said the words. She'd had a course in explosives. It was part of a Homeland Security program. She'd seen it before. Even felt it.

"In our house?" she said, trying to understand.

"In Sam's," he said, "but it would have destroyed the entire house."

Sam went still. "In the kitchen?"

"Yes."

A shiver of panic ran through Kirke. Momentary shock, then her heart dropped. She thought about her beloved house. Small as it was, it was hers. The only thing of any major value that she owned.

"Explosives?" Sam echoed in disbelief, then he turned on Jake. "You could have planted them yourself."

"I could have, but I didn't." He looked toward Kirke. "I think I cleared the house, but I'm not sure. I didn't have time to look outside."

"Listening devices?" Kirke said, glancing at Sam. Had they been there when she'd opened the envelope? Had someone heard them discuss the numbers? Had they meant more to that someone than they had to her?

Jake Kelly nodded. "I wouldn't be surprised if they haven't planted tracking devices in Kirke's car. I checked Sam's car. There weren't any, but after his performance I would suggest he change cars with someone before returning to the motel." He turned to Sam, who still looked stunned. "Can you do that?"

Sam nodded.

"How did you sign in?" Jake asked Sam.

Sam paced nervously the room. "As Malcolm Pierce and sister, Elizabeth," he said grudgingly. "I had to use my last name because of the credit card."

"Malcolm?" Kirke asked, startled.

"It's my middle name," he said defensively.

"You never told me that," Kirke said.

"Why do you think I would?" he replied, ignoring Jake Kelly.

She didn't answer. They were bantering, she realized, because their lives had just changed in a dramatic way. She felt like a fugitive, and he obviously felt the same.

Fear was there, too.

Because of one Jake Kelly, alias Mitch Edwards, alias David Cable.

"I'll give you free rent forever," she offered.

His frown faded, and he grinned at her. "Some promise. Then you couldn't pay the taxes, and we would both be on the street."

Jake had been listening impatiently. "I think you should move again tomorrow," he said.

Sam nodded.

"I'll get an untraceable credit card for you," Jake said.

"You had better go, Sam," Kirke interrupted as she glanced at her watch. "I don't want to be responsible for you losing your job as well."

"I don't get all this," Sam protested. Fear was on his face, but determination was there as well.

"I'll explain everything when you get back," Jake Kelly said.

Sam cast a quick glance at her. "Not good enough. I can't leave you together."

Jake shrugged. "It's up to you."

"Please go, Sam. I'll be fine," Kirke said. She wanted him to go. She wanted to talk to Jake, and she knew that he wouldn't say much in front of Sam.

And she had to know. She had to know everything. By God, someone was trying to kill her. Trying to kill Sam and Merlin and even Spade.

Fear crawled up her spine and constricted her throat. No. This couldn't be happening.

She darted a look toward Jake. He didn't try to reassure Sam.

"Go," she said again. "If it will make you feel better, I'll call Robin and tell her where I am."

Sam had met Robin several times. She'd attended several parties before her marriage, and Sam had liked her immediately. "Call now," Sam said.

She started for the hotel room phone.

"Use the cell," Jake ordered.

Kirke punched in Robin's number. She wasn't available, but Kirke left a message. "I need to talk to you. Call me at this number." She gave the number of Sam's cell. She glanced at Sam's glowering face and added that she was staying at a motel, mentioned its name but no telephone number.

After finishing, she turned back to Sam. "Now go, or you'll be late. Later," she corrected herself with a look at her watch.

"I'll call when I get there," Sam said. "I'll call during every break. If you don't answer, I'll call the cops." He grabbed his sax.

"Bye, Sam," Merlin said cheerily.

The door slammed behind Sam.

"He's right," Jake said slowly. "You should go to the police."

"Can they protect me?"

"Maybe," he said. "It might scare him back to whatever hole he left."

"But you don't think so."

"I think the fact that he left that hole to come after the man you knew as Mark Cable says he's desperate about keeping his past a secret. He saw you take something from the man he'd come after. He saw that same man whisper something to you. He must know you haven't passed it on to the police.

"How could he know that?"

Jake didn't answer immediately. Instead, he walked over to the window. For the first time she saw his shoulders slump. His fingers balled into a fist.

Tension radiated from him. Until now he'd seemed so sure of himself.

"How could he know that?" she repeated.

"I expect he has a friend, or friends, in high places. He could certainly afford it."

She thought about telling him about the visit from the

FBI agent earlier that day. She'd almost forgotten it during the confusion after the shooting. Something stopped her. Money and diamonds, the agent said. She wanted to hear Jake's version before saying anything.

"Is that why Mark Cable said not to go to the police?" she asked.

"Did he?"

She remembered then she hadn't told him that. She nodded.

"And he didn't say why?"

"He couldn't say much. He was dying."

"What else?" Jake asked in a voice that had lost all softness.

She had come this far. She was in a room alone with a man that could possibly be a murderer. But she really didn't think so. His eyes could be like ice. His face hard. Yet he had been patient with Sam, with her. For God's sake, he had brought a parrot to her, and a cat and litter box.

She didn't think a killer would do that, even to disarm a victim.

But still, she wanted to know more. "Tell me what happened," she said. "Tell me everything."

He didn't answer. Instead, he studied her.

She definitely was not at her best. She felt like hell and probably looked even worse. Her arm hurt. Her eye was swollen and sore. She'd been running on adrenaline and hadn't had much sleep. Then there had been the fear for her partner, half explanations to the police, sitting with Ben's wife, and a painkiller for her own minor injury.

She went to the bed that dominated the room and sat down. Spade jumped up beside her, making small, uncertain noises. The cat, like her, was out of his comfort zone. She brushed her hand against Spade's fur.

Jake sat down beside her. She fought the strong awareness that radiated between them, the heat that suddenly raced through her body.

"I'm damned sorry you got mixed up in this," he said. The defeat in his voice went straight to her heart. She didn't think he was a person who was sorry often. About anything.

But neither was she. She had been really sorry about one thing, and that was her marriage.

"Don't be," she said. "I made the decision to take the letter, not you. I'm the one who decided to keep it."

"But you might have surrendered it after the burglary."

"Maybe," she said. "Maybe not."

She waited for him to ask for the letter. Instead, he touched her face with featherlike gentleness. "You need some rest."

"No. You won't get away with that. You owe me more of an explanation." She tried to ignore the waves of heat spreading outward from where he touched her. She wanted to lean into him, to feel his arms around her. She wanted to feel safe again.

He tensed. She felt it in the way his fingers stopped moving against her face. Slowly, he lowered his hand.

She wanted it back. In fact, she wanted more. Much more. Her stomach was fluttering inside. More than fluttering. Aching.

But she also had to know what was going on. She waited for him to continue.

"Some of this stuff is classified, but to hell with it," he finally said. "Most of it was in the court-martial record, but it's probably buried so deep it'll never be found.

"I've told you some of it," he continued. "Seven years ago, I was sent on a joint mission with two CIA operatives. We had word that a South American drug lord had branched out by selling arms to anyone but Americans. The weapons were American-made ground-to-air missiles. The most sophisticated we had."

She was silent, listening intently. His hand had, during the last few seconds, touched hers, and somehow their fingers had become entwined. She tried to ignore the warmth of his hand.

"Don't stop," she said.

He hesitated, then shrugged. "We were posing as terrorists wanting to buy them."

"Why?"

"The dealer had done some discreet advertising. We

contacted him and made a bid. It was accepted, but he wanted the payment by hand. He didn't trust banks, not even off-shore ones. I think he also wanted an ongoing relationship and wanted a look at us."

"And what was the price?"

"Altogether, five million dollars. A million in cash and the rest in uncut diamonds."

Her eyes widened. "You were carrying that much?"

"It was the price for bringing home those missiles and hopefully finding the supplier," he said. "We were supposed to have been handpicked very carefully.

"My job was to get them back even if we had to pay for them. Adams's job was to find out where the drug lord got them."

"What happened?"

"Cox was a pilot. He flew us onto a landing strip supposedly ten miles from the seller's camp. One man was waiting with a jeep. He drove maybe a mile, and Cox said he thought he saw something in the road. The driver stopped, and we all got out of the jeep. That's all I remembered until I woke several hours later."

Her fingers tightened around his. She knew something bad was coming. A muscle in his throat worked, and his lips had tightened.

"Ramos and Chet Michaels, my two guys, were both dead. Gene Adams and Del Cox had disappeared. So had the guide.

"The diamonds and money were also gone. I figured then that the South American dealer had ambushed us and proba-bly taken Adams and Cox to find out exactly who they were and why they were there. I thought they were probably dead.

"I managed to crawl to a road where some farmers found me. One of them took me to his home and cared for me. I finally got to a consulate and recuperated a few more days.

"When I reached the States, the military police were wait-ing for me. Someone had found an account in my name in an offshore bank. Half a million dollars."

"No one looked for the others?"

"They were dead. So said the military, and I supposedly

killed them. They would have a hard time proving it, and I would have a hard time disproving it. They were missing—I had reported two dead myself—and I had at least part of the money. A neat trap."

"Surely they wondered what happened to the rest of the money."

"According to their theory, I had the money distributed in different places. It was all very nice and tidy. I had a choice. Plead no contest or they would pursue a life sentence. They were willing to deal because they wanted to keep the thing quiet. Our SAMs in the hands of drug dealers and terrorists? The U.S. willing to pay a drug dealer five million?"

"You didn't fight it?"

"With what? Half the information was classified. It can be in a court-martial. I fought it up to the moment I knew I wasn't going to win. Then my JAG attorney made the best deal he could get. It was a good one because they didn't want the information to get out. Bad publicity to lose five million dollars and lose our own highly classified weapons."

"But who stole the money?"

Jake shrugged. "I thought it was the drug dealer. It was worth half a million to keep the United States from going after him. You just didn't kill our military without consequences. But then several days after I left prison, I received a phone call. No name. The caller just said if I wanted to know what really happened in South America I should be at a bar in Atlanta. That's where I was headed when I saw Gene Adams at the accident site. He'd had plastic surgery, but you can't fake certain mannerisms. I'm sure it's him."

"And Mark Cable?"

"Del Cox."

Kirke tried to digest it all. SAM missiles, CIA, Special Forces, drug dealers, diamonds, secret missions.

It sounded more like an action adventure movie than real life. But now the sniper made more sense. So did the plastic explosives.

*If* she chose to believe him.

What was that movie? *Conspiracy Theory* with Mel Gibson. Everyone thought he was crazy, and he was, but he was also right. There had been a conspiracy of massive proportions.

Her mind, already dulled by the day's events and the painkiller, whirled.

She knew he wanted to know what Cable had told her, and now for better or worse was the time to tell him. It might give him the piece of information that could stop this escalation of violence.

"The letter," she said, "is in Merlin's cage, under the newspapers."

His gaze met hers, thanking her. His fingers tightened around hers, then he stood and went over to Merlin's cage and opened it. Merlin flew over to the bed, where he perched next to Spade. "Goddamn bird," he boasted.

A new expression and one she didn't like. Probably harked back to the time he was with the drug dealers. She turned her attention back to Jake.

He reached inside, and his hand stilled for a moment. Then very carefully, he took out the top sheet of newsprint and placed it on the table. Then he continued to look for the letter.

Kirke saw his growing frustration as he took out one layer after another and looked into every sheet.

He turned back to her. "There's nothing here."

# CHAPTER 15

Disappointment swept through him.

No, more than disappointment. Defeat. He'd placed far too much hope in Cox's call, then in the letter.

"It's not there," he added.

She stood and went over to him. She double-checked the pages. Nothing.

"Whoever planted the plastique found the letter," he said.

She looked at him for a long, searching moment, then said, "It doesn't matter. I know what was in it."

He stiffened. Waited. He'd realized that pushing her would be a mistake.

"Numbers. Only numbers," she said. "I opened it yesterday to try to decide . . ." She shrugged slightly. "There was no name on the envelope, no words inside. Just a few numbers."

He tried to hide his disappointment. He was good at doing exactly that. He remembered the day when the sentence came down . . . his father hadn't been as stoic. Jake would never forget the silent tears that rolled down the cheeks of Retired Lieutenant Colonel Donal Kelly. He'd died a few days later of a heart attack. He'd believed his son. The fact that his beloved army had not, killed him.

Gene Adams hadn't killed just two men that day. He'd killed three.

"Jake?" Her voice was soft. It was the first time she had used it, and his name sounded different when she said it. Softer.

"What were the numbers?" he asked.

She told him.

They meant nothing to him. If only he could have seen the envelope, the letter itself, then maybe he might make some sense of it.

"Were they separated by dashes or spaces?"

She shook her head.

"And nothing else?" he asked.

"No name on the envelope, no words inside," she said. "Just the numbers."

"Did Del Cox . . . Cable say anything?"

"He said, 'Envelope. Take it.' Then 'Give to Mitch Edwards.' "

"What else?"

"Something like Mili . . . and Virginia."

Her brows furrowed together as she thought. He hated to even ask. For someone usually so energetic, she looked exhausted and wounded. And ever so vulnerable.

Military? Virginia? He had hoped for more.

He went back to Merlin's cage, looking through it once more. Then he picked up a news sheet.

"What is it?" she asked.

"Blood. Your Merlin must have bitten him. That must be why he's been parroting 'Goddamn bird.' " He paused, then added, "That new tune he's been whistling? Adams used to whistle it all the time."

She looked stricken. "He could have killed Merlin."

He shook his head. "If anything had happened to Merlin, that would have been a pretty big clue that someone had broken into your house. That might have led us to the plastique."

Kirke ran a hand gently over Merlin's feathers as he preened. "Brave bird," she said.

"Brave," Merlin crowed.

"We need some fruit for him," she said.

"There's a store around the corner. I'll get some. And some takeout for us."

"That would be good. I'm beginning to get hungry."

She looked grateful. She shouldn't. She should be damning him. He was the one who had brought the world falling in on her.

"Jake," she said. "What now?"

"Find a place for you and Sam to go. Somewhere safe," he said.

"And you . . ."

He shrugged, "I have to find Adams before he finds you."

"And then?"

He ignored the question. "Lock the door behind me," he said. "Use all the locks. Don't open it unless you hear three knocks, a pause, then two more." He took the Do Not Disturb sign, opened the door, and placed the sign on the outside knob. "I should be back within thirty minutes."

❧

After he left, the image of a vulnerable-looking Kirke Palmer stayed with him.

He knew his abrupt departure must have puzzled her. But he needed time to think, and she had a way of dulling his senses.

For a moment he put himself in her place. She had nothing now. Not a car. Not a home she could use. Not even many clothes, just those he'd hurriedly thrown into a suitcase. Yet he'd heard not one complaint.

Military and Virginia. It didn't make any sense. Not yet. Maybe she would remember something else. If not, he would have to try to build a plan based on two words.

He turned his attention back to the matter at hand. He'd seen a large discount store earlier. He stopped there first, purchased two new throwaway cell phones—he'd used his own too much now. He also bought a pocket knife, a tray of fresh fruit, and a bag of apples. At the last minute he added a bag of donuts. After prison food, everything looked good.

Then he stopped at the only fast-food place in sight. He bought one large pizza, half everything, including anchovies, and half pepperoni only. He had no idea what she would like. For all he knew she was a vegetarian. At least then there would be fruit.

He knew damned little about her, her likes and dislikes. He only knew that she was probably the most stubborn woman he'd ever met. The fact that she still hadn't gone to the police reflected either integrity or stupidity, and he didn't think it was the latter.

His ex-wife couldn't get away from him fast enough. She'd been miserable before the South American mission, unable to adapt to the long absences necessary for someone in his profession. Kirke knew he was an ex-con, accused of terrible crimes, and yet she had listened with an open mind. It had been a very long time since that had happened. He had a few friends left—a very few—and those had known him for years. They hadn't believed the charges and still didn't, but Kirke had taken a giant leap of faith with damn little reason.

If she paid a bigger price than she already had, he would not forgive himself, and yet he needed her now. There had to be something more than those numbers. There had to be another hint.

As he drove back to the motel, he thought again about the numbers she'd said were in the letter. If only he could have seen it . . .

He couldn't fault her. She thought she'd found a safe place . . . the bottom of a birdcage.

Gene Adams now had the same numbers. Jake would have to discover their significance before Adams did.

He continued to puzzle over them as he parked at the motel. It was one of those motels with a nice front lobby. He drove to the end of one of the wings, went in a back door, and walked through the interior to the room. Kirke's room was ten doors down. Sam's one beyond that.

He'd thought about renting a separate room, but at the moment he didn't want to leave her longer than necessary. He felt it vital, though, that he be at the nightclub where Sam played. He was probably more vulnerable now, and Jake realized if anything happened to him, it would be a terrible blow to Kirke.

Sam's attitude didn't help him, but the musician was Kirke's friend and obviously a good one, and Jake didn't intend to make him pay for that fact.

—

Kirke's heart had dropped several feet when Jake Kelly had failed to find the letter. She thought she had been so clever.

But then she'd never gone against an international criminal and traitor before.

She checked Merlin's cage once more. She obviously hadn't been clever enough. And now she had nothing to take to the police. Or any other authority for that matter. It would be only her word, and her delay in reporting what she knew would make that word somewhat questionable.

"Merlin hungry," the bird said.

She filled his dish with bird food. What was she going to do with him? How to make sure he was safe? She couldn't carry him from place to place. He did not do well with change.

Maybe Robin would take him? *If* she called back.

Weighed down with fatigue, she stretched out on the bed. Lord, she hurt in so many places. In her heart as well as her body. She had let Jake down. She'd seen the disappointment, even despair that flickered in his dark eyes when he saw that the letter was gone.

She thought briefly about a shower. She needed one after this day. But she probably shouldn't get the new bandages wet, not to mention those from the prior day.

And then she was too tired to do much of anything.

Except think. Her mind was racing with all that had happened today.

She turned on the television, trying to find news, but the offerings were skimpy. Nothing about the sniper today.

The cell phone rang, and she picked it up.

"Kirke, this is Robin. Sorry to be so late in calling. I've been out of town on a story. Just got back and heard that you had been shot. Then I got your message. Are you okay?"

"Just a flesh wound," she said.

"A sniper attack? That must have been terrifying."

"Understatement. My partner was wounded badly, but he's going to make it."

"Why? Who? The paper doesn't have many details."

"I don't think the police know," she said. It wasn't exactly a lie.

"Is there anything I can do?"

She couldn't very well say she called because Sam insisted that someone know where she was. That would mean too many explanations. But she now had another reason. "Can you do an enormous favor for me?"

"I'll try."

"Can you take Merlin for a few days? Maybe Sam's cat as well?"

There was a short silence, and she could guess at the questions running through Robin's inventive mind.

"Does it have anything to do with the shooting today?"

Kirke hesitated. She didn't want to lie, but neither did she want to alarm Robin. "I need to get away for a few days to rest and recuperate."

"What about Sam?"

"He might be going out of town, too."

"Of course, I'll take them," Robin said. "My cat will like the company, and you know I love Merlin. I introduced the two of you to each other."

"It might be a short-lived romance," Kirke replied wryly. She hesitated, then asked, "Where's your husband?"

"He's out of town, will be for another week or two, so I'll enjoy the company. Will you be dropping them by?"

She wasn't sure about that. Her hesitation apparently was noted.

"I can pick them up," Robin said. "You said you're at a motel? What kind of motel accepts a loudmouthed parrot?"

"A cheap one," Kirke admitted.

A pause. "Kidding aside, are you in trouble?"

"I just need some time. I haven't taken a vacation in two years."

"Probably a very good thing. Not to worry about Merlin."

"You're a lifesaver. With Sam's cat there, Merlin won't get too despondent."

"Where are you going?"

"I'm not sure. Maybe the mountains."

"Have a good time. I have your cell phone if there are any problems."

"Ah . . . mine is gone. I'll contact you with a new cell number," Kirke said. "This one is Sam's."

"Kirke, are you sure there's nothing wrong? If so, Ben might be able to help."

"No," Kirke said a little too quickly. The last thing she needed was Robin's FBI husband becoming involved. But it gave her an idea. "I met an FBI guy earlier. Name was John Davis. Do you know him by any chance?"

"No," she said. "Don't think so. Why? You finally dating again?"

"There are only so many Bens to go around," Kirke replied.

"I agree with that," Robin asked, "and I don't intend to share him." She paused, then said, "But why the question about this agent?"

"He interviewed me earlier this morning about a hit-and-run, and there was something a little off about him."

"Can't give up being nosy, huh?"

"No." Kirke waited a second.

"I'll ask a couple of friends if they know him," Robin said. "When are you planning to leave?"

"Tomorrow."

"You've lucked out. I'm off then. What about nine to pick up the feathered and furry ones?"

"That's great. I'll really owe you."

"Kirke . . . you can always stay with me, you know. Especially now that Ben is away. I would love some human company."

Kirke had no intention of putting anyone else in danger.

She was radioactive at the moment. "Thanks. I appreciate it more than you know, but I would really like to get out of the city."

"Okay, but if you change your mind, just call."

After she hung up, she sat on the bed, wondering whether it was right to drag someone else into this, even on the periphery.

As if knowing his fate was being settled, Merlin flew into his cage, his safe place. Spade jumped up and huddled next to her. He was not in his usual space and was distinctly disturbed about the fact.

She lay back on the bed, putting her arm around the cat. She wanted to stay awake and wait for Jake, but she was so tired. She hadn't had a good sleep in longer than she wanted to remember. Her eyes drifted closed.

She woke to knocking on the door. *The signal.* She dragged herself up and went to the door, blinking as she opened it. She knew she'd lapsed into a deep sleep, and she felt drugged with it.

Jake Kelly entered, in his hands and arms bags and a huge box. He piled everything on the small table.

"Fruit for Merlin. Food for you."

"Thank you," she said, hearing the unusual primness in her voice. She suddenly felt shy. Not like her at all.

"You're welcome," he answered, opening the box. "I'll get some drinks down the hall. Any preference?"

She named a soda and watched as he left. She'd thought she was tired. From what she knew of his past few days, he'd had far less rest than she, and yet there was an energy to each step. Prison had not dimmed his inherent confidence.

She sat up and went to the table to see what he'd bought. She raised the lid of the pizza box. Pepperoni on one side, anchovies, olives, onions, pepperoni, and sausage on the other.

The normalcy of pizza was comforting.

She took a big slice of the side with everything on it. One bite and she was ravenous for more. She looked at the other stuff. Fruit for Merlin. Donuts. Lots of donuts. Two new cell phones.

Then he was back, filling the room with his presence, just as he had from the first moment she'd met him.

His cheeks were shadowed, and his hair looked a bit ragged, but those dark eyes consumed her in a way none had ever done before. She put the slice of pizza down and held her hand out to him.

He took her hand and wrapped his fingers around hers for a moment. Warmth flooded her.

"We need to leave here in the morning," he said almost regretfully. "They'll figure out before long you won't be back, if they haven't already. They're smart enough to start checking at hotels."

"You keep saying 'they.' How many do you think—"

"I don't know. More than two. Adams was at the scene when someone drove the car that hit Del Cox. Then someone else picked him up. There might be more. Probably are. He took up to five million, and that's what he started out with. He knows some very valuable secrets. I imagine he's built a small empire by now, probably in a South American country. A guess would be Argentina or Brazil. Neither are very good about extraditing criminals, and it's easy enough to hide there."

"Then why did he leave?" she said.

"He knew I would try to find out what happened," Jake said, "that I wouldn't stop looking until I discovered what had happened that day. He probably tapped my phone, and when he heard about the call with Cox's intermediary, he had to come. No one else knew what Cox looked like."

Her stomach plunged. How could they ever hope to out-maneuver this Adams and his henchmen?

"You can still go to the police," he offered.

He'd tried earlier to dissuade her from doing just that. Now he was encouraging her. Was he giving up?

She wasn't aware of a tear running down her cheek until one of his fingers trapped it. Then she felt embarrassed. She was here because she chose to be here. No regrets. *Never have regrets.* She'd decided that long ago.

She knotted her fingers to hide her sudden emotion. And confusion.

She was so darn attracted to him, and she still wasn't altogether convinced he was a good guy. The deadly glint in his eyes a second earlier had sent shivers down her back. It was like looking into a black hole.

Then he sighed and leaned down. His lips touched her face as softly as the sweet touch of a breeze, barely touching her skin but leaving a heated impression. They stopped at her mouth and lingered there. His hand went to the back of her head and rested there.

The light kiss deepened. Fire ignited in her belly, and her hand went to his face. It was rough and yet seductive. Everything about him was seductive, including the aura of danger.

He backed away, and he looked startled. And rueful. One side of his mouth pulled up. There was tenderness in it. And lust.

She'd never felt such a pull to another person. Relationships to her had meant friendship first. Common interests. Compatibility. If the sex was good, that was a plus.

But love as a many splendored thing? Forget it. That stuff was only in films.

Now she wondered whether there was something to it after all. Fireworks were going off inside her. Her pulse was rapid, and waves of heat swept her. Most painful though was the raw need fermenting in the core of her.

Then she winced as he brushed her arm.

He backed away. "I'm sorry."

"I'm not," she replied quickly.

"Are you always so honest?"

"No."

He grinned then, and she realized it was the first time she'd seen anything more than a slight smile.

He cradled her chin with his hand. "I've never met anyone like you before."

"I can honestly say the same."

"I'm sorry I crashed into your life like I did. I don't understand why you're not running to the police now."

"I don't, either."

"You can remedy that," he said.

"I would lose my job. I broke every regulation there is."

"And that would be bad?"

"I got fired from one job. I don't really want another on my record."

"What was it?

"I was a reporter with the *Atlanta Observer*," she said.

A reporter! No wonder she was so good with the questions.

"Why did you lose it?"

"I voiced my displeasure over the way a story was covered."

"Doesn't seem to be a firing offense."

"It is, if the story was written by a close friend of the publisher, and I wouldn't quit complaining."

"Why?"

"It was my story, and she got it all wrong."

He laughed then. An actual laugh. A low rumble that started in his throat and grew. It even, eventually, touched his eyes. It was fascinating to watch.

"Do you always tilt against windmills?" he asked. His hand touched her hair and pushed back a curl.

"It's a fault," she admitted. "My mom used to tell me that once I got an idea in my head, not even a rocket could blow it away. It wasn't a compliment. She said I had a compulsive personality." She was rambling along like an idiot, and she knew it. It was just . . . he so disconcerted her. This guy was dangerous to her well-being, both physically and, she suspected, emotionally. Dangerous, hell. Hell with *suspected*. She knew he was pure poison. She'd always been an adrenaline junkie, but she'd never consciously invited danger before.

He was watching her with an intensity that made the air between them sizzle.

Then, with a small movement of a muscle in his cheek, he stepped away. "You need to eat," he said, his voice husky.

She did, but she yearned for a different kind of sustenance. She wanted more of him.

He picked up her slice of pizza. "It's cold," he said.

If so, it was the only cold item in the room.

"That's okay," she said.

"Anchovies?" he said with some surprise.

"What's wrong with anchovies?"

"I just didn't take you for an anchovies person."

"Then why did you buy it?"

"That was going to be my half," he said.

"You'll have to settle for pepperoni only now."

"Anything after prison food tastes good," he said quietly. She looked up at him.

"Why are we talking about pizza?"

When their lips met again, this time there was no gentleness, only white-hot heat.

# CHAPTER 16

Jake knew he should stop.

He'd never taken advantage of a woman before, especially a vulnerable one, and the fact that Kirke had almost died today made her extraordinarily vulnerable. Escaping death often made one reach out and grab a piece of life, wisely or unwisely.

But it had been so long since he'd felt the softness of a woman. Even longer since he'd seen passion glaze a woman's eyes. Even as he knew his marriage was going bad, he'd been faithful. He wasn't going to be like his father.

But he couldn't stop his fingers from carefully exploring the back of her neck nor the smoothness of her face. Nor could he stop kissing her.

It was Kirke who deepened the kiss, who responded with the same abandon with which she seemed to do everything. No shyness. Not even the hesitation any reasonable woman would have for someone playing such havoc with her life.

Her tongue flicked out, tasting him, and her lips invited and seduced. They opened to him, and heat rushed through him. She wanted, and he wanted.

His blood was like currents of liquid fire, searing and sensitizing every nerve, every muscle. She leaned against him, and pleasure coursed through him as she responded so completely to every touch. And then her hands were doing their own exploration, intensifying every sensation.

He knew he should pull back. That would be the right thing.

But a sound came from deep inside her, a purring, welcoming sound that aroused him more than any spoken words. He felt her hand entwining with his hair, and they clung together.

His hand accidentally brushed the bandage on her arm, and he heard the swift intake of breath.

It was like a splash of icy water. He moved away with a sudden jerk.

He rose. "I'm sorry," he said.

"Don't go."

"I hurt you. Again."

"*You* haven't hurt me at all."

He shook his head. "None of this would have happened if I hadn't come to Atlanta."

"Yes, it would. Your Mr. Adams would still have tried to kill that man, and I still would have taken the envelope. I just wouldn't have anyone standing between him and me." She blinked rapidly, though, and he knew she must be far more tired than she wanted to admit. She still wore the bloodied uniform shirt, which meant she probably hadn't washed yet, either. Her arm had to be burning from that gunshot wound. She'd ignored it all, but apparently it was catching up with her.

He stood and found the pain pills that had apparently been prescribed after yesterday's injuries. He handed one to her, along with a soda, and watched as she swallowed it.

"Here," he said, handing her another piece of pizza. "You need some food with that."

Kirke obediently took several bites. Her eyes were obviously struggling to stay open.

"I didn't see any night stuff at your house," he said.

"That's because I wear T-shirts at night," she replied.

He went over to her suitcase and found a large T-shirt. It

had been on the list she'd given him. He put it on the bed, then went into the bathroom. When he returned, he had two wet washcloths and a towel.

He turned back the sheet and cover.

"Lie down," he ordered and was surprised when she did. It said a lot about how tired she must be. He helped her off with her uniform shirt. She wore a bra underneath, and it, too, had bloodstains on it.

He'd soaped one of the washcloths, and he ran it over her skin. He took his time washing her, returning frequently to the bathroom to get a fresh washcloth or rinse one out. When he'd finished the upper part of her body, he helped her pull on the T-shirt.

His cell phone rang. He looked at the number, then handed it to her.

"Sam," she said fuzzily. "I'm fine. Jake got a pizza."

She listened for a moment. "Okay. Here's Jake," she said after he made a gesture with his hand.

He took it and asked, "When will you be leaving the club?"

"Around two a.m.," Sam replied.

"When you arrive, the connecting door will be locked," Jake said. "You can call to open it."

There was a pause. Sam obviously wanted to say something, probably something obscene, but he resisted and just hung up.

Jake went back to the bathroom. More hot water. More bath as he carefully avoided the bandages covering cuts from the purse snatcher. He cursed under his breath. By the time he had finished, her eyes were closed.

He turned off all but the bathroom light and left that door partially open, then he dragged the chair over to the window. He could see the back parking lot from here, though not the front, and the hallway was accessible from both the parking lot and the lobby.

He looked back at her. The bruise around her eyes was growing more colorful. Her injured arm was outside the sheet. She looked the ultimate innocent. He'd wanted to kill Gene Adams before but never as much as he did at this moment.

Jake glanced at his watch. Eleven p.m.

He would snatch an hour's sleep, then drive to the club where Sam was playing. He had a bad feeling about that. Adams was good at exploiting weaknesses, and he might know that Sam was one of Kirke's weaknesses. When Jake made sure both were safe tonight, then he would try to work with Kirke on those numbers that Del Cox had passed to her. Maybe she would remember something else.

Merlin watched him as he opened the plastic container of fruit. He offered the parrot some grapefruit. The bird had been unusually silent, as if he sensed that not all was right with his world.

When Merlin finished his treat, Jake put the cover over his cage, grabbed a piece of cold pizza, and sat back at the window.

The parking lot was quiet. He closed his eyes. An hour's sleep, and he would be okay for another day.

                                  ➤

Kirke jerked awake.

For a moment she panicked. Where was she?

Then she remembered. Remembered the sniper. The purse snatcher. Dear God, the plastique.

She remembered the feel of Jake Kelly's hands.

She'd never felt anything as sensuous as when he washed her. Sensuous and yet oddly gentle. She shivered deliciously as she relived those few moments. Perhaps it was the gentleness that stirred so many sensations and emotions.

She moved and saw his form in a chair at the window. He was sleeping, and yet she suspected at any second he would detect her small movements. He needed sleep as well, and she enjoyed watching him, even though she felt partially drugged by sleep and her reaction to the events of yesterday.

What time was it? What had wakened her?

She turned to look at the clock, and in that moment he woke. No sudden movement, just a quietness that she recognized. He rose slowly with an athletic grace that sent another set of shivers along her back.

"I'm glad you're awake," he said in a low voice. He walked over to her and sat down. "I'm going to Sam's club to make sure he makes it back here."

"You're afraid he won't?"

"Adams probably knows where Sam plays, and he can lead them to you. I don't want to take more chances."

His words sobered her. She had to remember why she was here, not drift back to those hands, to the tenderness in them.

He took her hand. "Promise me you will stay here. Don't open the door until you hear my knock. Not for anyone. Not for room service or a repairman or someone from the desk. Not even for Sam. I've locked the connecting door. If he wants in, he can call."

She nodded, her eyes intent on his face. Not quite as hard now. Yet she thought she saw more lines.

"The signal?" he asked.

"Three knocks, pause, then two more," she recited.

He nodded. "And if someone tries to get in, urge Merlin to make that siren sound of his."

"Merlin never does what he's told."

"Well, do something that makes him think it's his idea," he said with a hint of a smile.

"Okay," she said, snuggling back down in the bed. She didn't want him to go. She felt infinitely safer with him at her side. But he was right about Sam.

He picked up the clock and set it for three. "If we're not back by the time the alarm goes off, call the police. Tell them everything you know."

He leaned over and kissed her cheek. "I hate to do it to you, but get up and fasten all the locks on the door after I leave. Then go back to sleep."

Then he was gone.

Despite his order, she got up out of bed and padded to the window. She stood near the corner and watched him walk to his car. There was an alertness to his movements that reassured her. For a moment, she wondered about him. She'd never asked if he had a wife. Had children. Had other family.

What if he had all three?

She watched as he drove out of the parking lot.

Then she went back to bed, but she knew she wouldn't go back to sleep. She coaxed Spade up on the bed.

Something alive. She needed that.

But she really wished Jake was back. He and those gentle hands that had soothed and comforted and, for a while, chased away the cold shadows.

# CHAPTER 17

Jake used his map to find the nightclub in downtown Atlanta.

Once he arrived, he drove around the block. There seemed to be no private parking, only valet service.

He wore a light blue, long-sleeved shirt he purchased earlier in the day. Still, he wasn't sure he could get inside the club with blue jeans until he saw two jean-clad men enter.

Well, he hadn't gone to a club in fifteen years or so.

He gave the valet twenty dollars and asked to park his own car.

The young man in a tie didn't blink. Just gave him directions on where to park.

Jake drove through a narrow alley into the back. He almost instantly saw Sam's car. He parked and looked around. No one. He stepped out of the car and inspected Sam's.

No explosives. Jake heard the crunch of pebbles as a car was being driven in. He stood and brushed dirt off his new shirt as he strode down the driveway toward the front entrance. He noted a side door that was probably used by employees.

He went inside, paid an exorbitant cover charge, and wandered over to the bar where he could see the small stage.

Sam was playing sax with four other musicians. Jazz, and very good jazz at that.

Some couples were dancing, Others were sitting back and listening. The lights were dim, and he doubted Sam could see him.

Jake ordered a drink. He was one of the few patrons sitting by himself. The rest were mostly couples.

Maybe he was giving Adams too much credit. Except he couldn't forget that C4 under Sam's sink. He sat there, his gaze roaming around the room again. Those working for Adams would be paid mercenaries, and there was usually something that set them apart from other people, no matter how much they tried to blend into the environment.

He listened to another song and glanced at his watch. They must be near the end of the set. He gulped down the weak bourbon and water, paid the bill, and headed toward the exit. He thought the musicians probably left by the side door.

"Don't like the music?" the guy at the door asked.

"I like it just fine," Jake said. "Just got a text message that the friend I was meeting can't come, and it's been a long day. I imagine the music's ending soon."

The man looked at his watch. "Another five minutes."

"I'll be back. That sax player's damned good."

The guy was looking at him. His gaze locked on the scar above Jake's ear. "You military?"

"Used to be."

The guy grinned. "I can always tell. I was in Nam. Marines."

He waited for Jake to declare his branch.

"Army," Jake said.

"You come back again, and I won't charge you."

"Thanks. I'll do that."

"If I'm not at the door, just ask for Sarge. Everyone calls me that."

Jake hesitated. "You see any other military here tonight?"

"None I recognized. Why?"

"Just wondered whether it might be a gathering place. Anyway, thanks, Sarge."

Jake left without leaving his name or giving Sarge a chance to ask more questions. He didn't like lying to guys who'd served.

Once outside, he glanced around. Two valets were lounging against the wall. One straightened.

"I'll get it myself," Jake said, handing the first one to reach him a five dollar bill. "I might be a few minutes. I have some messages to answer."

"Take your time," the valet said, "and thanks."

Not very dutiful of the valets. He could be back there stealing the contents of cars.

He made his way down the alley that led to the parking lot. He quickly checked his car in an abundance of caution. He'd left it unlocked, but he'd also left a dark thread in the door and trunk door. They hadn't been disturbed.

He stepped inside and waited.

Before long he saw a man slip out the side door. Different clothes than those Sam wore, but obviously one of the other musicians. He carried a saxophone case and placed it in a van.

Then Sarge appeared at the same door and went to the van. He got in the driver's side and drove it to the side door. Jake's view was blocked for a moment, then he heard a van door slam shut. The van started moving again.

He had a gut feeling Sam was in the van.

The musician was smarter than Jake had given him credit for. Jake waited as the valets both appeared and picked up cars. He followed the second one out.

Sam had done well, and Jake sure as hell didn't want to spoil it. He turned toward downtown Atlanta rather than toward the hotel. The traffic was thin enough at this hour so that he soon realized that no one was following him.

He turned onto the expressway and headed toward the hotel.

Kirke woke to the ringing of the room telephone. She looked at the clock. It was two forty in the morning.

She rolled over to pick it up and winced at the eruption of pain in her arm.

Ignoring it, she picked up the receiver and waited.

"Kirke."

*Sam. Thank God.* "I'm here," she said.

"Unlock the door between us."

She pulled on a pair of shorts and went to the connecting door. Jake had left the light on in the bathroom and the door slightly open so she wouldn't be entirely in the dark.

She was grateful for that as she opened the connecting door and faced Sam.

He grinned. "I decided I have a knack for cloak-and-dagger," he said. "Sarge helped me out. I think your friend was there. I didn't see him, but Sarge said he talked to someone who was obviously ex-military and who stayed only a few moments just before closing.

"He was worried about you."

Sam raised an eyebrow.

"He was," she insisted.

"Anything else happen?" He looked around the room suspiciously. He saw the food on the table and went over to what was left of the pizza. He grabbed a slice. It disappeared in two gulps.

She shook her head. "I talked to Robin. She's going to take care of Merlin for a few days. She said she would look after Spade as well if you want."

"I want," he said.

She hugged him. "I'm so glad to see you."

His cat leaped from the bed and wound in and out of his legs, meowing plaintively. Sam leaned down and picked him up.

"Poor Spade," Kirke said. "He's thoroughly confused."

"When will Robin be here?"

"Around nine," she said.

"And when will Kelly return?"

"I would think any minute."

"How are you?"

"Tired. Confused. And I hurt."

"Have you thought any more about going to the police?"

"Yes."

He waited.

"I would be admitting to withholding evidence. I would also be admitting to breaking any number of rules." She didn't add that she might also be sending Jake back to prison.

"Better than being dead," he said.

She had no answer for that.

The growing silence was broken by the knock she'd been expecting. She opened the door, and Jake Kelly entered, filling the room again with his presence.

Sam glowered at him.

Jake ignored it. "You play a mean sax," he said.

Kirke watched the conflicting emotions play across Sam's face.

He ignored the compliment. "What do we do now?" Sam asked.

"It depends on Kirke," Jake said.

Kirke looked from one face to another. Neither man trusted the other for whatever reason. "Tell him everything you told me," she said to Jake.

Sam perched on the table as Jake repeated his story. When he finished, Sam peered at him.

"You have no idea what the numbers mean?"

"No."

"He knew you as Mitch Edwards, but someone on his behalf called Jake Kelly," Sam said. "So why did he ask Kirke to give the letter to Mitch Edwards?"

That had been bothering Kirke as well.

"Maybe," Sam continued, "because the numbers had something to do with the man he knew best as Mitch Edwards. Something that was said when you were together. He was trying to tell you something that only Edwards would know."

Jake looked startled, then looked at Sam with new appreciation.

"I like puzzles," Sam said defensively, and Kirke could vouch for that. He'd always loved crossword puzzles along with many other kinds of puzzles. It had always amused her the way he would stir himself Sunday morning to listen to a public radio program that featured different kinds of word puzzles. Sam had sent in answers several times.

But she was taken back at his new cooperation. Maybe Jake's observation about his playing had disarmed Sam. Then again, it might have been the puzzle presented to him.

Sam turned to her. "Are you sure he didn't say anything beyond what sounded like *Virginia* and *military*?"

Kirke went back to that day in her mind. She'd been through it so many times, but she'd been so tired earlier. There was something else!

"Dallas. He mentioned Dallas. He said, 'Tell him . . . Dallas . . . ' I should have remembered that . . . I was concentrating on the last part of what he said, the part just before he lost consciousness."

She saw sudden recognition in Jake's eyes and knew it had meaning for him.

"You remember something?"

He nodded. "Maybe not without the other words. But combined with *military* and *Virginia* . . ."

He was silent, but she could see the wheels turning inside his head. Something was beginning to make sense to him. "Cox and I talked one night. He wasn't very communicative, but we had served in some of the same hot spots in the Middle East. Not together, but we had some common ground there. He got started on a bar near the Farm in Virginia. It's the not-very-secret training facility for the CIA. I underwent some specialized training there. He asked if I had gone to a bar called the Enigma.

"I had. It was after a grueling two weeks at the Farm, and a bunch of us from Special Forces were celebrating the fact we were through. A CIA instructor had recommended the bar. It was a spook hangout."

"Spook?" Sam asked.

"It's what we call a CIA agent," Jake explained. "Cox mentioned the manager. I think he really liked her. She looked after all the CIA recruits. Older ones, too. Word was she was the widow of a CIA guy who died early in Afghanistan.

"She was tough as nails," he continued. "While I was there, some drunk CIA types started in on us. We'd bested them on a challenge at the Farm, and their pride was hurt. The manager simply glared them down and threatened to bar them forever."

"Her name was Dallas, and it suited her. When she wasn't trying to restore order, she was warm and funny and had a southern accent that was pure honey. Cox appeared to have been smitten with her."

"When was this?" she asked, feeling a twinge of jealousy. He seemed a bit too fond of this Dallas.

"Nine years ago," he said.

Kirke didn't take any comfort in the memory. A bar in common? She couldn't stifle a yawn.

"And the numbers?" Sam contributed, now fully into the puzzle.

"I don't know," Jake said. "But Dallas might."

Kirke glanced at her watch. Three thirty.

They all needed sleep. Jake's face was lined with fatigue. She couldn't think any longer. Sam was a night person, but he, too, looked tired.

"I'm going to bed," she said. "I think we all should. Maybe it will be clearer in the morning."

Sam looked at her, then Jake.

"He going to stay here?"

"I am," Jake said without hesitation.

"Where are you going to sleep?" Sam asked truculently.

"In the chair," Jake said evenly, his gaze obviously weighing Sam.

She looked from Sam, the open, good-natured, musician who looked ten years younger than he was, to hard-edged Jake, whose enigmatic eyes sheltered every emotion.

Sam was being protective, just as she had been protective of him from time to time, but Jake didn't know that.

Awareness flickered across Sam's face. He raised an eyebrow, then picked up Spade and retreated to his room without another word. Despite Jake's suggestion, he closed the door, but she didn't hear it lock.

Jake turned to her. "You should go back to sleep."

"I don't know if I can do that when you're here," she said honestly.

"You won't know I'm here."

But she would. Even with her eyes closed, she suspected she would be aware of his slightest movement.

"Did you really like Sam's band?" she asked.

"I don't say things I don't mean."

She believed him. He had lied to her in the beginning, but she understood why. But small lies? She doubted it. He wouldn't care enough to do it.

She crawled back in bed and pulled the sheet over her. Her mind went over the conversation. Had Mark Cable included a clue in his few pained words? A clue that only Jake would understand?

Why not just tell her?

He hadn't known her, hadn't known what she would do. Perhaps he wanted no one except Jake Kelly to understand what he was trying to say. Maybe it was a Hail Mary pass on his part. He knew he was dying, and there was one last thing he had to do, but he didn't want whatever it was to fall into the wrong hands.

So what had he meant with those last words?

She snuggled between the sheets.

Maybe Dallas would offer another clue. A definitive one. With that thought, she closed her eyes and nearly instantly was asleep.

⟩

Jake sat in the chair he pulled next to the window. There were vehicles going by outside. In Atlanta, there were always vehicles going by. One car parked not far from the back entrance, and he watched as an obviously intoxicated couple stumbled inside.

They hadn't been found yet, but that meant little. Adams obviously had resources, probably even had them in the CIA. He'd managed to get himself assigned to that particular mission, which meant he probably had assistance.

How much had he taken away from that mission? If he'd

been willing to betray his country and slaughter his companions, he wouldn't hesitate to sell government secrets and take up arms dealing himself. He knew the major players.

All that would disappear if the government discovered he was still alive.

Too much thinking. He glanced over at Kirke. She'd resisted sleep for a while. Now he heard her soft, regular breathing.

He went over to a bag he'd tucked behind the TV while she'd been in the restroom. He opened it and took out the gun. He checked to make sure it was still loaded and then tucked it next to his shooting hand.

Then he closed his eyes. Two or three hours' sleep would do wonders.

What had Del Cox meant to say? Why now? Why not in the past seven years, while he was wasting away in prison?

Perhaps they could sort it out tomorrow.

He suddenly realized he was thinking in terms of *we* rather than *I*. He hadn't done that in a very long time, not since two good friends had been killed years earlier.

Atlanta could be just as deadly now. The C-4 proved that.

And, God help him, this time innocents were involved, and he wasn't at all sure he could protect them any better than he'd protected Chet and Ramos.

# CHAPTER 18

Kirke woke to daylight.

She tried to ignore it and buried her head in the pillows.

But the sun was filtering through the windows. She could feel it, and daylight always woke her.

She didn't want to acknowledge it. She heard a squawk. It was Merlin's demand for breakfast. She couldn't complain. It was far better than Merlin's scream when he was angry. She opened her eyes. The room was empty except for Merlin's covered cage.

She sat up and shook her head, trying to orient herself. Her gaze darted to the table with its jumble of boxes and other food items. Not a dream. These past few days had been no dream. Or nightmare.

Where was Jake?

She looked at the clock. Seven a.m. She hadn't gone to bed until after three.

She sat up and rubbed the sleep from her eyes. The door between her room and Sam's was slightly open.

She stood and went to the window. Jake's car was still there.

Kirke went into the bathroom and rinsed her face with cold water before glancing at herself in the mirror and wincing. Never much of a beauty, she was particularly appalling this morning. Her black eye had turned a rainbow of colors, and the bandage had fallen off her check, revealing a small red gash. Her hair stuck out all over, and her complexion was pale.

"Drat," she said in utter disgust.

She hated not being in control, and she was definitely not in control at the moment. She wasn't even in control of her own emotions. She felt as if she was a piece of metal irresistibly being drawn to a magnet.

"You're better than this," she scolded herself.

She looked longingly at the shower. Her hair was a disaster, and she wanted to feel icy water to wake her up, then warm water to soothe. But she didn't know where Jake was.

Safety was something she would never take for granted again.

She satisfied herself by splashing water on her face again and running a brush through her hair. She didn't even have any powder or cover-up to apply to the bruise.

She hated to feel so powerless. Even in that small matter.

A knock ended her momentary self-pity. *The* infamous knock, she thought.

She took one last look at herself. She still wore the wrinkled T-shirt and shorts, and her face was a still for a horror movie. She opened the door, and Jake stood there, three large paper cups in his hands. She smelled coffee.

She snatched a cup and put both hands around it, welcoming the warmth and smell. She lived on coffee. "Thank you," she said, suddenly feeling shy and awkward.

"It's black," he said, "but I brought some cream and sugar."

"Just black."

His gaze was as inscrutable as usual, but she saw it roam over her face and linger a second longer than necessary on her body. Heat rose in her, and she felt her cheeks blush.

Merlin squawked again. The fact he was using bird speak instead of people speak was telling. He was obviously disgruntled at being uprooted and neglected.

"He's not talking," Jake said.

She had finally decided to think of him as Jake. Just plain Jake. Until last night, she'd tried to think of him as Jake Kelly, or David Cable, or anything that wasn't as intimate— and friendly—as only his first name. But that was rather ridiculous now that they had shared a room together. Of a kind.

"He's frightened, I think," she said. "We believed he was passed around a lot as a young bird. He's okay in my house and Sam's, but this is a new place, and when he's upset, he doesn't talk. Only a couple of screeches so far. We've been lucky."

To her surprise, he went over to Merlin's cage and opened it. He stuck out his arm, and Merlin flew to it.

Jake seemed to know instinctively what to do. He ran his fingers along the bird's feathers as lightly as his fingers had touched her very early this morning. Merlin preened and spread his wings. Then he did something it took months for him to do with both Sam and herself. He put his head against Jake's neck.

"You've bribed him," she accused.

"No, I just brought him fruit."

It wasn't only that, Kirke knew. It was the quiet assurance about him, a steadiness that Merlin responded to.

"He's not going to like going with your friend," he said unexpectedly.

"No. But he'll be safe until all this is over."

"Tell me about this friend."

"She's a reporter with the *Atlanta Observer*." She paused, then added, "Her husband's with the FBI."

Jake didn't react, but then he seldom did. He always took things in, silently weighed them, then did what he wanted to do.

"He's out of the city," she added.

"And what are you going to tell her about me?" he asked curiously.

"I don't know. I probably won't say anything at all. No one knows about you."

"How much does she know?"

"Only that I need a rest."

"She must be a very good friend."

"She's always been intrigued by Merlin. In fact, I got Merlin from a friend of hers who works with animal rescue, so she kinda owes me on that one. She's also considering finding a rescue parrot of her own. This will be a good trial run."

"And will Merlin be equally as pleased?" he asked, his hands cradling the damn bird. Merlin was loving it.

Well, she had, too, a few hours ago.

She only hoped her eyes didn't reveal exactly how much. She glanced away and walked to the window. The view wasn't great. Parking lot and then the expressway. Already at seven, it was bumper-to-bumper.

"Have you thought any more about this Dallas?"

"Yes."

"And?" she finally said after he didn't add to his short reply.

He shrugged. "It's all I have to go on."

"You're going there?"

"When I know the two of you are safe," he said.

*The two of you.* She and Sam. There had never been the two of them, as far as any romantic interest went, and after today she and Sam may not even be friends. Except for those few exchanges earlier this morning, Sam had been nothing but hostile.

As if summoned, Sam wandered into the room.

He looked sleepy-eyed and as mussed as she felt. "I don't do dawn," he groused.

"There's some coffee," she said, gesturing toward the table.

"I'd rather have a Coke."

That she knew. He usually got up in the afternoon.

"There's a machine down the hall," Jake said.

"There might be bad guys out there," Sam said sarcastically.

Kirke realized that Sam's mellow attitude early this morning had faded with daylight. He was angry, and Sam rarely got angry. He was usually relaxed and took life as it came with a shrug.

"I checked earlier," Jake said evenly.

"I bet you did," Sam retorted, "Now that you've involved Kirke in whatever dangerous plan you have."

Merlin left Jake's arm and retreated back into his cage as if fleeing from the tension in the room.

"He didn't involve me," Kirke said. "*I* involved me."

"I let it get beyond control," Jake disagreed.

She shook her head. "The moment this Gene Adams, or whoever he is, saw me take the envelope from the hit-and-run victim, I became a target."

"The police might have helped," Sam interjected.

"Might or might not," she said, not waiting for Jake to reply. She was more committed than ever to his cause now. She believed him. She believed in him. An injustice had been done, and if there was one thing she hated more than anything, it was injustice.

"It doesn't matter now," Jake said. "You both are involved, and the cops don't provide twenty-four-hour protection."

"What do you suggest?" Sam said.

"Do you have someplace to go for a week or so?"

"And lose my job?"

Jake speared him with that hard gaze of his. "What happens when you get sick?"

"I don't," Sam replied.

"Then a family emergency?"

"Go, Sam," Kirke broke in. "You know Marshall will keep your place open. He thinks you're the best." She paused, then added, "Which you are. It's a good time to visit your brother.

"Where is he?" Jake asked.

Sam looked rebellious, even as he answered slowly, "Denver. He plays bass in a small club there. We used to have a small band together in high school."

"Anyone else know about it?"

"Some at the club know I have a brother, but they don't know where. Jeb and I parted under less than happy circumstances."

"Can you leave today?"

Sam hesitated.

Jake took out two of the prepaid credit cards he'd bought before leaving Chicago. He'd intended one for Kirke, but he thought Sam needed it more now. "There's $500 on each. Untraceable. Don't use any of your own credit cards."

"I can pay for it," Sam said, although Kirke knew he always lived on the edge of financial disaster.

"I don't doubt it, but you have to go because of me, and I don't want a trail. Can you take your friend's van?"

"I think so."

"Don't go back to the house. Buy what you need along the way."

Sam's eyes were very alert now. He wasn't happy, Kirke knew, but he realized they were out of their league here. Few people could match Sam's talent with the sax, but he didn't have a hostile or elusive bone in his body.

"Please, Sam, take them and go," Kirke said. "You've been saying you wanted to see your brother again."

Sam was slow in answering. "And then what?" he finally asked.

"I'll lead him away from you," Jake said. "I'll try to bring him out in the open."

"How?"

"I'll go by the house and pick up a few more things. He'll follow. You two will have disappeared. He'll have nothing but me."

"If it doesn't work?"

"It will. He wants to get rid of me in case Cox had managed to pass information to Kirke, and she passed it to me. He knows I'll come after him if he doesn't get me first."

"What about Kirke?"

Jake turned to her. "She has to disappear for a few days as well."

Kirke didn't reply. She had no intention of disappearing on her own. If she was going to be in danger, she was going to be in danger on her own terms, and that meant confronting it rather than running and waiting for disaster.

"Kirke?" Sam persisted.

"I'll be okay," she said. "There are places I can go."

"Why don't you come with me?" Sam offered.

Kirke looked sideways at Jake. His expression didn't change, nor did his eyes. He was the most outwardly emotionless man she'd ever met. So why was she so damned attracted to him? She'd always liked open people who laughed and cried and shared both joys and grief.

She shook her head. "I have friends. I've already asked for time off, and my boss said to take as much as I needed."

Sam hesitated.

"Get your cola," she said.

Sam looked rebellious but disappeared through the door, and she heard his outer door open and close.

She studied Jake for a moment. "I want to go with you," she finally said.

"Hell no."

"This man—this Adams—might not go after you. He wants me right now. He had a chance at you and came after me, instead. He might wait until I return, and I can't stay away forever." She paused, then said, "I'll be safer with you than I would be alone. I don't know what he looks like or what to look for. You do."

Sam returned with soda can in hand, cutting off the conversation. She turned silent. Sam would never leave if he didn't think she was doing the same.

Jake opened the package of donuts he'd bought last night and put several pieces of fruit in Merlin's cage.

Merlin didn't touch them, and Kirke was stricken. Merlin usually consumed everything immediately. His lack of appetite said everything he wasn't saying.

And now to save him, she would have to leave him for a few days.

At least Merlin knew Robin. Had reacted well to her.

Still, she hated to leave him. She didn't want him to feel abandoned again.

The phone rang, and she jumped. Robin. She was within ten minutes of the hotel.

"You said she would take Spade for a few days?" Sam said.

Kirke nodded. "She has a cat, Daisy. Probably would like the company."

"Is she familiar with Merlin's vocabulary?"

"Not entirely," Kirke admitted. "Merlin has pretty much been on his good behavior when she's been around."

She went over to him. "I'm sorry, Sam. I never thought you would be involved."

He gave her a quick hug. "You've cleaned up some of my messes." He moved away. "I'll get my things together and make a few calls." He glanced at Jake. "And no, I won't tell anyone where I'm going."

Jake tossed him the new cell phone she'd seen last night. "Use this from now on. Kirke and I have the number."

"And mine?"

"Keep it off. You can check messages on your old phone, but don't call from it."

"Kirke needs one as well."

"I have another one." He rattled off the number.

Sam's eyes narrowed. "Where did you get so much money if you just left prison?"

"My father," he said slowly. A flicker in his eyes told her he knew what prompted the question. "He left me what he had. Someone invested it for me."

Sam was thinking about the missing money. She knew it, because she'd had the fleeting thought herself.

She would have sworn, though, that there was something vulnerable in Jake's eyes. Then they turned as dark and implacable as always.

"Are you going to stay here when Robin comes?" Kirke asked.

"Would you feel better if I did?"

"No. Robin is curious. If she sees you, she might start putting things together. She gets a bone, and she doesn't let go. She was nominated for a Pulitzer Prize for a story she did last year."

With his usual economy of words, he just gave a brief nod and disappeared into Sam's room.

A few minutes later, Robin arrived.

Her friend stood back and looked at her. "My God, you look like you've been in a war zone."

"Thank you," Kirke replied.

"You know what I mean. It's been too long, Kirke."

"I know." Kirke stood back and let her in.

Robin's gaze ran over the three cups on the table, a half-eaten donut. The other bags. "Is there something you aren't telling me?"

"Just that the past few days have been a bit unsettling." She hoped Robin never learned what an understatement that was.

"That's not very helpful."

As always, Robin didn't ask direct questions. She made a comment, and sat back, waiting for answers to unasked questions. It was, Kirke knew, what made her a good reporter. She'd learned herself that she would get more information by listening rather than probing.

She shrugged. "It's really just what I told you. I need to get away." *Now, that wasn't an understatement.*

"Okay," Robin said good-naturedly, although there was a gleam of concern in her eyes. "But if you need anything, don't forget I have my own FBI agent and what I call 'my little old ladies detective club.'"

"I remember," Kirke said with a grin. Robin had had her own adventure last year and was aided by her eighty-year-old-plus neighbor and an elderly waitress.

"Goddamn bird," Merlin said in a man's voice.

Kirke felt a flood of relief as Robin chuckled.

"No," Kirke corrected, "Merlin's a very good bird. So good that Robin wants to keep you for a few days."

"Robin," echoed Merlin.

Robin went over to the cage. "I'll take very good care of the . . . blankety-blank bird," she said, mischief dancing in her eyes. "I'll try to edit his language."

In that moment, Kirke wanted to tell her everything. The purse snatching. The connection to the accident—no, murder—victim that started the nightmare she was living.

But it wasn't her story to tell. And Robin would feel honor bound to tell her husband and possibly pursue the story herself. That couldn't happen.

"I'll contact you," she said, mindful of the small window of time Jake said they had. She picked up Merlin's cage. "I'll help you with all this stuff.

"You're not going to tell me where you're going?"

"I'm not sure. I just need to get away for a few days."

"Okay. But if you need anything . . ."

Twenty minutes later, both Robin and Sam had left. The room seemed very empty without Sam next door, without Spade or Merlin.

Jake had watched them go, made sure they weren't followed.

Then he was back. "Time to go."

"Where?"

"Find you someplace safe."

"The safest place is with you."

"No, it isn't. For any number of reasons, it isn't. Adams wants me. The feds want me, and dammit, I want you. That's three reasons for you to run like hell.

She was stunned for a moment. Particularly by the third reason. Lightning had flashed between them since they first met, but she was shocked he admitted it in plain words.

"I don't want to run from you."

He regarded her with frustration, then without warning he pulled her to him and bent his head to kiss her.

There was nothing gentle about the meeting of lips. She felt the frustration and anger in them, then the need, and the world erupted around them.

She drank in the scent of him—the mixture of man and a spicy aftershave lotion. She tasted him as his tongue entered her mouth, and she felt a tingling sensation burn in the core of her body and snake through the rest of her until she was helpless to do anything but ask for more with eager lips.

The pressure of his hands changed from angry to demanding. She leaned into him, and his body hardened against hers. She wanted him. Dear heaven, she wanted him.

He suddenly released her lips and cursed. Softly.

"No good," he said. "I'm poison to you."

She looked up at him. His eyes weren't shadowed now. They were roiling with emotions she couldn't define.

"I want to go with you," she said. "I can help."

"You already have. I don't want you hurt again. Too many people have already been hurt because of me."

The pain in his voice pierced her. She'd started thinking he was immune to emotions, but now his words were raw with agony, and she realized she really didn't know anything at all.

"Either take me, or I'll stay here," she said. "I don't have anywhere else to go." It was the only weapon she had. She sensed that threat was the only one that would work.

"You have friends. This Robin?"

"I won't lead the bad guys to her."

His eyes searched hers. Heated. Frustrated. And tired. She wondered how much sleep he'd had. Not very much.

"I can drive," she offered.

He raised an eyebrow.

"I'm a good driver." She pressed her case. "And I have a *valid* license." She paused, then asked, "And you? Which of the licenses are you going to use? What if you're stopped, and someone follows up on it?"

He ignored the logic. "You don't know Gene Adams."

"No. That's why I'm safer with you."

"I don't know how many men he has with him. I count at least three now, but there could be more. Mercenaries."

"You said you needed him to come to you. He won't do that until he gets me first. You said that, too. You need me."

"I can fool him into thinking you're with me. One of your credit cards. That's all I need. In the meantime, you can go somewhere safe. A room in any city in the country."

"My credit card was stolen, and I have only the one. And how can I avoid this Adams if he comes after me? I don't even know what he looks like. What any of them look like."

She hoped she didn't sound like she was begging. "I will be safer with you," she concluded.

"You're a distraction," he said bluntly.

"Wouldn't I be one if you were worrying about me?" That was, of course, if he gave a damn.

He was silent a moment, then said, "You have to promise to do everything I tell you when I tell you."

"I will."

"If I tell you to leave, you leave."

She nodded.

"Swear. Just as you did to Del Cox."

"I swear."

"God help me if it turns out as badly as your first oath did," he said.

# CHAPTER 19

*What do the damn numbers mean?*

The question was driving Jake nuts as he drove through the afternoon and early evening with Kirke asleep beside him.

He glanced at Kirke. He'd continued to do his damndest to change her mind about coming with him until the moment they both got in the car, and even after.

How many lives was he going to disrupt, if not destroy?

They were traveling light. She'd packed the few items he'd fetched from her house. He had three pairs of jeans, one pair of washable slacks, four shirts and two T-shirts, shaving gear, a toothbrush, and not much else. Well, he'd had less in prison.

Kirke didn't have much more.

"There's no place to go," she'd insisted when he'd offered yet again to send her someplace. "Robin and Sam are the only people I'm really close to, at least to barge in for a week or more with few explanations. Sam's gone, and I wouldn't lead anyone to Robin. Besides, I would have to explain things to her, and that wouldn't be good for you. I could go to a motel, but . . ."

"No family?"

"No one but Sam," she said.

His heart was touched by the admission. He also realized how very little he knew about her. The one thing he did know was her vulnerability. She'd been right about that. She had few skills in evasion. She'd probably be easy to find, and she had an uncanny talent for attracting danger.

He hadn't wanted her with him for any number of reasons, among them the effect she had on him. She stirred emotions in him he thought long dead. Lust, of course, was natural; he'd been without sex for a very long time. But it was the other emotions that bedeviled him, the ones that touched him in unexpected places.

She was brave and scared. She was smart, street shrewd, but an innocent where someone like Adams was concerned. She couldn't even imagine what the man was capable of, though she was learning fast.

So in the end, he'd agreed to bring her along.

"Where are we?" she asked suddenly, and he glanced over at her. She'd straightened up in her seat, and one hand rubbed her eyes.

"North Carolina."

"Where in North Carolina?" She glanced down at a map that lay between them. It was a southeastern United States map he'd found at a convenience store. Before she dosed off, she'd marked their progress.

"Almost to Virginia."

She glanced at the clock. "I didn't sleep that long."

Through the corner of his eye, he saw her frown at his poor attempt of humor. "What about you?" she asked. "I can drive while you sleep."

"I'm fine," he said.

She sat up straighter in the seat. "Tell me about that bar you and Cable had in common."

"Cox," he corrected her.

"I can't stop thinking of him as Cable," she said. "Too many names here. He was Mark Cable and Del Cox. You were David Cable and who else?"

"Daniel now," he said, "Daniel Davis. Remember it, if you can. It's on my driver's license."

"You don't look like a Daniel."

"Maybe because I'm not."

"You *do* look like a Jake. Or is it Jacob?"

"I'm afraid to ask what a Jake looks like, and yes, it is Jacob." He was talking more than he had in seven years and longer. He'd rarely indulged in small talk, even when he was married, but now he felt a baffling pleasure in bantering with her. It dulled the cutting edge of loneliness that had been a part of him since he left the service, maybe even before that.

"No nonsense," she said slowly. "No pretense. Direct."

Impersonal stuff. All of it, but wasn't that what he wanted? No, he wanted a great deal more. He just couldn't have it without destroying both of them. No distractions now. People who care made mistakes.

He didn't answer. Nothing to say that wouldn't continue a conversation that was becoming more intimate than he could afford.

"You're changing the subject. Tell me more about that bar," she persisted. "That's where we're heading, isn't it?"

"Yes."

"This Dallas, she made an impression?"

"Yeah. I liked her. And I was surprised when Del Cox mentioned her. He wasn't a man to share."

"Warm and funny? I think I would like her."

"I think you like everyone."

"You sound disapproving."

"It can be dangerous."

"And it can be interesting," she countered. She rested her arm on his knee.

Warmth flooded him.

A warmth that could prove deadly.

He tried to divert her thoughts. And his. "I called information for a number for the bar when I got the coffee this morning," he said. "There's no current phone number."

"Did you try to find Dallas?"

"Never knew her last name, but once I get there, I should be able to find someone who remembers her. Maybe she knows the key to this riddle."

"*We* should be able to find her, then," she said.

"*We?*"

"I used to be a reporter. I was good at it. Besides, I'm good at talking to people."

"And I'm not?"

"Not exactly."

He didn't doubt that for a moment. He always went straight for the jugular in a conversation. She, on the other hand, had a background that depended on extracting information from people in an entirely different way.

"How did you become a paramedic?"

"I owned the house. After I lost my job, I didn't want to leave Atlanta, and there were no journalism jobs. I didn't particularly want to go into public relations. I've always liked biology and even for a time thought about medicine. I thought this would be a good way to decide whether I wanted to pursue it.

"And you stayed with it?"

She shifted in her seat. "I didn't have the money for eight more years of schooling, and I've been thinking about writing a book. Nonfiction about being a paramedic. Maybe fiction later."

He digested that. He suspected she didn't mention the real reason. She obviously liked the adrenaline of her job. He'd noticed that when he'd been in her home, then when she was at the hospital.

"Okay," she said, as if embarrassed about the direction of their conversation. "Back to the problem. We have a bar in Virginia. Maybe. We have a waitress/manager, maybe. We have some numbers, but no idea what they mean. We're making progress."

In addition to being stubborn, she was an optimist. Or just being sarcastic.

"Maybe," he replied.

She laughed. She seemed to do that a lot. It was amazing, considering their circumstances.

He liked the sound of it. Throaty and rich. He liked having her in the seat next to him as well. The sparks between them excited him in a way he'd almost forgotten, yet their silences were companionable. It was an odd and intriguing combination.

"What about the numbers?" she said after he didn't answer. "Any more thoughts on that?"

He had many, but none of them seemed to offer much help. He shook his head. "Not any we didn't discuss." He paused. "I'm trying to put together my conversations with Del. There weren't that many."

"How long did you know him?"

"Four weeks planning for the mission, then a week going in. Usually there's more training for something this complicated, but there wasn't time. A South American drug lord had made it known he had U.S. missiles for sale to the highest bidder. We couldn't let them get in the wrong hands, and we had to know the source."

"What happened to those missiles?"

"I heard they were taken out by an air strike. I don't know the details."

"Then they never discovered who and how they were acquired."

"Not as far as I know."

"Did this drug lord have a family or close associates?"

He glanced over at her. "A brother," he said. "He handled the business end."

"Maybe he would like to know what happened."

He liked the way her mind worked, exploring every possible angle, letting one clue lead to another. Hell, he liked everything about her.

And the last place she should be is here beside him.

"You're thinking of catching a thief with another one."

"Something like that."

"The CIA would do well to recruit you," he said.

"I take it that's not entirely a compliment."

It was growing dark, and he was hungry. She must be as well. All they'd had were the rest of the donuts he'd bought yesterday, and coffee.

"Hungry?"

She nodded. "I also need some makeup. Maybe dark

glasses. People will think you're beating me and call the police."

He took his eyes off the road and glanced at her. Her eye was no longer swollen, but the area around it was several different hues of purple. She still had a small bandage on her cheek and one large one on her arm. There were a few other small healing abrasions. "God, I'm sorry about those injuries."

"You shouldn't be. You didn't have anything to do with it. I really don't like someone else to take responsibility for my actions."

"I think that's what they call independent to a fault."

"Can you ever be too independent?"

The way she said it surprised him. Combative. Challenging.

"You're divorced?" he asked.

She stared at him. "How did you know that?"

He didn't want to lie to her. He'd done too much of that already. "I did a search on you."

She shrugged. "For a short period. I got sucked into the 'everyone should be married' philosophy. I soon discovered my husband had a very different idea of marriage than I did."

Before he could ask her more, she turned the question on him. "And you? Were you married? Or *are* you married?"

Touché. He usually didn't let people get into private places. Yet he'd asked her. Damn hypocritical of him to ask without being willing to discuss his own personal life, or lack of it. Still, he never talked about his father or his ex-wife.

The silence lengthened between them.

"You were, then?" she said finally.

"Yes." The curtness of his reply didn't invite more questions.

"No more?"

"No more."

To his surprise, she dropped the subject. "The numbers," she said. "Any more thoughts about what the numbers mean?"

"Telephone number, foreign bank account, safe-deposit

box numbers, post office box numbers. Or none of the above. Del never mentioned numbers."

"Could it be a pin number for a computer program? A password?"

He took his eyes off the road for another second to glance at her. There was little traffic, even on this heavily trafficked interstate highway, and he couldn't resist. She kept surprising him with that quick mind. He supposed she was a good paramedic. She soaked up information like a sponge and seldom became rattled, even when her own life was in danger. She also had an empathy for people—and parrots—that made them trust her.

"I don't know," he said frankly. "At this moment, anything seems possible."

"I'll help."

He was reminded again that he wasn't alone, that whether or not he liked it, she intended to be a partner and not a damsel in distress.

He nodded and felt her sense of surprise rather than saw it.

"Good," she said, as she sat back.

He didn't want to go back to the silence. 2He liked the sound of her voice. He liked the companionship.

"Where did you come by the name of Kirke?" he asked. He'd never heard the name before, but somehow the uniqueness of it fit her.

"Ah, something you couldn't find on the Internet," she said. "I'm amazed."

He shrugged.

She was silent a moment, then said, "My grandfather's last name. He didn't have sons. My mother thought he would like it. At least enough to get some money out of him."

"Did he?"

"He never said."

"And your parents?"

"Never knew my father. He split when I was born. My mother died of a drug overdose." She said it without rancor. More matter of fact, and he hurt for her.

"Then who raised you?"

"My grandfather. He was rather stern, but he knew his

duty. I was mostly farmed out to boarding schools."

"Is he still alive?"

"He died just before I finished college. He paid my college tuition and left me enough to buy the duplex. I've always been grateful for that."

He heard the affection in her voice. And, for the first time, a hint of loneliness. Small tidbits about her that didn't really didn't tell him why she was sticking out her neck such a long way for him.

He noticed a sign for a restaurant and left the interstate. "Choices," he said. "A hamburger chain or a truck stop."

"Truck stop," she said immediately. "I love them, and they might have some makeup."

"A truck stop?"

"There's lots of women truck drivers these days," she said.

"Truck stop it is." He concurred. He'd always found the truck stop food far superior to chains, but the ambiance usually sucked. He drove into the huge parking lot, passing at least twenty long-haul trucks and several passenger cars.

As soon as they stopped, she got out and stretched. She was still clad in shorts and T-shirt, and he admired her athletic legs and curves.

The restaurant was one of those rambling structures with showers in the back for truckers. Even at ten p.m., the restaurant was more than half-filled.

She slid into a booth, and he sat across from her. A waitress appeared with two menus she handed to them. Her eyes rested on Kirke's face, and he saw cold hostility as she turned toward him. "Coffee?" she asked.

Both of them nodded, and the waitress hurried back to the counter.

Kirke scanned the menu. "Can you order the hot roast beef sandwich for me? I'm going into the restroom."

Before he could stop Kirke, she was out of her seat, and the waitress was back with two cups. She set them down, blocking his exit from the booth. Then her hand brushed the coffee cup and it turned over, the hot liquid running over the table and down his jeans.

"Oh I'm so sorry," she said. She grabbed some napkins and tried to wipe up the coffee dripping off the table onto his lap, apologizing profusely all the jeans.

"It doesn't matter," he said, standing. He didn't want to leave Kirke alone. Not even for a minute. But then a second waitress joined the first in sopping up coffee from his pants. Together they blocked the way out, unless he wanted to leap over the table.

"You aren't burned, are you?" said the first waitress.

The coffee was hot but not steaming. "No."

"Your meal will be free, of course," the second one said. "And we'll pay the cleaning bill."

"That won't be necessary," he said, trying to see the hall Kirke had walked down.

Then someone who said he was a manager joined the crowd. More apologies.

"Look," Jake finally said. "I don't care about the cleaning bill. I'm not going to sue, but I do want to get to the restrooms."

He finally managed to push through the growing crowd and headed in the direction Kirke had taken.

"Where's the restrooms?" he asked someone.

"Down the hall and to the left," said the manager.

Jake ran down the hall and saw a sign saying Office. He retreated and went to the right.

Two doors across from each other. One said Guys, the other Dolls.

He knocked at the latter door.

No one answered.

He opened the door.

It was small. And empty.

# CHAPTER 20

Kirke stepped into the small, old, but scrupulously clean facilities.

She glanced at her face. Didn't look any better than it had this morning. No wonder she was getting some strange looks from people in the restaurant.

She rinsed the sleep from her eyes. She felt refreshed after her nap and, she hated to admit even to herself, looked forward to more time with Jake.

She'd never been with a dangerous man before. And he was that. Everything about him shouted *danger* and *beware*, and not only because of the present threat.

From the fitness of his body—how many push-ups did he do daily in prison?—to the dark, impenetrable eyes to the quiet efficiency with which he seemed to handle everything, he radiated warrior. She was far more fascinated with him than she wanted to be. And she was trusting him far more than she probably should.

A persistent knock came at the door. She frowned, but it continued. She started to open it to give someone a piece of her mind.

The waitress peered inside. "Just wanted to make sure you're okay, hon," she said.

Kirke nodded.

The woman's eyes went to the bruises on her face. "You in any trouble, I gotta bunch of truckers who will help."

Kirke winced at the thought of being considered a battered woman. "Thanks, but I'm okay. A purse snatcher did this two days ago. The guy I'm with . . . he's one of the good ones."

The woman didn't look convinced. "He doesn't look the type, but you never can tell . . . My friend . . ." Her voice trailed off.

"Thanks for caring," Kirke said and meant it. Too many people didn't bother to help when they saw something off-kilter.

"Okay, you need anything, hon, just let me know."

Kirke closed the door again and decided to take another look at her face. Terrible. They should have sunglasses at a truck stop. And a cap. She would look while waiting for her meal. Which reminded her how hungry she was.

Another knock.

Good Samaritan or not, this was getting ridiculous.

She opened the door again. A big burly guy was waiting across the hall for the men's room. Before she could react, he pushed her back into the restroom and shoved a cloth to her face.

She instantly knew what it was and tried not to breathe in the fumes. She was dragged several steps while she desperately held her breath. The door opened, and she slumped against his body as if unconscious.

He loosened his hold, released the cloth, and started to pick her up. She swung around and kneed him in the groin. He grunted and released her right arm but kept an iron grip on the other. She screamed as loud as she could.

"Bitch," he yelled, and threw her against the side of the wall. She was barely aware through a growing mental fog that she was now somehow outside the building. The chloroform was working.

She heard a car engine, the crunch of tires spitting up gravel.

"No!" she screamed as loud as she could before a hand clamped on her mouth again.

She bit down hard. The man roared with rage, and she heard a shout. Jake's voice. She was tossed like a sack of potatoes and landed in strong arms.

There was a slam of a car door, then the revving up of a car speeding off.

"Kirke?" *His* voice. Jake's voice.

She tried to focus.

He leaned over her. His face looked blurry, but his words came through clear enough.

"Gone? Is he gone?" She suddenly felt sick. The chloroform. She turned and threw up as he held her.

She was mortified. But grateful, too. She was *alive*!

"God, I'm sorry. I was coming after you, and a waitress spilled coffee and . . . I shouldn't have let you out of my sight. Then I heard you." His voice was raw. There was an emotion in it that she hadn't heard before.

"Someone knocked at the restroom . . . held a cloth to my mouth. Chloroform . . . I tried not to breathe it in . . ."

He continued to hold her, even cradling her as she became aware of the many eyes on them. Her scream had apparently emptied the restaurant, and everyone who had been inside was now watching avidly.

He looked up. "Her ex-boyfriend," he explained. "Almost killed her a few days ago. I was helping her get away. I don't know how he found us."

"Had to be two or more of them," said one whip-thin trucker dressed in jeans and a New York Mets ball cap. "There was a driver."

"Must have been his brother," Kirke said. "Just got out of prison."

"Wish I got my hands on them," the trucker said. Others nodded.

"He must have had some kind of tracking device in my car," Jake said.

The waitress who'd knocked at the door of the restroom kneeled beside Kirke. She was ashen. "You shoulda told me someone was after you. We thought it was the guy you were with . . ."

Kirke was having a hard time keeping up with her lies, especially in her muddled state. To her surprise, they just came bursting from her mouth. She'd never had to balance them before, not before Jake. "I . . . was ashamed," she said. And she was. Lying was becoming all too easy.

"I'll call the sheriff," the waitress said.

That, Kirke knew, was the last thing they needed. She shook her head. "I just want to get back to my family. They'll see that I'm safe." She didn't have to fake the tears that formed in her eyes. She couldn't forget her terror as she was being dragged away.

A trucker nodded. Then another. They obviously didn't want to hang around to give statements. She knew truckers were on tight schedules.

"Anyone going to Richmond?" Jake looked at the assembled truckers. "I can't risk taking the car. I can't put Jenny into more danger."

Her earlier wounds were evident. She saw belief on faces and regretted the subterfuge. Her hand dug into Jake's. It was big and strong, and his fingers tightened around hers. "Gutsy girl," he said in a voice so soft she doubted anyone else heard it.

"I'm going there, and I own my own rig," said the guy in the baseball cap. "No rules to say I can't take passengers."

"I'm going that way, too," said the one who'd threatened violence to the attacker seconds earlier. "I'll follow part of the way. Make sure no one's trailing you."

"I still think we should call the sheriff," the waitress persisted, but a man next to her shook his head, and she went silent. The owner? Whoever he was, he didn't want any trouble.

"What about your car?" the waitress asked.

"I'll move it to the back and have someone pick it up, or pick it up myself later. If that's okay."

The manager nodded. It was obvious to Kirke he wanted

no trouble. Or police on the premises. It occurred to her that some of the women who'd gathered behind the men weren't motorists but working girls who offered services out of nearby trailers.

The manager nodded. "You want me to keep the keys?"

Jake nodded. "I'll park it, then give them to you."

"How do I know whoever comes is legit?"

Jake glanced down at her and said softly so no one else could hear, "He, or she, will say Merlin sent him."

The man's eyebrows raised, then he shrugged.

"Ready to go?" the trucker who volunteered the ride interrupted. "I'm on a schedule."

Jake nodded. "I'll move the car and get our belongings."

She tried to stand, but her legs were unsteady, and she sat back down on the ground. She was still woozy, and her head hurt. She wasn't going to say that, though. She wanted to leave this place.

"You didn't have time to eat," the waitress said. "I'll throw some sandwiches together."

Another waitress crowded near her, guilt evident in her face as she looked at Jake. "I'm so sorry about the coffee. We thought it would give her a chance to get away if . . ."

The manager joined them. "Damn if I'll let them convince me to sabotage a customer again," he said. "You see, Lily was abused and stalked by her boyfriend for years. He nearly killed her."

Jake gave him a crooked smile. "That's quite a defense team you have. I don't envy anyone who wants to rob the place." Then the smile was gone. "Don't worry about it. It's nice to know there's people who care enough to risk themselves."

The first waitress looked relieved. "I'll get those sandwiches." She hurried off.

The drivers stayed with her while Jake went to move the car. One of the women who'd gathered on the edge went inside and came out with a wet paper towel and offered it.

"Thank you," Kirke said and rubbed her face with the cold towel. To her surprise, she felt better.

She saw Jake step out of the car he'd driven around the

corner of the building and parked among the sixteen-wheelers. He had his duffel and her suitcase in his hands. The truck driver who'd offered to take them broke away and led Jake to a huge eighteen-wheeler. After stowing the baggage, they both came back toward her.

Without so much as a question, Jake lifted her as easily as if she were a pillow rather than a 128-pound female and carried her to the cab, setting her inside. Then he got in next to her.

The waitress appeared with a huge sack bulging with sandwiches and a small foam ice chest. "Sodas," she said. Jake took a twenty dollar bill from his pocket, but the woman refused it.

Then the driver took off, and she took comfort in the steel underneath and around her.

"Name's Cook," the driver said. "Tim Cook. Have a load of new furniture heading from north Georgia to Richmond. What are you folks gonna do when we get there?"

"Rent another car, one they don't know about."

"Be careful. Lots of these new cars with agencies have a GPS that can be tracked in case a car is stolen or isn't returned."

"Thanks," Jake said. "I'm Ed Metcalf, and this is Jenny. I'm a friend of her family, and she called me after her ex did this. She's finally leaving the bastard. Didn't think he would go so far as to follow us."

"What do'ya do?" Cook asked.

"Just got out of the military after twenty years. Looking around now to find something."

"You in Iraq?"

"Afghanistan."

"I served at Fort Campbell in Kentucky before this war. Never did get overseas. I admire you guys. Bet that coward back there never served a day." He paused. "You might think about taking up trucking. If you can buy your own cab, you have lots of freedom. I bought mine when the interest rates were low. Be paying on it forever, but it's mine."

Kirke opened the ice chest. She asked if anyone else

wanted a soda and passed one to the driver before selecting one for herself. Then she leaned against Jake and listened.

For a man who didn't talk much, Jake held his own with the driver. He just asked questions, seldom offering much information of his own. Her head pounded. She had inhaled enough chloroform to make her sleepy as well as queasy. Remembering her attacker's hands on her sent shivers through her.

Jake's arm went around her. She didn't know whether their benefactor noticed or not. She didn't care. She snuggled there and finished the soda. Some of the turmoil in her stomach settled.

She looked at the clock on the dashboard. Eleven p.m.

She closed her eyes, letting herself be cocooned in the safety of Jake's arm. Ever since she met him, she'd been wandering around in an unmarked minefield, stumbling from one mine to another. Yet at this moment, there was no place she would rather be. The warmth of his body radiated through her own. She heard the regular beat of his heart and occasionally his arm would tighten around her as if to ensure himself she was there.

They would be in Virginia before long. Then it would just be a few hours to Richmond. She wished she had the map from their car to follow the way.

"Where's the map?" she asked suddenly. "The one in the car."

"I didn't see it," he replied. "I brought everything in the car."

"I marked it," she said slowly. "Whenever I go on a trip I draw a circle around the destination. When I stop at a rest stop or gas station, I trace how far I've come."

His body stilled, then he said, "I locked the car, but I left one window open slightly because of the heat. We sat where I could keep an eye on it, but then there was the coffee . . ."

"Ja—" she started to say, then remembered he was Ed now. "Ed, he must have taken the map."

His arm tightened around her shoulders.

"I'm sorry," she said.

"There's no way you could have known he could follow us. I was sure there was no tracking device on the car. If anyone has blame, it's me."

"He knows where we're going."

"We'll just go somewhere else," he said.

But they both knew there was only one place for them to go.

＊

Ames's fingers clutched the cell phone.

"You let them get away?"

"I saw a chance to get the woman. I figured once I got her, then we could get him when he came after her."

"You figured? Well, you figured wrong. You should have waited until you could run them off the road and get them both. Now they know we've been tracking them, and they'll be more careful."

He listened to more excuses, then replied curtly, "Get the hell back to Argentina. I'm tired of incompetents."

"I do have something." The man sounded as panicked as Ames meant him to be. He paid well, and he expected results. Bad things happened to those who couldn't get the job done.

"What?"

"A map. While I was trying to get the damn woman, Diego took a look inside the car. He can get into anything. It has Williamsburg marked."

"Williamsburg, Virginia?"

"Yes, sir."

"I still want you in Argentina. You might have been seen. Take the first flight out."

He hung up before his employee replied.

But now he knew where they were heading, even if they did find the bug he'd planted. *What could be in Williamsburg? Damn little to interest them but the Farm.*

Whatever they were after was there.

What in the devil did Del tell the woman?

That was the question he couldn't answer, couldn't even start to answer.

And now the paramedic had obviously teamed with the one man he feared.

They'd already outmaneuvered him several times. And he was chagrined he'd not killed her on the street yesterday. He'd made the rifle shot himself, having more faith in his abilities than in that of his associates. The fact that he'd missed unnerved him.

And made him more determined.

Williamsburg was a small city. More a tourist town than anything else. It was not far from the Farm, and there were several watering holes used by instructors and students. There was one . . .

He looked over at the man who was with him. He trusted Drake more than any other person.

"Rent a small plane," he said. "We're going to the closest airport to Williamsburg, Virginia. And reserve us two rental cars.

He didn't have to say more.

Maybe he could salvage something yet.

They hadn't gone to the police, probably because Jake Kelly had no credibility. He wouldn't risk going to authorities without proof. He would be back in Leavenworth faster than Ames could say "Gotcha."

And if they did? Ames still had someone in the CIA who couldn't afford another probe into the matter. That person would step on any local official who asked questions. The words *national security* covered any number of sins.

It shouldn't be long before he had both of them.

# CHAPTER 21

The truck driver dropped off Jake and Kirke at a motel on the outskirts of Richmond.

It was three in the morning.

They thanked him effusively. Jake tried to pay him, but the man refused to take anything.

He registered as Mrs. and Mrs. Gregory Evans. Kirke was getting tired of all the different names. She couldn't keep any of them straight. How did he?

This time he asked for only one room. Two double beds. They waited patiently while the clerk explained that it was a suite hotel, and they had a small fridge as well as a sitting room.

She didn't want a sitting room. She *only* wanted a bed.

They waited as the clerk made another card key. She'd always wondered how safe those keys really were. When she was on the newspaper, she'd intended to do a story about it someday.

When they reached the room, Jake inserted the card to unlock the door. He carried in his duffel and the small ice chest that still held a few sodas along with the remaining sandwiches. She carried her suitcase. They dumped everything in the small outer room that made the room a suite, and she sank into a chair.

He didn't sit. Instead, he eyed her purse.

"Is that the purse that was taken a few days ago?"

She nodded.

Jake picked it up and dumped the contents out. There wasn't much there. Her driver's license. A comb. A compact. Lipstick. A pen she'd picked up in the lobby.

He ripped out the lining. Dug deeper.

She watched in unsettled silence. She had few possessions with her, and that was her best purse, the one she'd paid what she considered an exorbitant price for. It was large enough to contain a notebook and host of other stuff. She particularly liked the long strap that she could wear swung across her shoulder. And it was a neutral tan that went with almost everything.

His fingers came up with what looked like a tiny hearing aid battery. "No wonder they found us," he said. "Damn it!" he said.

He went to the phone and called the desk for a cab.

"I hate to make you move again, but we can't stay here now," he said to Kirke. "I don't know how far behind us they are, or how many there are."

"What do we do with that thing?" she asked, staring at the tiny instrument as if it were a snake.

"Leave it here. Hopefully, they'll think we're here for the night. We'll take the cab to the airport and get a car rental."

"If they are right behind us, can't they follow us to the airport?"

"Not if we leave before they arrive. Without the bug, I can lose them."

"They have the map."

"But they don't know what our destination in Williamsburg is. Or why."

He was putting all their belongings at the door. All she wanted to do was lay her head down on the pillow. She waited for the adrenaline to kick in again. It didn't.

She was tired of being helpless. Of being completely

dependent on anyone. Maybe especially him. She didn't want to be a clinging female.

"I want a gun," she said.

"Can you use one?" he said, his eyes showing no surprise.

"Yes. Sam made me take lessons with him."

"Do you have a permit?"

She shook her head. "I never wanted one in the house, not after being a paramedic."

"Do you think you can actually shoot?" he said dubiously. "If you can't, then it's more dangerous than helpful."

"Yes," she said. "I've had it with being mugged, shot at, burglarized, and kidnapped."

"Then we'll have to get one illegally."

What was shocking was her own acceptance of such illegality. She, the always law-abiding one. Now she was running around the country with a convicted felon fleeing the law and plotting to buy an illegal gun.

Jake gave her a piercing look she couldn't interpret. She'd never met anyone so adept at hiding everything he felt.

"I'll get you one tomorrow," he finally said.

"Just like that?"

"Not quite that easy. But I'll do it.

"Am I going with you?"

"No! I'll find someplace safe for you for a few hours. I have to go into dangerous neighborhoods and deal with dangerous people. I've put you into enough danger. I'll be damned if I'll do it when it's unnecessary."

"I'm in danger if I'm alone."

"It will be for a few hours. No more. And then I'll take you to target practice."

"You don't believe that I can shoot."

"Oh yes, I believe you. I would be afraid not to." A smile tugged at one side of his lips.

Just then the cab arrived, and he quickly threw their belongings in the trunk. "Airport," he said. "Any of the car rental offices." She saw him glance around, and she did the same. Nothing unusual. No men sitting like vultures in a car.

But she was beginning to learn that meant nothing. Nothing at all.

She was silent as they rode to the airport and picked up a rental. She waited outside as he went into the office. While waiting in line, he checked text messages on the phone. One from Sam, saying he was almost to Denver and wanted her to know he was okay. Was she as well? Another was from his friend in Chicago. "Arrest warrant issued for you. Federal marshals all over. Know you're aren't at the cabin. I'm being watched. If you need money, I've made arrangements to get it to you. This phone still safe for text messages."

He snapped it shut.

Minutes later, they were on the road.

Dawn wasn't far away, and neither of them had gotten any sleep. He drove fifteen miles, found a motel, registered, and went to the room. Two double beds. Good. They both needed sleep, and separate beds reduced the temptation for anything else.

She stood, looking out the window as he dumped their belongings in a chair.

She turned around to face him. "Can you really afford to pay for all this?" she asked suddenly. "Sam's trip. Airplane tickets. Hotels. Phones. Throwaway rental cars. I know you said you inherited some, but . . ."

He felt a heaviness in his chest. "You're thinking I might have taken some of the cash or diamonds?"

"If I did, I wouldn't be here. I thought you might need help. I have a little saved . . ."

The heaviness lifted. He should have known better. "I'm fine financially," he said. "Prior to the South America fiasco, I had a good income as a captain with special duty pay. I invested it, then I inherited money from my father."

"You said you were married. Wasn't there alimony?"

"We didn't have children, and she earned as much as I did. We had an amicable divorce after my conviction." He hesitated, then added, "She didn't desert me, if that's what's you're thinking. She'd been ready to go for some time. She hated the long absences and the fact I could never talk about where I'd been or what I'd done."

"And now?"

"Last I heard she was happily married to a CPA."

Her gaze never left his. Up until this moment, events had unfolded at dizzying speed, and now, for the first time, they were slowing, and more critical questions were forming in her mind.

He owed her a complete answer. "My father was a colonel. He never wasted a penny and invested regularly. He left me over a half million dollars. That, combined with what I'd saved, gave me a cushion."

"When did he die?"

"A week after I went into prison. The doctors said it was a heart attack. I knew it was a broken heart. The military was his life. And *his* father's. He got me into West Point. I'm the only blot on an illustrious military history."

"But he didn't believe the charges?"

Jake shrugged. "No. I don't think so. But it broke his heart anyway. His beloved army prosecuting a son he believed innocent. I think he wanted me to use the money to clear my name." He paused for a moment, then added, "During the past three years, my accountant has been squirreling funds into various safe-deposit boxes. Nothing illegal. Taxes were paid. But the feds can't track it.

"No brothers or sisters?"

"One older brother who died in Nam."

Her face didn't change. Her eyes were red-rimmed but alert. It was obvious that the last twenty-four hours had made very clear the danger she'd put herself in.

"How do you get more money if you need it?"

"A friend has power of attorney for several accounts. He can take out money, but I suspect that those accounts are now being monitored. I still have one safe-deposit box I don't think they know about."

"Have you talked to him?"

"I've had a text message. I've been declared a fugitive."

"What if they find you?"

"I'll go back to prison, possibly for another eight years."

"But now we know that one of the men who was with you is still alive."

"You know what I told you," he said. "There's no proof he is still alive."

"The DNA from the newspaper?"

He shrugged. "Since no one found Del Cox's fingerprints, I suspect the same thing would happen with Adams's fingerprints and DNA. Someone made them disappear."

"But still, it should be enough for them to reopen the case."

"Why should they?" he said bluntly. "Just because I say so? The mission was a bag of snakes. Everyone was running for cover. The case is closed, and no one wants it reopened."

"I know people who can."

"Only if we find more than we have up until now."

She leaned against him, and he folded his arms around her. "Anytime you want out," he said, "just say the word. You've already done far more than anyone has any right to expect.

"I just want to say that I want to go to bed."

He led her to the bed and undressed her. Slow and gentle. He felt a tightening in the groin, but he'd felt that far too often in the past few days. Now, though, he wanted only to be next to her. To hear the rhythm of her heart, and feel her skin and breathe in the perfume of woman.

He wanted her to feel safe. He wanted her to *be* safe. He'd done a damn poor job of making her that way.

After he'd finished pulling up a cover over her, he watched as her eyes closed. No longer the reporter of several moments earlier when she'd grilled him. No longer the warrior who had tried to foil someone twice her size. Now she looked vulnerable and wounded.

He'd answered some of her questions, most of them honestly. But not all. Maybe that would come later.

Maybe.

# CHAPTER 22

Jake took a shower, first with steaming hot water, then cold. Very, very cold. It didn't help. He still wanted her.

He was in desperate need of sleep. He was also in desperate need of her. But the latter was self-indulgent. He had to have sleep. Carelessness came from its lack, and he'd let it go far too long.

She was already asleep when he finished. Not knowing whether they might need to make a fast exit, he pulled on a clean pair of jeans and slipped between the sheets of the second bed. He wanted to slide in next to her, but he doubted either would get much sleep if he did.

He woke to a cry.

Then another.

Dawn filtered through the heavy dark curtains. A light was on in the bathroom. He'd left it that way in case she woke. He knew the disorientation that people had after a trauma, particularly when waking in a strange place.

He looked at the clock. He'd been asleep three hours.

She cried out again. He slipped out of bed and went over to her.

He touched her shoulder gently, and she jerked.

"It's okay," he said in a low voice.

She jerked upright, into his arms. "I had a nightmare . . . I was all alone and . . ."

"I know," he said. "I've had some myself."

She looked startled, then comforted.

If only she knew the times he'd been scared shitless. "Something's wrong with you if you don't get scared or have nightmares. I sure as hell wouldn't want a partner who didn't know honest fear."

"How do you get through it?"

"Adrenaline while it's happening. Before and after are the bad times."

"How many bad times have you had?"

"Too many."

"You never look scared," she countered.

"It's a skill you learn," he said. His arms tightened around her. If only she knew. Probably the worst moment he'd had was when he realized how neatly he'd been trapped by someone unknown.

The thought brought back the darkness, the utter despair he'd felt. For the first time in his life, he hadn't been able to fight back.

He was fighting back now, and he was using a woman to help him. Damn his soul.

He started to pull away, but her hand kept a hold on him. "Don't leave," she said, and he knew she was reading his face. No one else had been able to do that.

He touched her cheek and ran his finger up to the corner of her good eye. The swelling had gone down on the other eye, but the colors were more pronounced. He knew it had to be sore, along with the bullet wound in her arm.

"I won't," he said, not knowing whether it was a promise he could keep.

She sat and looked at his face with disquieting intensity as if she could read every emotion in him. Her fingers ran down his chest, stopping at an ugly scar on his side, just above his waistline.

"What happened?"

"An explosion."

Then she touched another on his shoulder. "And this?"

"Compliments of my friend, Mr. Adams, I think," he said. "Or your Mr. Cable."

Then her fingers moved upward to the small scar near his hairline. "This, too?"

He nodded.

"And still they accused you?"

"According to the JAG prosecutor, I shot myself. Or had a falling-out with my accomplice, the drug lord. Take your pick."

"What do you remember?"

"Not much. Our jeep stopped. I got out. So did the others. That's all I remember. I came to—I don't know how long after the shooting—feeling as if all the demons in hell were stabbing me with pitchforks. Chet and Ramos, the other members of our team, were both dead. There was nothing on them. But the two CIA guys accompanying us were gone. So was the plane Del Cox had brought us in on. My first thought was an ambush by the drug lord we were to meet. My second was to get the hell away before someone returned to make sure I was dead."

"When did you suspect Adams?"

"Not until I saw him on the street when Cox was hit."

"You'd never considered . . . ?"

"In the past seven years, I considered everything, but there was no indication that Adams or Cox were involved. Maybe I didn't want to believe one of ours could kill his own."

Her expression was so full of understanding and compassion that his heart slammed into his ribs. Ignoring the voices of warning in his head, he leaned forward and touched his lips to hers.

An instant. A moment to feel again.

But it wasn't an instant. A sound came from deep within her, a sleepy, welcoming sound that aroused him more than any word. His mouth moved to her throat, then back to her lips. Her lips met his with a ravenous need of her own, and the kiss became raw, hungry, desperate.

*It's only the aftermath of fear,* he warned himself. The

reaction that took hold once the adrenaline faded. The need for human contact, for evidence that she was alive.

He would be an even worse bastard for taking advantage of it. That's what he told himself, but seven years of intense loneliness told him something else. She was offering herself. And he couldn't resist.

The questions in his mind, the reasoning of his brain all disappeared as the sparks between them ignited. He smothered her lips with his mouth, his tongue darting inside with voracious, searching need.

His hand moved up and down her back, and her body shuddered, but not with fear. He regretted the T-shirt that remained between them, but he soon discovered there was nothing else to keep him from exploring her body. Her body reacted to his touch, trembling slightly, then he touched her breasts. They were perfect. They grew taut under his fingers.

"Jake," she murmured. "Oh, Jake."

He should stop now, stop until the puzzle was solved, the riddle answered, and he was free. But he no longer had control. He was astonished at the intensity of his feelings, of the aching need he had for her.

His lips went to the pulse in her neck, which he nuzzled, feeling every movement of her body as it reacted to his hands, to his mouth. He wished his own body wasn't reacting in the same fundamental, undisciplined way, then thought, *To hell with that*. It had been so long . . .

When a soft purr came from her throat, he was undone. All his good intentions fled. Her lips nibbled his, her tongue reached into his mouth, and he was consumed with fire.

He thought about the packet he'd picked up in the men's restroom in a gas station where they'd stopped for gas. It had been a spur-of-the-moment thing. Hope. Need. Even fear.

"I have something with me," he whispered. It was a question more than a statement.

She nodded, a tremulous smile curling her lips. He stood and took a small packet from the pocket of the pair of jeans he'd worn earlier. Then he slipped his jeans off, along with his briefs.

He was only too aware of her gaze following him. He sat down again at her side. "Are you sure, Kirke? I have damned little future."

"Yes," she said simply and held out her hand to him.

"Your arm . . . ?"

"It's the rest of me that's hurting now."

He was aware that his lips were curving into a smile. He'd never met a woman with so little guile or pretense. He searched those large hazel eyes that interested him from day one. No doubts. No demands.

He opened the packet and slipped on the condom. Then he very carefully removed her T-shirt and took pleasure in looking at her. Enough curves to make any man sweat. Her nipples were hard, the breasts still tight from his touch.

His hands roamed over her body, memorizing every curve, every one of her shuddering reactions to his touch.

Her body strained toward him. His fingers went to the triangle of hair between her thighs, then to the moist area beneath. He'd never been good at foreplay, but now he wanted to give her as much pleasure as he could.

She gasped suddenly, and he knew she was ready. He lifted himself on his arms and moved over her.

"Are you sure?" he asked again.

"Yes," she said simply.

He fought his impulse, his need, to plunge inside, to take her hard and fast. His body wasn't interested in niceties. It was burning, the ache as painful as his wounds had been.

Still he forced himself to go slowly. He entered deliberately, reminding himself to hold back, to allow her to come as he did. He felt some resistance. He stilled immediately.

"Jake?" More plea than question.

He needed no more invitation.

He probed deeper. With her first cry, her first compulsive motions, he moved faster, rhythmically, each time thrusting deeper and feeling her warm moisture embrace him and ask for more. She met him stroke for stroke, but it wasn't the easy mechanics of an experienced woman. Her raw passion was too spontaneous, her cries too surprised.

He climaxed and knew she did as well, almost at the same moment. Waves of satisfaction flowed through him, satisfaction and exultation. For the first time in years he felt alive.

Waves of sensations rushed through Kirke as warmth and power reached into her, plunging deeper and deeper as if seeking the very core of her. Then spasms . . . each growing in strength until they climaxed in one magnificent blazing explosion.

She clung to him, savoring the intimacy of sharing such rare pleasure. But there was also a certain desperation. Kirke felt it when his mouth closed once more on hers with a kind of bittersweet resignation.

He relaxed on top of her, although his elbows balanced the weight. She didn't know how long their wordless communication continued before he gently withdrew from her and pulled her body against his chest, holding her there for magical moments before he released her.

Her eyes met his, and Kirke marveled at the turmoil in them, the expressiveness of eyes that were usually expressionless. They were like storms, boiling with turbulence.

Her left hand caressed his neck, and her lips brushed his, saying things neither had been able to put into words. Her other hand touched his cheek, feeling the slight roughness of new beard, relishing the intimacy of tracing the tiny lines that arched out from his eyes.

She did not have long to relish. His lips touched her cheek, and flames broke out anew. His mouth captured hers in a kiss that refreshed all the glorious feelings she already felt. Her body arched against his, and she felt him grow hard again. His eyes asked the question.

"Oh yes," she said.

He rolled away and left her for a moment. When he returned, he pulled her to him, and suddenly there was warmth and power again, reaching into her, plunging deeper and deeper as if seeking the very core of her soul, and then there were spasms again, spasms even more wondrous than the previous ones.

They clung to each other, savoring the aftershocks.

Then he lay back, and she took his hand. In the dim light that filtered through the curtains from a streetlight, she saw pain etched in his face. Kirke recognized his quiet hopelessness and, because now whatever hurt him hurt her, she shared it. She lingered in his embrace until he sat up.

"We have to move on," he said regretfully.

"I know," she replied. By now she expected an unfriendly face to pop up any moment. She realized they had probably stayed too long. But she wouldn't give up a second of it, no matter what the future held.

Kirke had thought she knew what sex was. She'd had no idea. She'd felt desire before, but nothing like the conflagration she felt now. Never before had she felt the primitive instincts that made her body respond in ways it never had before.

In fact, until now she'd always thought sex rather overrated except, perhaps, from the guy's point of view. Her ex-husband had been the "wham, bam, thank you, ma'am" type of lover. He hadn't cared if she felt anything, or at least his actions indicated that.

Not for the first time, she wondered why she'd married him. She had gone to bed with him before marriage, but it had been no worse, or better, than the one and only occasion she'd had sex before she met him. She'd thought it normal. And she'd liked him, even thought she'd loved him. They'd had so much in common, or so she thought. It just seemed to be the right thing to do.

How completely stupid that had been. There had been no one since then, not because she was a prude but simply because most of the men she met were either married or just didn't interest her in that way. She'd wondered whether there was something wrong with her.

But that thought vanished forever in the whirlwind of sensations that had raged through her.

Were still raging.

She took his hand, and he pulled her up. Their eyes met. He touched her face with such tenderness, she couldn't move. His eyes were masked again, but his fingers told her everything she wanted to know.

"I want you out of this," he said. "After last night I realized how selfish I've been. I wanted to be with you."

She was stunned by the admission. "I don't want out of it."

"You've had just a small taste of what these people are capable of," he said. Killing doesn't bother them. Neither, I suspect, does pain. They want to know what you know, and nothing is going to stop them."

"The old letter in the hands of my lawyer ploy won't work?"

"He obviously has vast resources," Jake said, ignoring her poor attempt at humor. "If he can't stop us, he merely has to move on. Neither of us know what name he uses or where he lives."

"Then why *doesn't* he disappear?"

"He's dead to the CIA, to the U.S. government. He would prefer to stay that way."

"You've already told me there is no out for me."

"I still have a few friends who can hide you."

"Why haven't they helped *you*?"

"They've done what they can."

She doubted it. She doubted that he'd let them. Jake Kelly was a man who obviously despised asking for help. He was willing to do it for her. Not for himself.

"No. We're in this together now."

"Things have changed. I'm a fugitive now," he said. "There's a warrant for my arrest. Before long there will be a reward. Help me, and you can be charged with aiding a fugitive. I'm not going to let that happen."

"We'll talk about it later," she said. "Don't we have to leave here?"

He cast her a look of pure frustration. "I'm not taking you to Williamsburg, not if there's a chance Adams knows where we're heading. He might have already alerted the police. If so, you can be held on any number of charges."

"He won't do that until he learns what I know. What you've told me. What we've put together. Or who I might have talked to. He probably wants to know what those numbers mean as much as we do. He may well think something else was in that envelope as well. It had been opened."

"Which is why it's important that you leave me and disappear."

She thought about that. And discarded it. "We're safer together. At least I'm safer."

His cell phone rang. He flipped it open, checked the phone number, then answered it.

He listened for a moment, then passed it to her. "Sam."

She took it. "Sam, are you okay?"

"That's my question," he said. "I'm in Denver. You okay?"

She decided not to tell him about last night. "I'm good." And she was. Her body still glowed.

"You'll keep me posted?"

"I will. How's your brother?"

"Surprisingly pleased to see me."

"I told you."

"I'll listen to you more often."

"No, you won't."

He chuckled. "I'll see you in a few days."

"You'll stay until we tell you it's safe?"

"As long as it's not more than a week. Then I have to be back."

"I hope before then."

"Me, too," he said. "You'll let me know if you need anything?"

"I will. Enjoy Denver."

She hung up before he could ask additional questions. She didn't like lying to him. She didn't like lying to anyone, but particularly to Sam.

"I need a quick shower, and I'll be ready to go," she told Jake.

"I'll make some coffee."

The tiny pot in the room made terrible coffee, but she would take anything she could get.

Before she went, though, she reached on tiptoes and

kissed him, then hurried into the bathroom before he could react.

While Kirke was in the bathroom, Jake dressed, then used the new cell phone to call an old friend from his Afghanistan days. Cole Ramsey had been back there again when Jake had been court-martialed. When he'd returned to the States two years later, he learned about Jake and had come to see him. He hadn't believed a word of the charges. He wanted to help. So had his father.

"Ramsey," his friend answered after two rings.

"Cole, it's—"

"Hi there, John. You gonna make that poker game this weekend?"

"I'm going to try," Jake responded, a sinking feeling in his stomach. Marshals were there, or listening.

"Bulldog will be there," Cole added.

"Good."

"See you then."

Jake closed the phone. Either the feds had been with Cole, or his line was tapped. So much for this phone. He would throw it in the nearest bin and get yet a new one. Maybe the feds wouldn't check out the number after hearing the conversation, but more than likely they would. They would know the call came from Richmond, but the trail would end there if he didn't use the phone again.

The colonel, Cole's father, was probably also tagged by now as well. He'd told Jake's supervising officer that Jake had gone fishing. No way to prove he knew otherwise, but Jake couldn't expect any more help from him.

But now he needed Cole, and Cole had offered a way for a contact.

If only he could keep Kirke safe long enough for him to meet with Cole.

As if on cue, she came out of the bathroom. Her hair was wet and curled around her face, her cheeks pink from the steam, and the towel did little to hide her curves. He grew hard again and wanted nothing more than to grab that towel from her.

He resisted. Instead, he picked up his duffel. "I'll wait outside," he said.

She nodded, her eyes wide and searching. She was irresistible. And that was dangerous. To both of them.

It took every ounce of his willpower to turn and walk out.

# CHAPTER 23

They lingered in Richmond, where Jake obtained a gun for her.

She'd debated herself about the gun. Although she'd learned to shoot as a reporter, years as a paramedic has shown her only too clearly what a bullet could do to the human body.

But then she remembered the fear hours earlier when that guy tried to chloroform her and drag her away. If he had succeeded, she'd be dead.

Jake accomplished the mission in an astonishingly short time. He'd left her at a large discount store with several hundred dollars to get, among other things, a cheap wedding ring, dark glasses, and a hat. He returned within an hour and nodded his head as she stepped into the rental car. It was scary to her how easily one could obtain an illegal weapon.

It meant, however, they had to be very, very careful drivers. She was with a guy who'd violated probation, who had a fraudulent license, and they had two illegal weapons in their possession. She took a long, deep breath as she closed the car door. She had crossed a line, and there was no going back.

He apparently noticed. "You can still leave," he said.

"You can catch a flight to anyplace in the country. You can join your friend Sam."

"No," she replied sharply. No way was she going to leave. His quest had become hers. She could leave him then. His life was far different from hers. He would go back to being a warrior, and she would return to saving lives. She realized the irony between their two vocations.

"You'll hamper me," he said bluntly. "I'll be worried about you."

"I'm good at talking to people," she said. "You're not."

He raised an eyebrow. "No?"

"No."

He didn't say anything else but started the car.

He turned off at a rural exit and drove until he saw a dirt road. No sign of a residence. No mailbox. No fences. "Hunting area," he said as he stopped. "Season's over right now."

He picked up the paper bag and got out of the car. She did the same. Jake handed the bag to her and watched carefully as she took the gun out. She immediately checked to see whether it was loaded, then she checked the safety.

She glanced up and saw his approval. He handed her a box of ammunition, and she loaded it, then took the safety off.

"Want me to shoot something?" she said.

He nodded.

She aimed at a tree forty feet away. Fired. Missed. She tried again. This time bark flew off.

"That's just fine if the bad guy is a tree and doesn't move," he said. "But could you fire it at a real person?"

"I think so," she said. "If someone was threatening you or me. If it was him or me. But I suppose no one knows unless it happens."

"No," he agreed. "I've seen trained soldiers unable to fire when it came down to another person. But someone who holds a gun and can't fire is dangerous to those around him. Or her."

"I understand," she said. "As a paramedic, I understand more than most what a bullet can do to people. But I'm also used to dealing with crises all the same, and I have a very high appreciation for self-preservation."

His lips twitched, but then said simply, "Okay, let's go."

She carefully carried the gun to the car and slipped it inside her purse, his question haunting her.

Could she really use it?

She had no idea.

⊸

Williamsburg had to hold the answer. Otherwise, everything he'd done in the past week, everything Kirke and other innocents had gone through, would have been for nothing. That knowledge ate at his gut.

He left the interstate and took a left, then a right.

"How far?" she asked.

"About five minutes."

He slowed as they approached the Williamsburg city limits.

It had been years since he'd been there, and he saw a lot of changes. Growth everywhere. "The phone number's no longer in service, so we may not find anything. But maybe someone around can tell me something."

Sure enough, the building that had once housed the bar was gone, and a strip mall had taken its place. The two-lane road had become a four-lane highway, and businesses lined it.

His heart sank. Still, he drove into the strip center.

Kirke's hand went to his leg. A touch of reassurance.

He stopped in front of a combination bakery and deli, the only food establishment in the center.

Kirke put on her newly purchased dark glasses and a wide-brimmed hat. The hat looked charming on her, but the glasses didn't quite hide the bruises that remained on her face. As usual, Kirke was out of the car before he could walk around and open the car door. They walked inside the shop, and he saw her nose twitch at the smells.

It was empty of customers. A smiling woman stood behind the display counter. "Can I help you?"

Kirke stepped up. "It smells wonderful in here. I think I could eat everything in those counters."

The woman beamed.

Jake's instinct was to step up and start spitting out questions, but he stood back while Kirke ordered a croissant chicken salad sandwich, and iced tea, and a box full of donuts.

Kirke looked at him expectantly, and he ordered a hot croissant ham and cheese sandwich. While it was heating in a microwave, Kirke asked about the bar that used to stand where they were standing. "My husband went there years ago when he—" She stopped suddenly as if she realized she was saying something she shouldn't.

The woman put their sandwiches on paper plates and slid them over the counter to Jake. Her gaze ran over him, apparently approving, until they rested back on Kirke and her black eye.

"No," she said lightly. "It wasn't him. It was a purse snatcher, and my Oscar is taking me on a trip to forget about it."

The frown faded.

"In fact, he promised to bring me to the places he used to visit," she rambled on. "He told me how much he loved the area. All the history. The rolling hills. He mentioned this bar that he thought was around here . . ."

"The Enigma," the woman said.

"You know it."

"I grew up around here. Used to go there with a girlfriend. Met my husband there. Broke his heart when the owner died, and his son sold the land for development. Made a huge profit," she said with disdain.

"Is this your business?" Kirke asked.

"Yes. My husband works for Old Williamsburg and often works late. I was bored and always liked baking, so we decided to invest what we had in this business."

The door opened, and two women walked in. Kirke and Jake took their food to a table.

"Oscar?" he said softly.

"I kinda liked the sound of it," she replied. Mischief danced in her eyes, and he was beguiled by it. She'd almost been killed last night, and she still had that quirky humor.

The newcomers ordered a cake, then left, and the woman returned to their table.

"How is everything?"

"More wonderful than I'd dreamed," Kirke said. "I think I want a piece of pastry from the second counter."

The woman looked even more ecstatic than Kirke. In seconds she presented them with a plate containing several pastries. "The other two are on the house," she said.

"Will you join us for a moment?" Kirke asked.

The woman hesitated for a second, then nodded. "The noon rush is over. Won't be much business until four. I'm Edna Caswell."

Kirke thrust out her hand. "I'm Betty Sewell, and this is my husband, Oscar." She picked up the pastry and took a huge bite, chewed, then said absently, "Oscar told me about a woman who used to manage the Enigma. A widow. Redhead. Name of Dallas. She gave him some really good advice, and I wanted to thank her."

"She told me to marry Betty," Jake said without a beat. "Best advice I ever took."

"Dallas. Haven't heard that name in a while. She left several years ago," Edna said. "Say, how long you two been married?" Edna asked.

"Ten years."

"You look so happy together," Edna said.

"How long have you been married?" Kirke asked

"Twenty years. Just sent our oldest kid to college. The youngest is a senior in high school."

"Do you know where Dallas is now?" he asked.

"I heard she went back to Texas with her son," Edna said.

The door opened, and Edna got up.

"Do you know where?" Jake asked.

She shook her head.

"Her last name?"

"Haley, I think, or something like that."

She flashed them a smile, then went to wait on the new customers. When she finished with them, another customer entered.

"I don't think we're going to get anything else," he said.

"I don't, either. But maybe now we have enough to Google her or go to a search site."

He pushed out his chair and stood. He still had to pay for the pastry she'd ordered.

He waited until the other customers received their food and sat down. It looked like a one-woman business at the moment. He left her a big tip, then paid the bill at the counter. "Thank you. The food was great, and I really appreciate the information. I've thought about her often. Thought I would send a note. Tell her what great advice she gave me."

"Hope you find her. Everybody liked her."

He nodded, took the box of donuts Kirke had ordered, then they left.

Outside the door, she turned to him. "Should we check with anyone else here?"

He considered asking the other merchants, then discarded the idea. He didn't want undue notice. Kirke had done a good job in disarming Edna. But too many questions would raise suspicions. "Let's see what we can find out now that we have a last name."

"She wasn't sure Haley was right. And there's a dozen different ways to spell it."

"It's worth a try."

"Okay."

He went back inside. "Can you tell me where the nearest library is?"

"Turn right leaving the parking lot, then left at the third light and right again and . . . I'll draw you a map."

He waited as she found paper and a pen and drew an elaborate map. She looked at the map, then handed it to him.

"Thanks again," he said.

"Come back. I bake every morning."

"We'll do that."

After he joined Kirke in the car, he remembered the call he was going to make. He didn't really want to talk in front of Kirke. The one thing he wanted from Cole Ramsey was a way to take Kirke somewhere safe. With or without her consent.

He had to admit, though, she'd been helpful in there. He probably would have come on too strong and aroused suspicions. Suspicions would mean police.

Kirke had been perfect.

Maybe they should leave Williamsburg now. Adams had that damned map. And Dallas was in Texas. Texas was a damn big state to find someone. But the more he thought about it, the more he believed that Dallas played a part in this puzzle. Why else would Cox have mentioned her to Kirke?

He started the car and headed out of the parking lot just as two men turned into it. As they passed, he saw the driver's face. Crew cut. Hard. Even brutal. The man looked startled, then instantly braked. A car behind him ran into him, blocking him from going backward.

The driver ignored a woman stepping out of the driver's side and sped ahead, barely missing a mother and toddler trying to cross the lot. Jake didn't wait any longer.

He put his foot on the gas and ripped out of the parking lot, leaving screams and chaos behind. The other car was seconds behind him.

Kirke was looking behind. "Tell me what he's doing," he said. "I can't look back."

"How did they find us?"

"It doesn't matter now."

Jake swerved in between two cars and said a prayer as he caught the tail end of a yellow light. The other car would get caught in blocked traffic. He had a few seconds to disappear.

He maneuvered again to get in the left turn lane, knowing it would be more difficult for the driver of the other car to follow him, then he turned left, right, then right again for a block, then a left. He heard cars honking behind him and it told him how far back the opposition was.

No pattern. The opposition would expect a pattern. Instinct. Find another major road and hide in a full parking lot. A grocery store. A shopping center, anything.

Then he saw signs to Williamsburg Village and started following them. There would be crowds there, and parking lots, and he doubted whether the opposition would think he would head there and chance getting trapped.

He swung into one of the parking lots and maneuvered

into a tight space between two cars with dark colors like theirs.

"Move over to the driver's seat," he said. "If you see anything, get the hell out of here. Go to the nearest police officer. Tell them you were kidnapped."

He got out, and she shifted over to the driver's seat. He took out his pocket knife and within seconds changed license plates. He didn't replace the one he took, just left an empty spot. Hopefully whoever owned the car would be at the village the rest of the afternoon.

After they left Williamsburg, he would put back the original plate and toss the stolen one.

The bad guys undoubtedly had the old plate marked. He just needed enough time to get the hell out of the area.

He got into the backseat. "You drive," he said. "Take off the hat. Follow the signs to the interstate and head south to Portsmouth."

She didn't ask any questions, just started the car and headed out of the parking lot. He ducked down on the floor.

A new license plate and a lone driver should be enough to get them out of town. He wondered how many men Adams had looking for them.

Adams was desperate. And dangerous.

But so was he.

# CHAPTER 24

Kirke drove almost to Portsmouth. They stopped at a rest area not far from the city limits.

At Jake's direction, she parked in a secluded area, and he quickly changed license plates again. He discarded the stolen one in a waste can.

When Kirke went into the restroom, he located a pay phone between the two restrooms.

When he'd called Cole Ramscy earlier, his friend had told him that Bulldog was expected at the poker game. Bulldog could be no other than Dane MacAllister, who'd served with both of them. Bulldog was his service nickname, but Jake had always called him Mac. Jake knew Cole and Mac were friends and lived within miles of each other in Oregon.

It had been obvious that Cole's telephone was tapped, and possibly there had been someone else in the room. Jake hadn't talked to Mac since before his imprisonment, and he doubted the FBI or marshals or whoever would tap him as well.

He should have called Mac earlier, but he hadn't wanted to use the cell phone, and he really hadn't wanted Kirke to hear the conversation. He called operator assistance and quickly had Mac's number.

Mac answered immediately. "MacAllister," he said.

"Mac?"

"Yeah. Good to hear from you. Not so good to hear of your trouble."

"Cole talk to you?"

"He lost a tail and used a pay phone to call me. He wants to know what he can do. I do, too. I didn't believe those charges for a second."

"Have a family yet?"

"A wife and a kid. A boy."

"You shouldn't get involved."

"If I was in trouble," Mac said, "what would you do?"

That stopped him. His throat went dry and tight.

"One of the men I supposedly killed is alive," he said. "He seems to have an army behind him, and he wants me dead. Unfortunately, I have a civilian with me. He wants her dead, too."

"A pretty civilian?"

"Yeah."

"What do you need?"

"Do you still have contacts?"

"A few."

"First I need to locate a Dallas Haley. Not sure of the spelling. I think she's a CIA widow. She managed a bar in Williamsburg called the Enigma. Catered to the spooks. A friend of hers says she's probably in Texas.

"Betcha it's Dallas for Dallas," Mac said, then chuckled.

Jake sighed. Unfortunately Mac, in addition to being a great soldier, was also a jokester.

"You can't narrow it any more?" Mac asked, obviously aware that Jake didn't share his amusement.

"I hope *you* can. Oh, and she has a son."

"Age?"

"I don't know that, either."

"Anything else?" Mac replied.

Jake realized time was slipping away. Kirke would be back any moment. He glanced toward the restroom. The door was closed, and his attention was caught by two men entering the building. But they showed no interest in him as they went to a counter and obtained some maps and tourist information.

"I want you to protect my civilian."

"Is that going to be difficult?"

"Probably, but I don't care how difficult it is. I want her out of this. Any way you can."

"No deadly force, I take it." Mac's voice was amused.

"No, dammit."

"Where do you want to meet?

"The city of Dallas."

"Okay, I'm on the way. I'm sure Cole will follow as soon as he knows he's not followed. When will you be there?"

"We're driving through. We're in Virginia now. I estimate eighteen to twenty hours."

"I'll try to meet you between two and three at Bob's Barbecue. If either of us is running late, call this number and ask for Bob. He's my brother-in-law." He gave the phone number and directions, then hung up.

Jake was loath to put anyone else in danger, legal or physical, but now he had no choice. If nothing else, he needed them to take Kirke safely off his hands.

He hung up and turned. Kirke was behind him.

Had she heard anything? He hoped to hell not.

She looked at him with a question in her eyes.

He shrugged. "An old acquaintance. I thought he could help find Dallas."

Her face didn't change. He couldn't tell whether she'd heard more of the conversation or not.

"Time to get going," he said, starting for the car. Damn but she got to him. He wanted to reach out and touch her hair. Hell, he wanted to do a lot more than that. He also hated deceiving her, but it was more important to get her out of harm's way. "You look tired," he added. "I'll drive for while. Try to get some sleep."

"Where are we going?"

"West. Texas."

"That's a long way. A plane . . ."

"We can't risk that," he said more curtly than he intended. "Driving day and night, relieving each other, we can get there in about twenty hours. Are you up for it?"

She nodded. "I did it a lot of times in college."

Jake got in the driver's side, turned the key in the ignition, and they drove out of the parking area.

⟡

Kirke knew she shouldn't jump to conclusions. She'd already separated the good guys from the bad ones in her mind. Yet when she'd left the restroom she'd stopped at the sound of Jake's voice as he talked on the phone. It was low, but she heard one phrase: *I want her out of this. Any way you can.*

Did he mean her? Or, God help her, Dallas?

She pretended sleep and actually slipped into it. *Gunshots. Merlin's siren. Hands grabbing at her.*

"Kirke!"

She heard his voice from a distance and tried to understand. Then slowly she emerged from the fog of sleep. Nightmare. It was just a nightmare. The same as last night except for Merlin.

She shook her head and peered out of the car. It was dark. He'd stopped on the side of the road, and vehicles were ripping past them.

"I'm okay," she said. "Just a bad dream. What time is it?'"

"Around ten."

"I should drive."

"Can you?" He asked.

"With some coffee and cold water."

"We need gas. I'll stop at the next likely looking exit, and we'll switch."

He started the car again and returned to the road. She looked down at her hands. They were shaking slightly.

*Merlin.* Ten o'clock. It wasn't too late to call Robin. She knew Robin stayed up late.

"Can I use the cell phone?" she asked him. "I want to call Robin."

"The feds might have this number now," he said. "They can trace it."

"We're in the middle of the country," she said. "If we don't use it again, they'll have no idea where we're heading."

He hesitated.

"I won't be long."

He handed her the phone. "We'll get another prepaid as soon as I can. We won't have to be so careful."

She nodded and punched in Robin's number.

"Hey, I hope it isn't too late," she said when Robin answered almost immediately. "How's Merlin?"

"Chatting away and whistling a weird melody."

"He's eating?"

"Oh yes." A pause. "You okay?"

Not really, but she wasn't going to tell Robin she was nearly kidnapped last night. "Yes," she lied. "I have to ask another favor."

"What is it?"

"Information."

Jake glanced at her but didn't say anything.

"I'll do my best," Robin said on the other end. "Okay, what or who do you want me to find?"

"A woman named Dallas Haley. Probably H-a-i-l-e-y or H-a-l-e-y. She used to live in Williamsburg, Virginia, and was manager of a bar named the Enigma some ten years ago. It's closed now, occupied by a bakery/deli." She gave Robin the address.

"How do I reach you?"

Kirke gave her Jake's cell phone number.

"Oh," Robin said, "I checked on that agent you asked about. He just came to the Atlanta office."

"Thanks," Kirke said, hearing the strain in her voice.

She glanced at Jake. He was driving easily, concentrating on the wheel. She quickly tapped the keys to see his call list. Two. She memorized them in her head, then turned the cell off.

Had he noticed? If he did, he wasn't reacting.

A few minutes later he turned off on an exit road. They stopped at an all-night gas station and convenience store. She went inside as he pumped gas into the car. She bought a cup of coffee and scarfed down a cold corn dog. Pretty awful, but she was used to grabbing food on the quick. Jake came in and selected an even more evil-looking piece of fried chicken and ate it on the way back to the car.

She got into the driver's seat and steered the car back on the interstate.

"Take I-85 to Atlanta, then we'll take I-20 the rest of the way," he said.

"Where do we go when we get to Texas?" she asked.

"Hopefully, your friend Robin will come up with some ideas," he said.

It wasn't what she wanted to hear. She wanted to ask him who he'd talked to at the rest stop, but he would probably lie to her again, just as he'd lied to her then.

She kept hearing the federal agent's words. *He's dangerous, and he'll do anything to get to the diamonds.* She hadn't liked him. Hadn't liked his arrogance. Was that why she hadn't listened? Much less believed? But now there was the mysterious phone call Jake hadn't shared with her.

Still, this was a man who'd saved her life twice. That gave him the benefit of the doubt.

And, God help her, she wanted to be with him.

But she would be more cautious when they reached their destination. She glanced over at him. He appeared to be asleep. So quick. But then she'd learned that about him. He was obviously trained to grab sleep whenever he could. She knew, though, that he would waken at the slightest unusual sound. He was uncanny about that.

She turned all her concentration on the road.

# CHAPTER 25

Jake checked his primary cell phone at a rest stop just over the Texas line. He no longer kept it on nor would he make calls on it, but he could receive messages with no risk of being pinpointed.

He had a new phone, purchased in Louisiana, to make necessary outgoing calls.

Among the messages was one from Kirke's friend Robin. The other was from Sam.

He handed the new phone to Kirke and walked away so she could have privacy.

She called Robin first.

"Kirke, I tracked down the bar and found its address. It closed five years ago. I Googled Dallas Haley's name. Went through about a million of them and finally had a hit. Wouldn't suspect there were so many women named Dallas, or so many other Dallases of one kind or another. It was Haley, spelled H-a-l-e-y. Finally found a story in a local Williamsburg paper on her. It's one of those small, neighborhood newspapers. I can e-mail it to you, or just read the pertinent parts."

"Pertinent parts," Kirke replied.

"It looked like one of the paid news stories about a business, the ones that look like a news story but is really a paid advertisement. Interviewed several people. Never mentioned CIA, but did say the majority of its customers came from surrounding military bases. The name, of course, is a dead giveaway to anyone who knows CIA history and the breaking of the Enigma code during World War II." Kirke heard the glee in Robin's voice when she talked about the name of the bar. Robin loved history.

"Anyway," Robin continued, "the story mentioned the manager named Dallas. Last name Haley. It quoted her as saying the bar was like a big family, that everyone looked after each other.

"I called down to the paper, said I was doing an article for the travel section and found the article. The writer of the article was editor of the paper, and she remembered Dallas. She'd gone to the tavern several times with friends, and on one visit the owner said business wasn't so good. She thought she would help by writing the story."

"Did she know it was a CIA watering hole?"

"I asked her that. She said it was rumored, but then they also got some military people in there. Said maybe the powers that be at CIA heard the rumors and made it off-limits. Not good for security to have CIA agents drinking in a place everyone knew about. Business dropped off, hence the story. She said this Dallas managed the place until the owner sold it. When she was writing the story, she asked Dallas if she'd been born in Dallas, and Dallas said no, Denton, Texas. Her mother had the habit of naming the kids after places where they were born, but the father said no to Denton. So she was named for nearby Dallas."

Kirke was awed. Robin always had a way with people. She obtained information no one else could. Politicians would spill the damndest things to her. "Much more than I expected," she said. "Thank you."

"I couldn't find anything on her after she left Williamsburg, though. No property or tax records. No wedding license. No records at all in Texas." She paused. "There's something else."

Robin's tone warned her. "What?"

"There was a murder at the shopping center you mentioned yesterday. As I was talking to the reporter, she was working on the story. A woman was killed in the shopping area where the Enigma used to be. Police believe it was a robbery. A Closed sign was on the door during business hours, and the woman was found in the kitchen. She'd been stabbed."

"What was her name?"

"Edna Caswell," Robin said, then, "I don't know what you're mixed up in, but I would like more information."

Kirke's heart beat rapidly, and she stifled a cry. Edna. The cheerful woman who'd met her husband at the Enigma. She and Jake had stopped there, and now she was dead. She could barely breathe for a moment. When it was only her life, she could justify trusting Jake.

Could she still justify it?

"I'll call you back," Kirke said.

"Where are you? No, you don't have to tell me. Texas." Robin's voice held resignation. "Do you know what you're doing?"

*No.* "Yes," she said, ignoring the other voice in her head. She needed to talk to Jake. Then she would decide.

"Kirke, if this is something illegal . . ."

Kirke decided to hit beneath the belt. "Remember when you were breaking a few laws on the officer slaying story?"

"You've broken laws?"

"Not unless helping someone is breaking a law."

"Except sometimes it's called being an accessory. Be sure you know what you're doing. Murder's involved now."

If only she knew. Not one murder but, to her count, four now. Maybe more.

She ignored the comment and, instead, she tried to divert Robin. "When it's over, you'll have the biggest story since your Pulitzer nomination. Might even win this time."

"I would rather have a live friend."

Kirke had no answer for that. "I have to go. I'll call you tomorrow. I swear. Everything might be over by then."

"What about your job?" Robin asked.

"I have a few weeks' leave after the sniper incident."

Silence.

"Got to go, Robin. Thanks. I owe you." She hung up before Robin said anything else to her, but her heart was still pounding.

"What's wrong?" Jake was next to her. "Kirke?"

"Edna from yesterday is dead. Stabbed. A robbery, police said." She looked up into his eyes. "But we know otherwise."

He closed his eyes. He reached out to touch her, then dropped his hand to his side. "God, no," he said.

"Robin has offered several times to talk to her husband. He's a good guy, Jake. A really good guy."

Jake opened his eyes, and his gaze met hers. "He might want to help, but I'm a convicted felon, Kirke. And I'm now officially a fugitive. My reasons for breaking the release conditions won't matter to the government, not unless I can prove I was innocent. But I want you out of it now. I have some friends. They'll take care of you."

"You're not going to stop?"

"I can't. I'm getting close. Adams might know about Dallas now. If they do, she's in as much danger as Edna." He gave her a searching look. "Did she tell you anything else?"

"Our Dallas's last name is H-a-l-e-y. She comes from Denton, Texas. Robin couldn't find any records for her. No marriage records. No property records."

She found herself swaying. She was still stunned by the news about Edna and filled with grief for the woman and her husband.

Jake put his arm around her and held her close for a moment. "I'm sorry," he whispered in her ear. "If I could go back in time . . ."

She heard a slight break in his voice. Maybe no one else would realize, but she knew him now. He felt Edna's loss as much as she. One moment she would feel that strong attraction, even a closeness she'd never felt with anyone else, and then he turned into a stranger.

He did that now. He walked a few feet away and made a call with the new phone. She heard only a few yeses and nos, then, "I'll be there."

*Not we. I.*

"You want to tell me about that?" she asked when he finished.

"No," he said, and this time the side of his lips moved upward in a sexy, tantalizing smile. "But I will. We're meeting two people I know. Both were in Special Forces with me. One's been doing his damndest to help me these past years. I asked them to come down and take you somewhere safe."

"That was the conversation you had yesterday?"

"I was afraid you'd heard," he admitted. "I didn't think you would agree. I thought you would try to find some way to avoid them."

"You didn't think I should have a say in it?" she said, outraged now. "Were you going to kidnap me? Is that why you said, 'Whatever it takes'?"

"Yes, dammit."

"Why tell me now?"

"Edna Caswell is dead because she talked to us. I figured that would scare sense into you."

She hauled off and hit him. Not as hard as she could but hard enough to make a point. She had given him everything she had. Her trust, her friendship, even her heart. She had put her life on hold. She had put friends in jeopardy. She might have lost her home. She'd been assaulted, shot, and almost kidnapped. All the while he was planning to take decisions away from her, to dump her with friends like so much unwanted baggage. She wanted to hit him again. Instead, she struggled to keep her dignity and stepped back.

He looked stunned.

Heads turned their way. A man did a double take. A woman grinned. Another looked concerned.

Still another couple approached.

She stepped away from Jake. "Nothing to be concerned about," she said as lightly as she could. "He just said something really stupid."

Jake straightened and tried a grin. "I should have learned," he said. "Unfortunately she's smarter than I am."

The women chuckled. Two men looked uneasy.

Kirke went to the car and got in the passenger's side. He followed.

"Did it occur to you," she said, "that I have a job? That I have to return to Atlanta? I have, at best, ten days? You can't just haul me away and store me like a piece of meat. What if you don't find this Adams or whoever he is? I can't live in fear the rest of my life. I won't live in fear. And right now I'm the best chance you have to draw him into the open. He wants me because he doesn't know what I know. He needs me more than he needs you. As you said, no one will believe you."

"I'll turn myself in then," he said. "My life isn't worth yours."

"And just how will that help me?" she asked, not bothering to hide her anger. "I'm still a danger to him until he knows what I know, or what I have or what he thinks I have."

She didn't mention her doubts, her questions. Even her fear that he, too, wanted the missing diamonds. Maybe he thought he deserved them. But she was going to be there when he met Dallas.

Back in the car, she fastened the seat belt. "Now where are we going?"

His silence was louder than any words.

"I want to be there to talk to Dallas. I'm going to be there. You brought me on this trip. Now I'm going to finish it."

"God help me," he muttered, just loud enough to hear.

"I doubt it," she said, still infuriated that he had gone behind her back, still not entirely sure of his intent.

"If they killed Edna Caswell, they might well know where we're headed." he said, his breathing a little heavier than usual. He moved in his seat and winced. "You throw a nasty punch."

"If you're a woman, it's the only kind to throw. And I *did* figure that they are probably on their way. That means we'll have to find her before they do."

"Tell me everything your friend said," he said, surrendering for the moment, although she knew the subject wasn't closed.

She thought about withholding some information, then shrugged and told him everything.

"Your friend says she couldn't find any legal records,"

Jake said when she finished. "If she did return to Denton, maybe she's using another name."

"Or she married again," Kirke said.

"Or she isn't there," he said. "She could be anywhere in the world."

"But if we can find her maiden name, perhaps we can find relatives who know where she is," she said. "You said it was rumored she was married to a CIA agent killed in the field. Wouldn't she be receiving some kind of benefit?"

He nodded. "It would be classified, though."

"You said Gene Adams might have help in the CIA."

She could tell from his face he'd already considered the possibility. Which was why they crossed half the country without stopping.

"So he has resources we don't?"

His silence again told her he was miles ahead of her.

"And you think Edna told them what she told us?"

"Yes," he said simply. "They must have seen us leave and went inside to see what we wanted."

"We're in a race to beat them to Dallas then."

He nodded.

"What about college?" she suggested, trying to think of every possibility. "Maybe she attended a college around Denton. She married a CIA agent. She probably had more than a high school education." She looked at the map they had. "Looks like there are two colleges in or around Denton."

"We don't even know what she looks like now. Or when she graduated."

Jake was a warrior. She'd been a newspaper reporter. She'd always had an instinct for finding what she was searching for. It had been part of the job. She supposed that he, on the other hand, had a more direct approach to confronting a problem.

"Robin said she would e-mail a copy of the article, or we should be able to find it. Maybe there's a photo." She looked at him. "Could you pick her out of a crowd?"

"I don't think so. It was ten years ago. I was drinking. Mostly I remember the red hair."

"So we have the name Dallas and the color of hair," Kirke said. "Not much to go on. But we have two options. Yearbooks, if we can narrow down the years she might have attended. Second, alumni associations. They might have a current address on someone named Dallas Haley." She glanced at him. "Is either of your friends a good hacker?"

"Just so happens Cole is."

"Then I suggest he check alumni records. Maybe he can do that while we check yearbooks. The university libraries should have copies, and most are open to the public."

The look he gave her sent rivers of heat through her. There had always been heated attraction between them, almost from the very moment they'd met. There had been respect. But now there was much more than that.

"Thank you," he said simply.

She didn't think he had ever said that before. It didn't sound natural on his lips, but the look in his eyes made it real.

His hand went to hers for the first time since they'd left the deli, and she realized he'd been trying to put a distance between them, just as he had when they first met. He'd been preparing to say good-bye.

"Did you mean what you said? Get rid of me any way they could?"

"Yes. I still do. You've almost been killed several times now because of me. I can live with a lot of things, but you being hurt is not one of them." He paused, then added, "Adams is a chameleon. He's CIA-trained and can be anyone he needs to be."

She swallowed hard. His voice was low and husky, almost aching with feeling. She had no doubt he meant it.

He would try to protect her. She knew that. What she wasn't sure of was his end objective.

It wouldn't matter if they didn't reach Dallas Haley before the bad guys did.

# CHAPTER 26

Kirke felt immediately at home inside Bob's Barbecue Barn. The restaurant was similar to one she liked in Georgia. Emphasis was obviously on its barbecue, not ambiance. Seventies music blasted from a vintage jukebox in the corner, and wooden picnic tables provided the seating. Table decorations were mostly hot sauce bottles.

After days of fast food, the aroma of smoked meat was heavenly.

She and Jake didn't have to identify themselves. The moment they entered, a burly man approached them and nodded his head toward the back.

"Go through the door in the back. The one that says No Admittance."

Jake simply nodded, and together they walked to the office. Jake knocked once, then opened the door.

Two men lounged in chairs, looking as if they had not a care in the world, yet she didn't miss the immediate alertness that flickered across their eyes as she entered. It was obvious they trusted the owner of the restaurant, but caution was as much a part of them as the color of their eyes.

Kirke had become all too familiar with the same quality in Jake. Even when he slept he was alert, strange as that sounded.

"Cole Ramsey . . . Dane MacAllister—everyone calls him Mac—meet Kirke Palmer," Jake announced.

The man named Dane made a mock salute to indicate which one he was. The other just studied her, head to foot, as Jake had done on their first meeting. It didn't have the same hot impact as Jake's perusal.

Both were lean and trim and looked as if they did the Iron Man competition every month or so. They were also attractive. Not traditionally so, but with that same self-assuredness that Jake possessed. They had that pantherlike caution and lethal quality as if danger lay behind every corner.

"Miss Palmer," Dane acknowledged the introduction. "I understand you've had something of an eventful week."

Jake had obviously filled them in during one of his calls. "You could say that," she said.

Cole offered his chair.

"Thanks, I'd rather stand," she said. "I've been in the car for more than twenty hours."

Cole leaned across a desk that was covered with papers. "Hungry? Bob's barbecue is the best ever. You'll think better on a full stomach.

"I could eat a buffalo," she said. "We've been surviving on donuts." As the words came out, a lump formed in her throat at the memory of who'd sold them the donuts. She didn't want the same thing to happen to Bob.

"Bob can take care of himself," Mac said, obviously reading her face. "Used to be a cop. A damned good one. He's aware there might be danger. But practically the entire police department is over here sometime during the day. There's five cops in the other room as we speak.

Kirke darted a look at Jake. Had he told the two about Edna Caswell? Or had they learned in some other way?

Dane caught the look. "We backtracked you two to Virginia. It was all over the news there. Murder is not common in Williamsburg. It was easy enough to connect the address to the info you gave us on the Enigma.

"Find out anything else?"

"Dead ends. It's like Dallas Haley tried to get lost. She *was* married to a spook. A friend in the CIA was able to discover that, but he couldn't get any info on a settlement or her current address.

"Will anyone else find the same brick wall?"

"Depends on how high it goes."

"High enough that I was neatly trapped," Jake said. "That job had to be planned way in advance by Adams. I didn't want him on the mission, and my superiors said the CIA insisted on it. Maybe he was just waiting for an opportunity, but I personally think he planned that mission for a long time. I doubt now whether there ever were any missiles.

"And you think this Dallas has information. Maybe even proof of what happened?"

"All I know is that Cox died trying to reach me, and he asked Kirke to tell me something about Dallas."

Kirke listened as Jake told his friends all that had happened. In about ten terse sentences, starting with the hit-and-run, then the numbers, the sniper, the explosives in Kirke's home, the attack at the truck stop, and finally the visit to Williamsburg.

When he finished, there was a silence. Then both looked at Kirke with new interest.

"A paramedic?" Cole asked.

She nodded. "But a journalist before that. I can't seem to stop letting curiosity get the best of me."

Jake broke in. "Kirke has some ideas about finding Dallas. She thinks that Dallas may have returned to Denton because she grew up there and possibly has family there. Also, there's a strong possibility she might have gone to one of the colleges around Denton. If so, the name Haley may be on alumni lists as her married name, or we might try finding her photo in college yearbooks. If we can find her maiden name, maybe we can find family, then her. We can divide the tasks. You guys take the alumni lists. We'll take the yearbooks.

"I can also search marriage licenses in Virginia and in Texas," Cole said. "If she married a CIA agent, there's a good chance the marriage took place in Virginia.

"Or in Texas," Kirke said. "We don't have her maiden name, but we have his name. Haley."

"What's his first name?"

"We don't have that," she admitted. "Her husband died twelve, thirteen years ago. The woman we talked to just knew Haley."

"There has to be a godawful number of Haleys getting wed in both states," Cole said. "And how are you going to get a photo of her?"

"Kirke's reporter friend found an article in a local newspaper. Maybe there's a photo. She can e-mail it to me if we have an address."

"Reporter friend?" Cole interrupted.

"I used to work with her," Kirke said. "She's great with research. I asked her to try to find something about Dallas. She's the one who came up with the right spelling of the last name, along with the Denton connection."

Dane stood. "If she's made queries, she might be in danger, too," he said. "My contact says there's been a flurry of interest there about Mitch Edwards and Dallas Haley. More than one query about the wife of a dead agent might ring some alarm bells."

Kirke's heart stopped. She'd thought that Robin's search for a former bar manager innocuous. Could her queries have attracted the notice of Adams's contact in the CIA? Her eyes met Jake's.

Jake stood, a muscle in his throat throbbing. It was obvious that he, too, had not thought Robin's queries would be noticed, much less tracked. And perhaps they weren't, but after Edna . . .

"I have to call her," she said. She looked at Jake. "That probably means alerting the FBI. She most certainly will call Ben."

"Do it," Jake said without blinking. He handed her the phone.

"Ben?" asked MacAllister.

"Her husband's an FBI agent."

"That gives us even less time to find Dallas," Jake said,

"but she has to know. She may not be on their radar, but I'm not willing to take that chance."

Kirke used the new prepaid phone to call Robin. She could take risks for herself, but she wasn't going to get another person killed. Especially not Robin.

"Robin, this is Kirke," she said when Robin answered. "You might be in danger. A friend of . . . my friend said queries about Dallas Haley have been noticed in the CIA. There could be a bad guy there. I think you should join Ben if you can."

"CIA? They don't operate within this country."

"They're not supposed to, but there could be a maverick who's helping a killer."

"What is this all about?"

She looked at Jake. He was close enough to hear.

He nodded.

She quickly capsuled the recent events.

When she finished, there was a silence. "You're convinced he's innocent."

"I wouldn't be here if I wasn't. Until I heard about the woman in Williamsburg, I didn't think you were in danger. I'm not so sure now."

"Why don't you go to the police?"

"Jake is on parole. He violated it to come to Atlanta to meet this man. The army wants the matter closed, and unless he gets some evidence, they'll put him back in prison. We think this Dallas Haley has information that can help him."

"This is what you meant about a big story? Did your Jake agree to this call?" Robin asked.

"Yes."

A silence, then, "I'll be careful, but they're probably concentrating on you now. I think you should consider talking to Ben's FBI friends."

"I can't. Not yet. We have to find Dallas before the bad guys do."

"The FBI—"

"Could be stopped by national security concerns."

An audible sigh came from the phone. "I'll be withholding

information about several murders," Robin said. "So will you."

"And you haven't done that before?"

Silence. Then, "You think you can find her?"

"Yes."

"If you don't call in the next twenty-four hours, I'm going to tell Ben everything. He just finished his assignment and is due back day after tomorrow. I don't keep secrets from him."

Kirke didn't say anything.

"Any longer," Robin amended.

Still silence.

"Well, not many," Robin amended again.

"Twenty-four hours," Kirke finally said. "I'll get back to you. Just be careful. Is there anyone you can stay with?"

"With a foul mouthed parrot and two cats?" A hint of a smile came through.

"Is he still whistling that song?"

"Incessantly." Robin said. "But Ben made sure we have the best protection system available. And I have an attack parrot in residence."

Despite Robin's light words, Kirke heard the concern behind them.

One last question. "Did that article have a photo?"

"Yes." Robin gave her the Web address where she'd found it.

"Thanks, Robin, for everything." She paused. "Be careful."

"I'm not sure I should be thanked. I should be running to Ben."

"Just take care." She hung up before Robin had second thoughts.

"We have twenty-four hours," she said to the others in the room.

Ames Williamson, alias Gene Adams, landed at the Dallas International Airport at 3 p.m.

Everything was falling apart. He'd received word from his contact in the CIA that queries had been made about

Mitch Edwards, Jake Kelly, and himself, as well as Dallas Haley. Some questions had been raised only a few hours earlier.

He knew the latter name. He'd been in the Enigma when he'd been instructing recruits but thought it far too obvious for his taste. He'd disapproved. Anyone hearing the bar's name would think of the CIA. People in that part of Virginia most certainly would.

But when one of his men said Williamsburg had been marked on the map stolen from Jake Kelly's car, he remembered that Del Cox had mentioned the Enigma more than once. He'd even heard Cox talk to Kelly about it one night when he'd been listening in. Cox always talked too much.

A goddamn bar. Yet it was the only thing he associated with Cox and Williamsburg. He immediately sent a two-man team to check it out.

He was getting low on men. He'd recruited an army of ex-servicemen and paid them well enough to ensure some loyalty, but most of them were in Argentina. In any case, he never completely trusted mercenaries. Certainly none had shown much competence during the past week. Three had been sent home since they'd allowed themselves to be seen.

He could fly back to Argentina. But then he risked leaving behind evidence that would keep him on the run forever. It certainly would dry up his current business. He'd been selling old information for six years. He didn't have that much left, and his CIA contact was sidling away from him. If his names, both former and present, became known, he would become radioactive. His mansion would go. His women. His power.

Damn Cox. The man had kept more than a few secrets from him. He wished Cox had died in a more painful way. And Kelly was slippery as an eel. That had surprised him. He'd considered Kelly just another grunt.

He walked out of the restricted area of the airport and saw a driver holding a sign for a Mr. W. Williams. He nodded to him, and the driver rushed up to take his carry-on. Ames followed him to a limousine. "I don't want that," he said. "I specifically asked for a nondescript car."

"But I was told—"

"I don't care what you were told. I want a standard sedan, one that won't be noticed."

"It'll take a few moments."

"I don't care how long it takes," Ames said.

The man disappeared. Ames found a public phone and used an untraceable credit card to call his contact at the CIA. The contact didn't answer, but he didn't have to. Ames simply left a message, "An old friend from the neighborhood is in town." Caldwell would find a safe phone and call back within an hour.

The man who'd met him reappeared. "I have a new car. It will be here in ten minutes."

"A rental agency?"

"No. Someone who specializes in providing special needs for discriminating clients. The registry is untraceable."

Which was a way of charging more. Still, though he hated to admit it, he had little choice at the moment. The longer this lasted, the more he risked, not to mention the money pouring out of his bank account.

The man who'd greeted him drove him to a hotel he'd selected and handed him the keys. "I'm Temple," he said. "I can stay with you or be at your call."

"I'll call you," Ames said.

Temple gave him a card, and he glanced at it. No name. No address. Only a phone number. Ames suspected that number changed frequently.

He'd just reached his room when his cell phone rang.

He listened to a tirade about the risks incurred by being called at his office, then interrupted his caller, "I don't give a shit about the risk to you. Remember, I know about all that money you haven't reported. An anonymous call will send you straight to jail."

The man on the other end of the line swore, then said, "This is getting too damn hot for me. Leave me alone."

"Forget about that. You're in this as deep as I am. You help set up the South American mission. You've been getting money all these years. Don't forget I have the account numbers. Now, I want everything you can find on a woman named

Dallas Haley. I don't know if Dallas is a legal name or not, but she was a hostess or manager at the Enigma, a bar in Williamsburg."

"Why?"

"She must know something about what happened that day in the jungle. Maybe where the remainder of the diamonds went. There's a connection between Del Cox and her. I have to get to her before Kelly does, and I want to know what Kelly is doing."

"We can't operate in the U.S."

"Tell me another joke," Ames said. "I'll be in touch." He hung up.

The cell phone rang again. He answered it.

"We have something," one of his men said. He was the best hacker that money could buy.

"What?"

"A credit card Kelly is using. It's a prepaid one, but now we have the number, I should be able to follow any use he makes of it."

"Right." He hung up and smiled. Jake and the damn interfering woman were his.

# CHAPTER 27

❦

They checked into a hotel near the barbecue restaurant.

Jake was even more of a stranger since they'd heard about Edna Caswell. He hadn't touched her, not the slightest pat, or even his hand brushing hers. Everything had been about finding Dallas.

She was having her own attack of conscience. Maybe she should have asked Robin to call her husband. Maybe they should alert local authorities to the danger to Dallas.

Then all the reasons why she shouldn't do any of those things crowded out those thoughts. They had little information and even less proof. They had the word of a convicted thief and possible traitor and seven numbers. They had a dead body, but given everything else, Jake might well be charged with that as well. He'd been inside the restaurant. She was an accomplice in helping a fugitive. Their credibility would be nil.

Meanwhile, the bad guys could get to Dallas.

Did Jake feel that way as well? Was that why he seemed to be withdrawing from her?

Or was it something more? Was he not telling her something? He'd said little about his life. He said he was divorced but little about why or when or where. He seemed to have an endless source of money, and his explanation of a inheritance was, well, convenient.

All those warnings ran through her head, even though she felt no fear of him, at least not physically. Emotionally was another matter altogether. Her reactions to him frightened her. She had plunged into this journey wholeheartedly. To right a wrong. And, to be honest, to save herself. But she feared she was falling in love. That would be disastrous with someone like him. Even if he was cleared, he was a warrior. She was a healer, or close to one. He was the wandering type, and she just wanted a home of her own, preferably with a house full of pets and children.

She said none of these things as he requested a double room. They were both exhausted, but she would dearly love to have his body next to hers. That idea was scotched when he asked which bed she preferred.

"The left," she said for lack of a better answer.

"Why don't you take the first shower," he suggested.

She wasn't sure she would survive one without falling on her face. She'd napped a little in the car, but she'd not really slept. Yet she really needed a shower. Her washing for two days had been quick splashes of water on her face.

She headed for the bathroom, discarded her clothes on the floor, found little soap bars, shampoo, and conditioner, and turned on the water until it was as hot as she could stand.

She reveled in the flow of hot water. Still, exhaustion slowed her movements as she washed her hair, then rinsed it and just stood there letting the water wash off layers of grime and internal doubts. Finally she forced herself to turn the water off.

She dried herself, then wrapped another towel around her and stepped out.

Jake was standing at the window again. He could be so still. No movement and yet she sensed the energy raging inside him. How had he ever survived prison?

She wanted to go to him, to touch his face, his hair. She wanted to fit her body into his.

Instead she went to the bed. He'd placed the bag containing

her few possessions on top of it. One clean T-shirt left. She pulled it on. If they were going to the college tomorrow, she would need some clean clothes.

That was the last thought she had as she closed her eyes.

———

Jake spent more time than he needed in the bathroom. Another cold shower was mandated, though he didn't feel he needed to stay awake tonight. Cole was on one side of their room, Mac on the other. The rooms had been reserved by Barbecue Bob. No worry that any of the names he'd used would be on record.

Kirke was dead on her feet. Her eyes were red from exhaustion, and her movements lacked that vitality that was so much a part of her.

He didn't want to be tempted by her, and God help him, her just being alive tempted him. Even if he did clear himself—and the chances were getting slimmer that he would—he had damned little. His career with Special Forces was over. Not only had he led his team into a trap, but he'd lost seven years of training. Seven years for a special ops officer was a lifetime. He might get back pay, but in the past few weeks, he'd run through a fortune in forged documents.

He toweled off, slipped his jeans on, and returned to the room. She was asleep. One hand stretched out as if asking him to join her.

It took everything in him not to take it and slip into bed with her.

Her hair was still damp and curled around her face. Her long legs were outlined under the thin sheet. He pulled the spread over her.

He would give nearly anything if he'd met her ten years ago. But then he'd been married. Not happily, but married.

He stepped away from her and quietly went to the door. He opened it softly, exited, then closed it gently behind him. He went next door to Cole's room. It opened immediately when he knocked.

"I didn't think you would get here," Cole said.

"She took a shower, then I did."

He caught the question in Cole's eyes.

"Alone," he said.

Cole's eyes met his. "She's smart. And pretty."

"She's too damned curious," he said gruffly.

"What about Nancy?" Cole asked.

"Divorced me right after the court-martial."

Cole didn't comment.

"You never liked her," Jake said.

"I didn't dislike her. I just didn't think she could survive the loneliness. It takes a special woman to put up with the long absences."

Jake was silent. He'd discovered that about Nancy as well, but that realization came too late. She'd liked the image but not the reality. He knew more about Kirke in a week than he'd known about Nancy in six years. Unfortunately, the opposite wasn't true. Kirke knew damn little about him, and he had to keep it that way.

"Let's get on with it," he said. He hated taking favors. He never would have gotten Cole and Mac involved if Kirk's life wasn't at stake. He hadn't really expected them to run to his aid as they had. After losing his best friend on a mission, he'd tried to keep others at a distance. Yet Cole had been supportive as soon as he'd learned what happened. He'd protested and tried to reopen the case, even knowing it could destroy his own career.

"You're going to have a devil of a time removing her from the action," Cole said. "She has the light of battle in her eyes."

"Very tired eyes, and she's never been in battle. She has a gun permit. She knows how to shoot. But I'm not sure she could fire it at a live human being."

"I think she could," Cole said, "but I understand you want her out of the line of fire. I felt the same way about my wife, though she could outpilot any guy in her squadron."

"You'll get her away then?"

"I'll try. Now get the hell to bed, or you'll be useless."

Jake left reluctantly. He doubted whether he would get any sleep knowing that Kirke was inches away. Forbidden fruit. She was that, and more. But if he had any integrity left—any at all—he would stay the hell away from her. And that meant hurting her like he'd never hurt anyone before.

～

Bob had showed at the hotel with a copy of the article and photo he had taken from the Internet. He also brought breakfast. She'd liked him yesterday when he'd welcomed Jake and her to his restaurant. She loved him now as he revealed the contents of several large boxes: bacon, biscuits and gravy, and omelets. He also carried a pot of steaming coffee.

"You have a friend for life," Jake told him. "She lives on coffee."

"Food, too," she protested, inhaling the smell of the bacon.

Bob beamed at her. Then he went to Mac's room, followed by one of his employes loaded down with more food.

They ate quickly. She finished first, then watched Jake. He was slower, obviously savoring every bite. As if, she thought, it might be his last good meal. It might well be, if they didn't find Dallas.

They arrived at the library after stopping at a twenty-four-hour discount store where they both purchased new clothes. She bought a pair of navy blue slacks and a fitted blouse, and he found a light brown shirt. They changed in a service station restroom, then they drove to Denton and found the library of the most likely university.

They were directed to the university history section and quickly located the yearbooks. A century of them.

*Where to start?*

How old was Dallas?

She guessed from what Jake had told her and the photo they'd received from Robin that she'd been in her late thirties at the time Jake had met her. That would put her in her mid-forties now.

"Let's start at 1983 and go forward. Work to 1989. If we don't find anything, we'll go backward from '83."

Everything depended on Dallas being her given name and not a nickname.

Jake's friends would hack into the college alumni files at the same time. If they had no luck, then they would go to plan B. Federal benefits records. It would be more than a little difficult and dangerous, but it might be the only way.

Two hours went by, then four. Her eyes grew blurry, but one thing kept her alert: the murder of the nice woman at the Williamsburg bakery. The killer might have exacted the same information she had. If the bad guys had someone still in the CIA, they might obtain Dallas's whereabouts far quicker than they.

Jake finished the last in his series of yearbooks with a bang that startled other readers. She had taken a chair on the other side of the table. Proximity to him always seemed to cloud her judgment and her concentration.

"Dammit," he swore in a low tone. "Nothing."

"It was always a long shot," she said, picking up the last of her pile. After this, they would go backward five years, then go to the other college. This one, though, had been the most likely, the one most local kids attended.

Nothing in the next one. A slow panic was beginning to set in. What if she and Jake had set up Dallas for death? They *had* to get to her.

She prayed that his cell phone would ring, that Jake's friends had found something, but it was silent. She started on the group of yearbooks that went from 1984 down to 1980.

Kirke tried not to flip through the '83 volume. Her mind was already moving ahead to the next step when she saw it. Junior year. Dallas Gallagher. Small photo. Long hair streaming over her shoulders and a bright smile.

She went back to the '84 yearbook's senior class to see if she missed something. No Dallas Gallagher. She must have dropped out or finished at another college.

Silently she pushed the '83 yearbook over to Jake.

He saw it, closed his eyes for a moment, and she realized he felt the relief she did.

"Check the phone book for Gallaghers," he said. "I'll go outside and call Mac."

She quickly replaced the volumes on the right shelf, thanked the librarian on duty, and asked about a phone book. In minutes she had twelve Gallaghers. She rushed outside.

For a second, she didn't see him. Then she saw Jake leaning against a wall, talking on his cell phone. She stopped, conquering that momentary fear of abandonment. At the same time, she warned herself. He'd never said anything about sticking around if he did discover the truth. He'd never said anything about love. They'd gone to bed together, but he'd just been released from prison. Anyone would have looked good to him.

He glanced up, his eyes as emotionless as the first time she'd met him. "Mac and Cole will start Googling Gallaghers in this area. Shouldn't be too many."

"Twelve," she said.

He gave her that rare half smile. "I really didn't think we would find anything."

From him, it was the supreme compliment.

She went over to the car and got in the passenger's side. "Where to?"

"To find a public phone."

Objective: find a Gallagher who knew Dallas Gallagher Haley. She agreed with him now that a public phone was far safer than using the cell.

She was looking for one when he suddenly made a right turn into a large convenience mart with a deli. He parked and turned to her. "They might have a phone inside."

It did. The interior had a small sitting area, along with a counter containing the required fried chicken along with hot dogs and other sandwiches. He grabbed a plate and selected a piece of chicken and a biscuit. She took a hot dog.

Then they sat down and went over her list.

"Dallas told the reporter her mother named her children after the place they were born. Here's a Dayton."

He started to rise.

"Let me do it," she said.

He sat again, took a handful of change from his pocket,

and handed it to her. "He may not be any relation to Dallas," he warned.

She knew. She took the change. And said a small prayer. *She* needed one. *She* needed it.

She went to the phone, inserted the coins. And dialed.

# CHAPTER 28

—➤

There was no answer. Not even an answering machine.

Kirke slumped in disappointment. For a moment, she'd thought they were so close.

She saw it in Jake's eyes as well.

"Back to the list," he said.

She started at the top of the list with a Thomas Gallagher. This time she got a telephone answering machine asking her to leave a message. Same reply for the second. The phone was disconnected on the third.

A woman answered the fourth.

"Mrs. Gallagher," Kirke said. "You don't know me, but I'm a friend of Dallas Gallagher . . . she later became Mrs. Haley . . . and I'm trying to reach her. I was hoping you might be able to help me."

"I don't know anyone named Dallas."

"I'm so sorry to have bothered you," Kirke said soothingly. "Thank you for your time." She hung up and went to the next.

Another answering machine reply. She looked at her

watch in frustration. How close was Adams and his pack of jackals?

An elderly voice answered the eighth attempt. "Hello."

Kirke started her spiel.

"Dallas?" came a cautious response. "You're a friend, you say?"

Shock stopped her for a moment. She had almost given up. Shock and an incredible thrill of success. "More a friend of a friend. He has a message for her."

"Why isn't he delivering it?" Suspicion had hardened her voice.

"He died," she said simply. "Can you tell me how reach her?"

A hesitation, then, "Who are you?"

"My name is Kirke. Kirke Palmer." From the suspicion in her voice, Kirke knew she had to tell the truth. Something was going on here.

She saw the frown on Jake's face and chose to ignore it.

"And who is the friend?"

Dear God, which name had the man she knew as Mark Cable, and Jake knew as Del Cox, used when he knew Dallas. "He was CIA," she finally said. "I knew him as Mark Cable. He also used the name Del Cox."

"You said he died?" came the slow reply.

"He was killed a week ago," Kirke replied.

"Give me a number. I'll see if she wants to call you back."

"Just a moment," she said. She gestured to Jake, and he hurried over to her.

She covered the speaker part of the phone. "She knows Dallas, says she'll ask if Dallas wants to call me back. She needs a number."

"The new cell," he said.

She took her hand from the speaker, then gave the woman the number. "Please ask her to call me. It's urgent."

"I thought you were just delivering a message."

"It's an urgent message. It could be a matter of life or death."

The woman hung up.

Kirke leaned against the wall. "I don't think I handled that very well."

"I think you did," he said.

"I was afraid she wouldn't contact her immediately. I pushed more than I should."

"You had to do it."

"Should we call the others?"

They exchanged glances. To her surprise, he said, "Your call. You have more of an instinct for this. I can be . . . too blunt."

Understatement, but she let it go. "Let's wait an hour. If we don't hear anything, we can finish the calls and visit this Dayton Gallagher."

They ate the lunch, which was now cold. He drank coffee, she a diet soda. The cell phone lay between them. They willed it to ring.

"Why would she be so cautious?" she asked.

"Maybe she's frightened of something. Or someone."

"Del Cox?" she asked.

The cell phone rang.

He picked it up and handed it to her. His confidence filled her with a warm glow. He was not a man to trust others. She'd discovered that.

"Hello," she said into the cell phone.

"This is Dallas. My aunt said you were looking for me. That a Del Cox had given you a message." Her voice was slow. Halting.

"Yes," Kirke said. "Are you at home?"

"Is it important?"

"It could be," Kirke replied.

"No," Dallas said. Her voice was pleasant. Throaty and warm.

"Good," Kirke said. "Can you meet me?"

"Not until I know more."

"I'm a paramedic from Atlanta." She'd decided only the truth would do now. Obviously Dallas was hiding from something. Or someone.

Dallas waited for her to go on.

"A week ago I received a call. A hit-and-run. Man down. When we arrived he was near death, but he thrust an envelope into my hand and asked me to give it to a Mitch Edwards. He mentioned Dallas."

"And he's dead?" The words were little more than a whisper.

"Yes. I'm sorry." She paused, then said, "It's a long story, and you might be in danger. Please meet with me. In a very public place, if you wish."

Dallas hesitated.

"You can check me out," Kirke said. "Call the Atlanta Fire Department." She gave Dallas the station number, then its phone number. "You might want to call information," she said, "and make sure it's the number. Don't take my word. Don't take anyone's word."

"A public park," Dallas agreed and gave directions. "Seven p.m., near the refreshment stand by the softball field. If you check out, I'll meet you there. If not, then don't wait."

"How will I recognize you?"

"You tell me how I'll recognize *you*," Dallas replied. "And anyone with you."

Kirke thought of the T-shirt they'd bought along the way. "I'm five feet nine inches," she said. "I have short auburn hair. I'll be wearing a T-shirt with Tennessee on it."

"Will anyone be with you?"

"No," she lied. It was safer if no one knew Jake was with her.

Dallas hung up before Kirke could say anything else. She suspected Dallas knew she was lying. Would that keep her from coming? She wanted to kick herself.

Kirke turned off the cell and repeated the conversation to Jake.

"She's scared about something," she said. "At least we know what she looks like."

"Maybe," he said. "The newspaper photo is eight years old, the college one nearly thirty."

Jake asked the store clerk for directions to the park. He purchased a map, thanked the clerk, then they left.

She looked at her watch. Four hours to kill.

Four hours for Adams to find Dallas before she and Jake did. Had she issued a strong enough warning?

✦

Ames prepared to leave the Dallas hotel for Denton. His man from the CIA had come through. Partly.

"The check goes to a bank account in Denton, Texas," his CIA contact said.

"What name?"

"No name. Just an account number."

"Goddamn," he said. "That's worth nothing to me. I need her address. Go back and get it. Government has so many damned papers, the address has to be there somewhere. If I fall, you fall, too. Remember that." He cut the call off.

He called one of the men waiting in his suite. He gave him the name of the bank, as well as the photo his hacker had found on the Internet. "I want someone there. Make sure they have a photo. I want them to look at whoever goes in and out. If the woman does, then I want her followed."

That would take too long, and he knew it. Maybe she never went into the bank. Wasn't necessary these days with checks automatically deposited and ATMs everywhere.

She probably lived in the neighborhood around the bank. Most people did. He gave orders to three other men to circulate in the immediate neighborhood, particularly in neighborhood restaurants and shops, to see if anyone could identify the person. They should say they were looking for the sister of a dying sibling. People were very sentimental about things like that.

Six men. That's all he had with him now. One at the bank, three in the neighborhood, and two with him. Too bad they didn't get more from the woman in Williamsburg. All she knew was Texas.

Ames took out an expensive cigar and lit it. He'd acquired the habit in Argentina and couldn't give it up.

He had to get to this Dallas person before Kelly did. Preferably he could take them all out together.

They'd proved wilier than he'd expected. The woman was

a civilian. Jake was military. And so far they'd run rings around him. No more. He'd taken his time in the beginning. He wanted to be sure nothing came back to him, but now he couldn't risk finesse.

He wanted them dead, and he wanted them dead now.

➤

Jake's plans had gone awry again. Dallas would be looking for a woman. He couldn't send Kirke away as he planned.

He and Cole had planned to drug her drink. Something that would put her out of action for a few hours. Nothing strong or destructive or addictive. Only a small headache the next day.

He'd listened as she spoke into the phone and couldn't grab it from her. He should have done it himself. Yet he realized that she was striking pay dirt where he—

Then she'd announced where they would go and what the woman had said. Whether she planned it or not—and he suspected she did—she had become indispensable.

She'd done well. Better than well. She'd been superb. He knew she didn't like to lie, and mostly she'd told the truth, but she'd lied about being alone. In that one transgression, she'd also placed herself in even more danger. He hoped to hell she didn't regret it.

He didn't like it. Yet he had no choice. From what she said, Dallas might run if she didn't see an auburn-haired woman wearing a Tennessee T-shirt. He had the disquieting feeling that maybe Kirke had planned it that way.

"Let's take a look at the park," he said after they left the convenience store.

He found it within minutes. It appeared to be a sprawling facility with picnic areas, walking trails, lakes and athletic fields. He drove around until he found the concession area.

He parked at the restrooms and opened the trunk. He'd packed their belongings before leaving the hotel. He opened her bag and tossed her the T-shirt. "I'll wait out here," he said.

When she disappeared inside, he used his cell phone. He hated to use it again, but he had no choice. He didn't see a pay phone.

In minutes, he told Cole what had happened. "We need her, but I want her safe. Can you and Mac be here?"

Silence. Then, "Did you think we wouldn't?"

It was a rebuke.

"No," he said. "I'm just not used to—"

"Where do you want us?" Cole interrupted.

"Can you meet us out in the park in, say, two hours?"

"We can and will."

"At the concession stand," he added. His voice was a little rough. There was a lump in it. Three months ago, three weeks ago, he didn't think anyone gave a damn about him. He'd told himself he didn't care, that a man was far better off to rely only on himself. One wasn't disappointed then.

It was hard to admit he was wrong. Had been wrong.

If only Dallas appeared now. Maybe then the mystery of the numbers would be solved. Maybe he would know everything that happened that day in the jungle.

Maybe he would even have his name back. His life back. The one sorrow would be that his father would never know it.

Or was he leading his makeshift team into another ambush?

# CHAPTER 29

Two hours. They had two hours to wait.

The number of people in the park had thinned out. Friday afternoon, Kirke thought. Mothers taking their kids home for supper. And in a few hours? She recalled the softball fields. Were games scheduled tonight?

"Can we get some pepper spray?" she asked.

"You have a gun," Jake replied. "Better than pepper spray."

"It's a park," she said. "There are kids." She was having second thoughts about Dallas's suggestion. But the woman must have had a reason. She kept remembering what Jake had said about her. Tough as nails. She would have to be, to control a bar full of testosterone.

He didn't argue. "We should be able to get several small canisters at a gun shop."

"A florist, too."

He raised an eyebrow but didn't question her, and she didn't feel like enlightening him. Not yet.

In the meantime, she had to do something. She'd never been good at waiting. She was scared on so many levels, terrified on some. What if Dallas didn't show up? What if she did but didn't have what Jake needed to clear himself? What would happen to him then? And what if they had led Adams to Dallas? And ultimately to themselves?

But maybe what she feared most of all was losing Jake once this was over. To either prison or to the life he was meant to have. She wouldn't even think of the third alternative. That Adams would win.

And if Jake found what he needed to clear himself, he would be free to get on with his life. Back to his career. Back to the army. The sun would disappear. The warmth would leave her.

She could return home, the only real home she'd ever known.

To her job. To Merlin.

It should be enough. She should be giddy with anticipation.

She dreaded the very thought.

How could someone make such an impact on a life in such few days? She'd never believed in love at first sight, or second, or third. That's what happened to her mother, and it lasted three seconds, or as long as it took Kirke to be born.

She'd come to believe time, friendship, and like interests would ensure a happy marriage. She'd been wrong about that, too.

She stole a look at him, saw the worry lines around his eyes as they drove out of the park.

"Where are we going?" she asked.

"To a bank where I can cash out the credit cards," he said. "I want you to have some cash. If anything goes wrong, get the hell out of there and call your friend Robin. Don't try to help. You'll just be in the way. I'll be more concerned with protecting you than anything else. That's dangerous for all of us."

She froze. "You think it might be a trap?"

"I don't know what to expect," he said, "but I want your promise. No promise, we don't go." He gave her a crooked grin. "I know how you feel about promises."

"You think Adams has found Dallas?"

"I think he's close."

"How many people do you think he has with him?"

"Enough to do what he wants to do."

She was silent.

He glanced at her. "We have our backup, too. Cole and Mac will be at the park. I still want your promise, though. At the first hint of trouble, you take off. Otherwise we don't go tonight."

She nodded.

"Say it!"

"I promise." She crossed her fingers at her side.

She concentrated instead on the cars around them. Adams seemed to prefer dark sedans. To match his soul, no doubt. Denton had a population of more than a hundred thousand people, and the chance of glimpsing a bad guy was nonexistent. Still, she hoped to see the bad guys before they saw her.

⟶

Ames flipped open the cell phone on the second ring. "What do you have?"

"An address," his employee said. "You were right. Found the bank. It's in a suburban area. I asked around at restaurants, telling them about the sick sister. A waitress remembered her. She found a credit card slip. Jeffers was able to find the card holder.

"Good," Ames said.

"You want us to take her?"

"No. I want her to lead us to Kelly. I want several people on her. I do *not* want her to know she's being followed."

He hung up. The phone rang again.

"I found your woman," said the voice on the other end. "I was able to get into survivor records. Her married name is Crew. Her husband is Dennis Crew. He's a cop."

Another goddamn complication. One he didn't need.

He knew what happened if a cop's wife was killed. Just like when a Special Forces mate was killed. They didn't stop coming after you.

It didn't matter now. The woman obviously knew something, or Kelly wouldn't be here. He had to eliminate all three of them. That was the only way the trail to him would be erased.

"Ames?" the guy on the line said. "Get out of the country while you can. People are asking questions now."

"Who?"

"A reporter in Atlanta, for one. It's not contained."

Ames swore to himself. His contact was shaky. That was very bad news. Scared people made mistakes. Maybe it was time to eliminate him as well.

"I'll be gone in the morning," he lied.

---

Jake stopped at a bank first. They both went inside while he cashed out the prepaid credit cards. He used his David Cable identification to do so, and when they reached the car, he gave Kirke $3,000 in fifties and hundreds.

He watched as she carefully distributed it in several pockets of her purse. He was reminded that he should have done this in the beginning. She'd been little more than a prisoner without resources of her own. But he'd been so focused on his own objective.

He'd treated her dismally. He had drawn her into a web of danger, then taken advantage when she was vulnerable. He had convinced her that her life depended on him, when she might well be safer in the hands of the FBI or, better yet, in some faraway place.

He cursed himself. He'd lost any niceties he'd learned as an officer and gentleman at West Point. A combination of years in Afghanistan and other hot spots followed by seven years in prison had made him mistrustful, wary, and bitter. Not especially qualities any woman would want in a man.

He turned his attention to finding a gun shop. He accompanied her inside one, and they found both Mace and pepper spray. He chose several canisters of pepper spray, and the clerk instructed Kirke on how to use it most effectively. She gave one cannister to him and put the other in her purse.

He accepted it, knowing he would never use it. He preferred a more lethal type of defense. Especially for someone like Adams.

"Now the flower shop," she said.

He'd seen one earlier. He didn't question her reasons for

stopping but stayed in the car while she ran in. She reappeared a moment later with a corsage in hand. Carnations. Two of them. The type you buy for a prom date or Mother's Day or for some award ceremony. She plopped it down on the seat beside them as he drove away.

She offered no explanation about the corsage. Some feminine whim. Except that wasn't like her.

Finally he had to ask. "What's with the corsage?"

"You've never pinned one on a girl?"

"No." He'd usually been on the move as a kid. He'd been in Japan his junior and senior year. There had been no proms in the traditional sense.

"It comes with a very big pin," she said. "I could probably have talked her into giving me just a pin, but that would take explanations and—"

"A weapon," he said flatly. "A pin?"

She sat taller. An indignant—and stubborn—expression crossed her face. "I took a self-defense class. They said it could be very handy."

"Where do you keep it?"

"A place that provides the least chance to get stuck."

He couldn't help but grin at that. "I hate to tell you, but it wouldn't deflect a determined mercenary."

"You never know."

"You already have pepper spray and a gun."

"And now I have pepper spray, a gun, and a pin."

Dammit, she made him smile. Her combination of determination, guts, and naïveté continued to astonish him. At the same time, his earlier reservations about her willingness to actually shoot returned. *She wouldn't.* He had to recognize that.

He drove back toward the park. They had an hour before the meeting.

He saw Mac immediately. He was sitting on a picnic table not far from the softball field. He looked relaxed, with a paper plate of French fries in front of him.

Someone parked next to him. He stiffened as the occupants got out and started toward a softball field. Three of them wore baseball shirts with the words Police printed across the back. Two more people left a car on the other side of him and walked toward the field. Their shirts proclaimed them firefighters.

It didn't take a genius to realize a game between the police and fire departments was about to begin. *Great.*

Now he knew why Dallas had designated this place. She couldn't have picked a safer one.

But it was dangerous as hell for him. Every moment he stood there placed him in more peril.

He turned toward Kirke and saw the question in her eyes.

He nodded. They had little choice. If Kirke didn't show for Dallas, no telling how long it would take to find her again.

"I don't want you involved in this," Jake said. "You're helping a fugitive," he said. "That could mean prison time. Stay in the car. I'll meet her. Drive away if you see anyone approaching."

"There's no way I could possibly know you're a fugitive," she said, "and she won't recognize you."

"But now I can identify her," he countered.

"She's looking for a woman. You approach her with that scowl, and she'll likely scream for help. And she won't have to scream very loud."

He still looked dubious.

"I'll be be safe with cops all over the place. I have the gun with me. I have my pepper spray."

"And a pin," he added with just a little sarcasm.

"Besides, won't these police types scare off the bad guys, even if they did find out about Dallas and the meeting?"

Jake wasn't certain. Adams must be as desperate as he was.

The decision was taken from him as Kirke stepped out of the car. For the second time in his life, he was completely trapped. If he wanted what could save the rest of his life, he had to let her go. If he tried to stop her, they would be far too conspicuous.

He placed the baseball cap on his head and donned the dark glasses. Then he took the pistol and belt holster from the glove compartment and snapped it to his belt. After pulling out his shirt to cover it, he stepped out of the car. Doubly damned if he was caught carrying. As a felon, a gun was a very big no-no.

He headed toward the baseball field, passing the refreshment stand. Kirke stood there, munching on a hot dog, looking entirely at ease. Admiration flooded him. She had more damned guts than most men he knew.

He walked to the fence where family and friends had dragged up chairs to watch the game. A small bleacher section was already full. Good-natured catcalls were being exchanged as the teams warmed up.

He turned where he could watch the refreshment stand as well as see part of the field.

One woman came up to him. "Fire or police?" she asked.

"Fire," he replied.

"Good. Would you like to join us?"

"Thanks, but I'm waiting for someone."

The woman nodded and returned to her group. He wondered whether she could be Dallas, but the features were different, along with the age.

Then he saw a woman, man, and boy walk toward the field. The man wore the blue police uniform shirt. The boy held his hand.

He recognized the woman's features immediately. There was strength in her face and laugh lines around her eyes. Her hair was the color of rust and pulled back into a bun. Her skin was tanned against a sleeveless pink blouse and cream-colored slacks. She wore only a touch of lipstick and a simple turquoise pendant. He had the impression of a woman comfortable with herself. When they reached the fence, someone called to her, and she headed that way with the boy while the man headed toward the field.

She joined a group, sitting on one of several chairs already placed alongside the fence.

She glanced at her watch, then quickly at the refreshment stand. She whispered something to the boy, then stood.

The game started. The crowd came to their feet as the first

pitch was thrown. Jake turned so he could watch the woman as well as appear interested in the game. Mac and Cole were watching Kirke.

He felt a jolt at his side, and turned, his hand instinctively going toward the holster.

Someone had bumped into him while moving a chair closer to the fence. He quickly dropped his hand.

"Sorry," the man said.

He wore a patrolman's uniform.

"No problem," Jake said and stepped away.

"You got someone playing?"

"No, just like baseball."

He looked back to where the woman he thought to be Dallas was standing.

She was gone.

He whirled around to look at the refreshment stand.

Kirke was gone as well.

# CHAPTER 30

Kirke ate a hot dog and drank a soda, then ordered an ice cream.

People were still walking toward the field. She looked at her watch. Five to seven. The game was probably at seven.

She took her time licking the ice cream. Her stomach was rumbling, but she obviously needed to have a reason for loitering. She tightened her hold on her purse. She unzipped it so both the pepper spray and automatic were instantly available.

She knew, though, she wouldn't fire the gun. Too many people. Too many children. Nerves started crawling up her back.

A roar came from the baseball field as a woman in a pretty coral blouse touched her. "Come with me," the woman said.

Kirke followed her around the refreshment stand toward the restroom building. They went under a little roof and turned right into the women's room. The men's room was opposite.

Dallas checked the stalls, found them empty, then turned to her.

"I'm Dallas Crew," the woman said.

"I'm Kirke."

"I know. I found your photo on the Internet. The story about the sniper. I also called the fire station. They like you there."

"What did you tell them?"

"That I was a friend, but you weren't answering calls, and I was worried about you. They told me you were taking a few days off to recuperate." She raised an eyebrow as she studied Kirke. Powder disguised the remaining bruising around her eye, but Kirke knew it was still visible to someone with a good eye. "Doesn't look as if you're recuperating much," Dallas added.

"A South Pacific beach would be better," Kirke said wryly. "Thank you for coming." She paused, then asked, "Why here?"

"My husband's a cop. He's playing tonight. You startled me today. I didn't know what to expect, but you sounded so urgent. Then you said the right words on the phone . . . or maybe the wrong ones: Del Cox."

"You knew him then? As Del Cox?"

"I know it was one of the names he used. I saw the identification in his wallet when he got sloppy drunk once. I took money from his wallet to pay for a taxi, and an ID dropped out. I also knew him as Dave Lewis, which I think is his real name. I knew he was CIA, though he never said as much. Having been married to one, I recognized all the signs."

"You were close?"

"For a time after my husband's death. What happened to him? And why am I in danger?"

Kirke told her what she knew as quickly as she could. When she finished chronicling the events, she said, "We have these numbers and have no idea what they mean. Since he mentioned your name, we thought you may. You're our last chance."

"What is the name of the man you say was accused?" Dallas asked.

"His name is Jake Kelly, but his cover name was Mitch Edwards," Kirke said. Lying wouldn't help now. Dallas had obviously asked the question for a specific reason, and Kirke knew she was right when emotion flickered across her face.

Dallas nodded. "I might have something that can help."

Kirke waited.

"It's at my house. I can leave in about twenty minutes. I'll meet you there."

"Can I bring Jake?"

Another hesitation, then a nod.

"What about your husband?"

"He's out there playing. They'll be celebrating the outcome of the game, win or lose," she said. "It's a cop thing. And a friend is taking my son for a sleepover."

"Can you tell me anything now?"

"I want to hear from your Mr. Kelly first," she said. She sighed, "I'll be opening a Pandora's box. I want to be sure it's worth it."

"We'll follow you home," Kirke said.

She interrupted. "The tall, lean hunk out at the fence your guy? The one you want to help?"

*Your guy.*

Kirke didn't know how to answer that. The area was full of cops. Dallas's family was all cops.

She finally nodded. Jake had known the chance he was taking and had been willing to do it. "He met you years ago at the Enigma when he was taking some training course. He remembers you. Said you stopped a fight."

"I stopped a lot of them." She paused, then said. "Don't worry about me calling for help. Not now," she said.

"Why are you doing this?"

"My first husband was an honorable guy. He died doing what he did because he loved this country. I think he would want me to help your friend."

"It could be—"

"Dangerous? From what you told me, this Adams probably knew about me already, and certainly by now. Seems I'm in the same position as you are. Act now, or live in fear. Even my family may not be able to keep me safe."

"I have to get back, or Jake will tear this park apart trying to find me."

"I'll leave the park in about twenty minutes," Dallas said

as she glanced at her watch. It's seven thirty now. I'm driving a silver sedan. There's an American flag decal on it." She
gave Kirke the license plate number.

"Can I have your address, in case we get separated?"

Dallas handed Kirke a card, and Kirke glanced at it. It
had her name, Dallas Crew, and under it, Web Site Design.
Two phone numbers were in corners. No printed address, but
she'd scribbled it down.

"Thank you," Kirke said, a lump in her throat. She hadn't
known what to expect. She put the card in the pocket of her
slacks.

"I should probably thank you. I needed closure on this
long ago."

◆

Jake made a couple of rounds around the refreshment area.
No Kirke. Then he called Cole. They'd decided not to call
one another unless it was necessary. Jake hadn't wanted
Adams or his henchmen to realize he wasn't alone.

"I've lost Kirke."

"She went into the ladies' room with a good-looking, red-
headed lady."

Jake visibly relaxed.

"You haven't seen anything suspicious?"

"Nope. Oh, the redhead is coming out. You stay with her
while I stay with Kirke."

Jake nodded. Dallas was probably safe here, but he still
wanted to keep an eye on her until he heard from Kirke.

He returned to the fence and watched as Dallas approached
the people with her son. Before she reached them, though, she
made a call on her cell. Then she went over to her son, leaned
down, and said something to him. They both laughed.

For the first time today, he started to relax.

◆

Kirke waited until Dallas left.

As she turned out the door, she heard a whistle. A familiar tune. Merlin's tune.

She felt, rather than heard, someone behind her. He must

have been peering out from the men's side of the building. Before she could react, the barrel of a gun pressed into her side. "If you want to live, move around the corner. Quickly."

When she hesitated, he shoved the weapon farther into her back, and whispered in her ear, "I have a silencer. I can quite easily kill you and escape in the confusion. Don't expect your boyfriend. He's being taken care of."

It was the latter threat that made her move. She heard the deadly intent in her captor's voice. She couldn't see him, but she knew immediately he must be Adams. She had no doubt he would do as he said.

*Where is Jake?* Adams would have been expecting him, but he wouldn't know two other men were with her. Did Mac or Cole realize what was happening?

She decided to cooperate for the moment and wait for an opportunity. She took a step forward, then another.

"Faster," he said.

Adams put his arm around her as if they were sweethearts, but the gun still pressed into her.

Kirke noticed something red on the sleeve of her attacker. Blood. She also noticed the sleeve was the color of the uniform she'd seen earlier on a park employee. Her blood chilled. Who had he killed now? Was she next?

And no wonder he had been able to get close to her. He'd probably been emptying wastebaskets, hovering around while she was inside. Maybe he even heard some of the conversation. Jake had once called him a chameleon.

He had been quick. He must have located Dallas and followed her here.

The blood on the uniform looked fresh.

"Pretend, bitch," he said in a low voice as he forced her to move quickly around the building to its back, then to woods that backed the facility. He moved his face close to hers.

Step by step they moved among the trees toward the parking lot. She heard the motor of an automobile engine running not far away. She tried to turn her head, but he had a lock on her neck. To some, he might resemble a lover. She didn't see either Cole or Mac now. And Jake? *Someone's taking care of your boyfriend.*

Her heart pounded. She had to believe they were there.

He ducked to miss the branch of a tree, and she decided to scream. Better to be shot here than thrown into a car to an unknown fate. Maybe it would give her protectors an opportunity . . .

Then she heard the crunch of stones behind them. So, apparently, did her attacker. He started to turn, the gun now to her head.

Now or never. The strap of her purse was around her shoulder, the pepper spray just inches away. She purposefully caught her toe on the rise and stumbled away from him. He leaned down to grab her arm, and with the other arm free, she reached in the purse, grabbing the small canister from inside her purse.

At the same time, she heard a shout. Mac, she thought. Or Cole.

He twisted around, still holding her left arm as he aimed his gun toward the shout. She brought up the pepper cannister and sprayed.

He coughed and swore. His hand let go long enough to slap her across the face. She dropped the canister, then the gun was next to her head.

"Don't come any closer," she heard him say to someone else, "or I'll blow her head off."

Her head rang. She felt herself being thrown into someone else's arms. "Get her to the car."

In the distance she heard a roar of approval from the softball field. Didn't anyone hear? Or see? *Scream.* She opened her mouth, and a hand clasped over her mouth. Her new captor was jerking her along, dragging her. They obviously wanted her alive. Her left hand was free. She took the hatpin from where she'd tucked it into the waistband of her slacks and jabbed it through the hand holding her.

He let go.

She scrambled to her feet and started to run. She heard a pop alongside a tree. This time a scream did start deep in her throat as she ran into some arms. They closed around her and threw her to the ground, a body covering hers, sheltering her.

She heard the sound of a car screeching off, then Cole's voice, "It's clear now."

Jake cursed as he rolled off her and helped her up. His gaze went to her face. He closed his eyes for a second, then put his arm around her, drawing her close.

Cole looked at her face. Winced. "They got away," he said. "God, I'm sorry, Kirke. I couldn't fire without hitting you. When you got away, I didn't want to fire and draw all those cops over here. I have the license plate number, though." He looked at her closely. "You okay?"

She nodded, trying not to let the other two see that she was shaking. Inside and out. Her face smarted, and she suspected she would have another black eye just as the first was fading. But she was alive.

She looked around. They were shielded from the ball field by trees. Shouts from the game had masked any noise.

"What happened?" Jake asked softly.

"I was waiting where we planned," Cole said. "But she disappeared into the ladies' room with a woman. No one around but a guy emptying trash. When she came out, the guy grabbed her and put a gun in her back. I didn't doubt he would kill her if I charged him. Mac and I could only follow until we had an opportunity. She gave it to us."

"No way, though, were we going to let her get in a car," Mac said. "I was circling around toward the parking lot. I knew someone would be waiting for the guy." He looked at Jake. "Was that Adams?"

Jake nodded. "I saw that much. Dammit. Someone stopped me at the field. I should have known . . . expected . . ."

"I was caught off guard, too," Mac said as he approached. He held her purse out to her. "Here's your little bag of tricks," he said with a grin. "Damndest thing I ever saw." Then he sobered. "I'm really sorry I wasn't on him faster. After I saw all the cops, I didn't really expect an attempt . . .

"Probably why he did it," Jake said bitterly. "He knew I would be arrested if I made any kind of counterattack. Probably thought I would just let her go. He didn't plan on you two. Or," he added, "Kirke."

Cole's gaze went to Kirke. "I saw you use the pepper spray. What did you do to the other guy?"

"A corsage pin," she said, but her eyes were on Jake. "Dallas is going to help us. We're to follow her home."

"Why is she going to help?" Jake said flatly.

"I don't know. When I mentioned Mitch Edwards, the name obviously meant something to her. She said she might have something that could help. She said she would leave in twenty minutes, and we can follow." She searched her pocket and pulled out the card. "Her address."

Jake looked at Mac. "Mac, go ahead and get there as fast as you can. I want someone there before Dallas Crew arrives. The only way Adams could have known about this is if he'd followed her."

Mac glanced at the card. "I have a GPS in my car, and I know this city. I'm on my way. Cole, you follow them. I'll keep in touch."

The four of them raced back toward the parking lot, Jake and Kirke following Cole. As they ran, they heard some more yells from the softball field. They separated near the parking lot. Dallas was standing beside a silver sedan. When she saw Kirke, she stepped inside.

Kirke got inside their rental and collapsed. Jake reached out his hand, and she took it, realizing seconds later that she was practically draining it of blood. She shivered and couldn't stop shivering. Reaction. She was humiliated by it.

He started the car and pulled behind Dallas. Then he put his arm around Kirke. "When I couldn't find you . . ." His voice was ragged, and it faded away as if he couldn't finish.

*Brace up.* She was strong. She was woman. She was even Superwoman. Except she didn't feel like Superwoman. She felt like a mouse being stalked by a tiger. And that tiger had stepped on her tail and almost got all of her in his mouth.

Jake had to concentrate on following the sedan. He wanted to hold Kirke. Instead, he had to focus on the car ahead. He couldn't lose the woman now. Especially if Adams was waiting for her.

But he was only too aware of Kirke beside him. She was shivering despite the heat in the car. He'd begun to think she had ice water in her veins. She'd sailed through so many potential disasters in the past seven days, enough, in fact, to destroy lesser people.

It was beginning to hit home. He knew it would. He'd experienced it himself after several firefights during a compressed period of time. There was an accumulation of fear. She'd gone through repeated perils with an aplomb that had stunned him. Even a cat had only nine lives, and she'd used about four or five in a matter of a week.

He glanced at her. Her cheek was swelling, but she looked beautiful. God, he liked her. Even loved her, though he fought against that last word. He had no right to it. Not now. Maybe not ever.

It took thirty minutes or so to arrive at Dallas's home. A modest split-level, it was located at the end of a street and sat next to a wooded area. She drove into the garage, and the door closed behind her.

Jake looked for Mac. He saw the car, but it was empty. As discussed on their cells, Cole parked down the street. Dallas expected two people, not three.

It was only seconds before the front door opened. Dallas stood in the doorway. Jake and Kirke approached when he caught a movement behind Dallas.

His internal warning system raged. He'd assumed from what Kirke had said that Dallas would be alone. Obviously, she wasn't. He noticed Kirke stiffening as well.

What in the hell was going on?

Dallas stepped out; so did a tall man with his hand on a gun in a holster at his waist.

"This is Jake Kelly," Kirke said. "I think you met him years ago." She glanced down the street where Cole was waiting. "That's Cole Ramsey. Former Special Forces with Jake. He's helping."

Dallas raised an eyebrow. "Anyone else?"

The question was addressed to Kirke. The two women had, in a short time, apparently established trust.

Jake felt sidelined, but he'd been humbled more than once in the past few days.

Kirke nodded. "A man named Mac. He was going to make sure no one was lurking about."

Dallas nodded. She turned to the man next to her. "This is my brother, Dayton. He's the only one in the family who knows about Del Cox."

Jake hesitated. Yet he had no choice now but to play this out until the end. He stepped inside and wasn't surprised to see Mac sitting on the sofa. He sighed when he saw Jake and Cole. "Too long with computers," he said. "He was waiting for me."

Dayton regarded Jake and Cole warily. "Put your weapons on the table."

Jake took the gun from the holster in the small of his back and did as he was told. Cole followed suit. He noticed that Kirke didn't volunteer the gun he knew she had in her purse. Instead, her fingers clutched the purse to her.

"Take the weapons into the kitchen," Dayton Gallagher said to his sister. Dallas followed his instructions, and Jake studied her brother. Dayton was a big man but with little fat. He obviously worked out. His blue eyes were icy and his manner wary.

Jake had underestimated Dallas. He'd thought it strange that she'd agreed so readily to allow strangers in her house, especially after hearing Kirke out. But apparently she'd put those twenty minutes to good use.

Dallas returned. "I'm making coffee," she said. "There's something stronger if you want it." Then she looked at Kirke again, and her eyes widened. "What happened to you?"

Jake briefly described the attack on Kirke in the park.

"Why her?" Dayton asked.

"I imagine because they thought she was easier, and they knew I would do anything to get her back," Jake said.

"You weren't followed?" Dayton asked.

"I don't think so. But my guess is that they already know where Dallas lives and were following her."

"I'm going to call Denny," Dayton said.

"No," Dallas said. "You know Denny. Everything's black and white to him. If he knows there's a fugitive in the house, he'll shoot first and ask questions later. Listen to the man's story."

Dayton obviously didn't want to want to agree, but he did. Dallas, like Kirke, was apparently a force of nature.

"Go ahead and start," Dallas said to Jake.

Jake started with the mission, then receiving the letter. Kirke took it from there.

"And you two?" he asked Mac and Cole.

"They served with me in Afghanistan," Jake said.

"And we knew damn well he wasn't guilty," Cole said heatedly. "You fight with a man, and you know what he's made of."

Dayton nodded at that and relaxed slightly.

"Why you?" Jake turned to Dallas and asked. "Why did Del Cox mention you?"

Dallas hesitated, cast a glance at Dayton, then started. "We were lovers for a short time. Love wasn't involved. Loneliness was. My husband had been 'missing' five years. I couldn't get any information, but I stuck around the Farm for years, hoping I would hear something. I managed the Enigma. It was one way I could stay close to men like him. Maybe I would find out something." She sighed. "I couldn't let go. Then one day, I was told he was dead. No details. Nothing. That night I got drunk, and a customer named David Lewis took me home. He came in the bar often, and he was a loner. I probably paid more attention to him than I should have, but he always seemed so alone and I knew he was CIA. All the signs were there. Anyway, we both had too much to drink and slept together.

"I swore it wouldn't happen again, but then he went on an assignment, and when he returned he was a wreck. He'd helped me. I thought . . . damn if I know what I thought. Simple fact I didn't think at all. I'd never believed in sleeping around. I had to really care about someone to sleep with them, and no one measured up to my husband. But I was so damn lonely then. I knew Dave was in love with me, and I should have cut it off.

"To make a long story short, I got pregnant. I didn't tell

him. I never wanted to marry into the CIA again. Never knowing where your husband is, or what kind of danger he's in, is my definition of hell." She paused. "And I didn't love him. I liked him, but . . ."

She stood. Walked around the room.

"Then I heard David had been killed. There were whispers about a mission gone bad. Jeb was born six months later. I had planned to stay where I was. I had friends there, and memories. Then one night David showed up in my bedroom at midnight. He looked like hell. Somehow he'd learned about the baby. He tried to give me a hundred thousand dollars.

"I didn't want the money. I didn't know where he'd gotten it, and something felt all wrong about it. I had enough with my widow's benefit and my job. I told him that people thought he was dead, and he replied that it was better that way, warned me not to say anything or I could be in danger. Some supersecret government job."

"And you believed him?"

"I didn't know what to believe. And I didn't know where or how he'd gotten the money. For all I knew, his story could be true or he could have turned mercenary."

"He left abruptly, as if he was afraid. He wouldn't take the money back. I didn't know what to do with it, so I put it in a separate account in Jeb's name and just left it there.

"Then he appeared again one night six months later. He was drunk and frightened, and this time he really scared me. Said someone was after him and might come after me."

"I packed up the next day and left. It was time anyway. The Enigma was slowly dying, and my job wouldn't be there long. My father was a sergeant in the Denton Police Department, and he'd been urging me to come home. I didn't tell him what had happened, but he knew I was afraid of something. He made sure there were no records that led to me. I married a year later."

"To a cop?"

She smiled slowly. "I can't seem to get dangerous men out of my system."

"And he doesn't know any of this?"

"No. I was afraid he couldn't let it go, that he would try to find Dave. But I did tell my brother, Dayton. We were always close, and I knew I could trust him. I thought someone should know in case . . ."

The room was silent.

"The CIA never asked you about Dave Lewis after he disappeared?" Jake asked.

"No. But then no one knew about us. We were together only a few times, and neither of us wanted anyone to know about it. His name wasn't on Jeb's birth certificate."

Dallas turned to Jake. "The Del Cox you knew. What did he look like?"

"The last time I saw him—just before he was struck by the car—he'd changed his appearance. Seven years before that, he had dark hair and a dark beard. Wiry. Intense brown eyes. Smart as hell with explosives. Should I tell you his favorite expression?"

"No," she said softly.

Jake thought back to the boy he'd glimpsed with her. Slim like Del—no, David Lewis. Curious dark eyes.

Dayton broke in then. "It's not fair to open this now. There's Jeb to think of, and Denny—"

Kirke broke in. "Jake was accused of a crime he didn't commit. He spent seven years in prison, and now he's violated parole because Del Cox sent him a note asking that he meet with him. Jake's life has been destroyed, not to mention that two of his friends were murdered. Del Cox died trying to tell Jake something—maybe trying to make amends."

Dayton stood, then nodded to Dallas, who stood.

"I'll be back," she said and left the room.

When she was gone, Dayton turned to them. "This is going to turn her life inside out."

"What does her husband know about Jeb?"

"That he's the son of a CIA guy killed in action. That's all."

"She's at risk until the truth comes out," Jake said. "Once it does, Adams no longer has a reason to silence anyone."

"You're convinced it's this Adams?"

"I saw him right after the hit-and-run. I think he was going to try to finish the job, but then Kirke arrived. He'd changed his face, but I recognized other things about him."

Dayton paced.

Then Dallas returned with a box in her hands.

She put it down on the table and unlocked it with a key she had with her.

"He gave me this that last night I saw him. He was distraught and scared, and something else. He asked me to keep it for him. If anything happened to him, he wanted me to give it to a Mitch Edwards. I didn't want it. But when I moved back to Texas, I couldn't throw it away. He seemed so desperate about it. But it's been at the bottom of a box full of memorabilia for years. When you called earlier, I took it out and opened it. There was only an envelope and a key. She handed it to him.

Jake took it and picked up the envelope. Opened it carefully. A paper that looked like a lease agreement fell out. It was in the name of Mitch Edwards for a unit in a storage facility in Richmond. No number was mentioned.

He handed it to Kirke.

The numbers now made sense. Most storage facilities had codes to get inside. Otherwise one had to present all kinds of proof to gain entrance to a particular bin, or compartment, or whatever they called it.

A sense of elation filled him. Cox wanted to give him the numbers a week ago. The lease must still be valid. There was something there, something that would finally reveal the truth.

The lights went out. The room went entirely black.

# CHAPTER 31

Glass shattered on opposite sides of the house. It could only be windows breaking.

"Drop to the floor," Jake said in a tense whisper. "Guns. Where are they?"

"Kitchen counter," Dallas said.

Kirke reached for her purse, which had been next to her. She unzipped it and took out the automatic. She felt for Jake's hand in the darkness, then handed it to him.

She heard Dayton rushing into the kitchen. Mac and Cole were moving as well.

She was staying where she was. Next to Jake.

"Get behind the sofa," he said, spoiling that strategy.

She crawled behind the sofa. She saw a tiny green light above her and realized the invaders probably had night vision goggles. They could see. Jake and the others couldn't. There was a soft pop. Then another. Silencers. What were they firing at? She made herself as small as possible behind the sofa.

Then she heard a shot, so loud and so close her ears hurt. A bullet whizzed by, causing her to duck even farther down. Another. A flash of light. A curse.

Then a large flash of light flooded the room. She raised her head slightly to see. Dayton had set a large battery-operated floodlight on a table, then quickly ducked. It was just enough time for her to see three armed figures wearing night vision goggles. They clearly cringed when the glare of the light blinded them. Shots. One after another. One of the intruders went down, then another. A bullet smashed into the floodlight. It may have been a gutsy move, but it was too late for the attacker. His position had been marked. Another shot rang out, and she heard a thump as a body hit the floor.

Then silence except for a soft moan.

It seemed over almost as quickly as it had begun.

A pinpoint flashlight flickered over the room, and she peeked out.

Jake spoke first. "Kirke?"

"I'm okay," she said as she sat up.

"Dallas?"

"Alive."

"Cole?"

"Yo."

"Mac?"

"Yo. I don't think they expected quite as many of us."

"Dayton?"

"A superficial wound," he said. "Nothing serious."

The light moved from one figure to another, and she recognized Dayton's bulky figure as he moved among the fallen attackers.

Two were still. A third was moaning.

To her surprise, the latter had a knife sticking in his left arm along with a bullet in his shoulder.

Cole went over and kicked away the man's gun. He pulled out the knife none too gently. He then tied the man's wrists with rope from the kitchen.

"Kirke?" Jake's voice sounded harsh as he reached for her.

"I'm untouched this time," she said, though the tremor in her voice probably said something else. Reaction was setting in. Fast. Now she knew how the men at the OK Corral felt. She would never watch another Wyatt Earp film again in the same way.

The pungent smell of gun smoke permeated the air. A vase lay broken with flowers falling from a table. The steady drip of the spilled water added to the eerie stillness in the room as everyone took stock of the mayhem.

"I'll see if I can't get the electricity back on," Dayton said.

Someone handed Dallas the flashlight, and she guided it over the bodies, making a path between them with the light. The one moving body was writhing with pain.

Kirke moved over to him.

"Stay away," Mac said sharply.

"This is what I do," she said, ignoring his demand.

"Let her do it," Jake intervened. "She's a paramedic."

She quickly examined the wounded man. Painful wounds but not critical. She moved on to the other two. Definitely dead. A fourth was in the hall with a large hole in his leg. She improvised a tourniquet as the lights came on.

Dayton reappeared. Ignoring his own injury, he stooped down and tied the man's hands. Then he flipped open his cell phone and punched in a number. "Denny, get home fast. We've had a home invasion. Dallas is okay, but we have a few dead bodies." Then he called 911 and asked for an ambulance and police.

He took Jake aside. "You two had better get the hell out of here. Take your friends with you."

Mac shook his head. "Cole and I will stay. We both have gun permits."

Jake hesitated and addressed Dayton. "Kirke can take care of your wound."

"Paramedics can do that."

"I don't want you to get in trouble on our behalf."

"They broke into my sister's house with silencers," he said. "I don't think there will be a problem."

"Thanks," Jake said, his voice rough.

"As far as I'm concerned, they came after my sister, and by God, those who live will pay for it."

Jake didn't argue. Kirke knew why. There would be sirens all over the bloody place in minutes. They had to get out before Jake was apprehended. No telling how long they might be held if they didn't leave now.

"Go," Dallas said. "Let us know what you find out."

"Give me your gun first," Dayton said. "We need the bullets and guns to match."

"Kirke's and mine are not registered."

"Don't worry about it. I have a permit. I'll just say they were gifts. Go."

Cole threw Jake his car keys. "Use it as long as you need. Your car might have been tagged at the park. I'll take yours and return it to the rental agency."

She saw a muscle move in Jake's throat. "If you ever need anything—"

"I'll know who to call," Cole finished for him. "Now get the hell out of here and clear your name so we can go on a nice, peaceful fishing trip."

Jake and Kirke ran for the door, then to Cole's car. Lights were going on up and down the street. Jake put his foot down on the gas pedal, and they sped away.

It wasn't until several moments later when they were on the interstate when she could breath normally again. "Adams wasn't there, was he?"

"No," Jake said.

"Is it ever going to end?" she asked wearily. She sank against the cushion. No more adrenaline. She didn't think she ever wanted to feel it again.

"It's going to end," Jake said firmly. "It's going to end tomorrow."

They stopped at a car rental agency near the airport, and Jake rented a car with one of his aliases. They left Cole's car for him to retrieve.

Jake took the wheel and turned onto the main road, then the interstate.

Once again, they had no belongings.

She was exhausted, yet she was wired. She was beginning to feel like Alice in a violent wonderland, a universe so alien to her everyday life that she halfway believed it was all a dream.

Yet all she had to do was look at the mirror, touch the

bandage on her arm, and feel the bruises whenever she moved to know that it was very real.

"Why did Dayton protect us?"

"Not us," he said. "His sister and nephew. I don't think he wants the story in every tabloid in the country. His nephew is the son of a renegade CIA agent. A secret child with an honorable cop as a stepfather. God knows what else. What a news frenzy that would be. No, I think he can convince those two cretins that they would be better off as home invaders than traitors.

She nodded, then closed her eyes and feigned sleep. There was a lot to think about, a lot to consider. But then she realized sleepily that her head was nodding. She hadn't thought she could ever sleep again, but . . .

They stopped at a moderately priced motel in Oklahoma. He paid cash, and no questions were asked.

He half carried her into a room that was clean if unimaginative, then double locked the door behind them.

She was as emotionally exhausted as anyone could be. He pulled down the bedspread and laid her on the sheets. She let him pull off clothes that were sprinkled with blood. It almost seemed as if she was watching from a distance instead of being in the moment.

Her short hair was matted. Her face smudged. Her lips were bare of lipstick. Her skin was blotted with bruises, and she still had that black eye.

He sat there and watched as she curled up in a fetal position and thought he'd never seen a more beautiful woman. He leaned over and touched her face. So soft. She looked damned vulnerable, but he knew now she wasn't. She was pure steel.

Yet there was a softness as well. He saw it when she looked at him. He couldn't imagine why she looked at him that way when he'd been responsible for so much pain, so much terror. His heart contracted at the sight of her, and a painful tenderness—something he hadn't felt before—swept through him. She'd given up so much to help him.

She made a little noise, and he went over to her. He stroked her back.

She woke and yawned, then saw him. She held out her hand. He could no more refuse her than stop breathing.

He slipped off his shirt and slacks but not his briefs and slid into bed with her. He had no condoms, and he knew how fragile the situation was. He might well be back in prison next week. He damn well was not going to chance getting her pregnant.

Even if by some miracle he exonerated himself, this couldn't last. The last few days had been a roller coaster of emotions. Of hopes. And hopes crushed. Of a realization that he needed people and a wonder that they had readily risked so much to help him. For someone who had tried hard to avoid emotional entanglements, it was painful.

He had too many scars for an optimist like Kirke.

Kirke—a unique name for an equally unique person—stretched out beside him, her body fitting into his, absorbing his warmth. He remembered how cold she was earlier, and he put his arms around her and pulled her against him.

She uttered a purr of something like contentment, then her body relaxed, and he heard soft breathing. Nature was taking over. To his surprise, his own eyes started to close.

He let them.

✦

She woke to his warmth. His body heat flowed through her, and she didn't try to move. They were in the spoon position, and she knew the slightest move would wake him.

Instead she memorized the feelings, the emotions . . . everything she felt at this moment. He'd mentioned catching a plane in Oklahoma for Richmond. If they were successful, this might be all over this afternoon. He would be cleared and the government apologetic, if it ever was. He would be reinstated and return to adventures throughout the globe.

And the two of them? He'd never implied there would be anything beyond tomorrow. He'd never mentioned love.

If the impossible happened, and he did declare undying love, what was it that Dallas had said? That hell was being married to someone when you didn't know where he was, or whether he lived or not. Kirke felt a new appreciation for all the wives of servicemen.

But that was pie in the sky. Wishful thinking. And she'd given up that long ago. Instead she would take what magic they had together and cherish every moment.

She would go back to her life of giving temporary aid to victims of mayhem and violence and stupidity. And just plain life. She shivered. She had been content. Now she wondered whether she could be content again without Jake Kelly.

He moved, apparently waking at that slight movement of her body.

His lips moved along the nape of her neck, arousing every nerve ending in her body. A sound came from deep within her.

"Beautiful, brave girl," he whispered. "I've put you through hell."

She turned and looked at him. His eyes met hers, and she marveled at the turmoil in them, at the expressiveness of eyes that were usually so expressionless. The hard lines in his face appeared deeper with tension, yet his hands were incredibly gentle as they roamed across her skin, caressing and arousing at the same time.

"Lovely Kirke," he said. His words were like a drug to her, a heady aphrodisiac. She had never been called that before, nor had her name sounded so soft. Her body came alive, her nerves tingling with anticipation, a need growing inside her as he touched her breasts.

Just as she thought she would explode with delicious heat, his lips replaced his fingers against her skin. They nuzzled softly before reaching the taut nipple of one breast and resting there. His tongue ignited a string of fires that ran through her body like lightning.

Her hand entwined itself in his hair, and her lips touched his forehead with tender kisses. Her other hand touched his cheek, feeling the slight roughness of new beard, relishing the intimacy of tracing the tiny lines that stretched out from his eyes.

She felt his briefs and tugged them down.

"I don't have a condom," he said.

"I need you," she replied simply.

Suddenly, there was warmth and power reaching into her, plunging deeper and deeper as if seeking the very core of her. She felt spasms, one after another, until she felt she would explode. Then he pulled out and fell on top of her, and his seed spilled over her. They clung to each other, savoring those physical feelings as well as the emotional ones that danced wildly between them.

She didn't know how long they stayed that way. So many words unspoken. But she knew he wouldn't say anything to her until he was free of the charges that had trapped him. And even then . . .

He pulled away and went into the bathroom, returned with a warm cloth, and carefully washed her. Then he went to the window.

How many times had he done that? How many times had he tried to tame the restlessness and energy that was so much a part of him? How could any woman hold him, much less Kirke Palmer?

The sun flooded through the window, and she looked at the clock.

Seven thirty. Just twelve hours since someone had tried to kidnap her. Less since the shoot-out in Texas. She sat up and looked at her clothes with dismay.

He picked up the phone and called several airlines.

When he finished, he turned back to her. "Our flight leaves at noon. We get into Richmond at seven p.m. I think you should call your reporter friend. You said she can be trusted, and so can her husband. I want to surrender to him at the storage facility."

"What if there's nothing there?"

"Then it's over," he said flatly. "I'm not going to endanger you further. If we don't find what I hope we will, maybe your writer friend can write a story about the past few days. Once the story is in the open, Adams won't dare go after you. It will only confirm the fact that he's alive.

She knew from his tone he couldn't be dissuaded.
She made the call.

               ➤

Ames knew he'd lost this battle. Maybe not the war. Four men hadn't returned. One or two might well talk. There were enough people involved now that his existence would eventually be confirmed. He would be on the run.

He needed to get back to Argentina, take what he could, and disappear again.

First things first, though. He was going to finish the job that should have been finished seven years ago. There was also a chance that Jake Kelly and the woman knew where Del Cox had kept the diamonds he'd stolen from Ames. Not only would he close the loose end named Jake Kelly, he'd recoup any diamonds that might remain and any proof that might help condemn him.

He picked up the phone and dialed. He had one ace left in his hand. His contact in the CIA.

               ➤

Ben and Robin Taylor were waiting at the storage facility when Jake and Kirke arrived at ten p.m. Ben acknowledged introductions with a curt nod. It was apparent he was not happy, but Jake had sworn he would surrender immediately after opening the stall, no matter what they found.

Jake was gambling all or nothing. Being a fugitive on the run wasn't much more appealing than prison. He certainly wasn't going to draw Kirke into that kind of life.

Taylor obviously didn't like the rules, but he wasn't a fool. It would be a coup to bring in someone like Jake Kelly, and it wasn't unusual for a fugitive to surrender to a particular agent. As for Jake, he needed a witness to opening the stall.

"Do you have a weapon?" Taylor asked.

Jake shook his head and stood silent as Ben frisked him.

Once the formalities were over, the two couples faced the locked gate of the facility. Jake punched in Cox's numbers to open the gate. Instantly, the green light flashed that the code was accepted, and the huge iron gate began to swing open. Once inside, it was easy to tell the unit number was the last three numbers of the code.

Jake drove to the stall, and Ben and Robin followed in their rental car. Jake looked at Kirke before getting out of the car. She gave him a tremulous smile, reached over and squeezed his hand, then handed him the key Dallas had given them.

They all gathered around the lock, and Jake took a deep breath. He slowly inserted the key and tried to turn the lock. The lock hesitated for only a second before the tumblers caught and popped open.

Jake reached for a hanging light switch and turned it on. Despite the big sign outside that claimed climate control, the room smelled musty and dank. There were two cardboard cartons on the floor. On top of them were two envelopes, one with his name and one with Dallas's name. He picked them up, hesitated.

Letter? Or boxes?

He opened the letter for him. He was very aware of the FBI man next to him. A letter some two pages long came out into his fingers along with several diamonds.

*Mitch, or is it Jake?* it read. *I haven't had the guts to write you directly, and so I hope this might reach you not long after my death.*

*Long story. Long journey. Lots of mistakes along the way. The biggest was Dallas. The second biggest was you.*

*I want you to know I never agreed to the killing of Ramos and Chet. I was walking behind you when suddenly I heard gunfire and saw the three of you go down. Adams told me to finish you off. I couldn't do it and fired a shot into the ground.*

*I had agreed to help him steal the diamonds. It seemed like a way to get Dallas away from Williamsburg. He never said he was going to kill anyone, but I should have known. Maybe I didn't want to.*

*We would have enough money, he said, to change our faces and live anywhere in the world. He knew I needed money. Dallas had told me she wouldn't marry another company* man and, hell, I didn't know anything but explosives. The kind that kill people. I thought if I had enough money, I could buy a ranch.

After he shot the others, I knew it was only a matter of hours before he killed me as well. He wanted no witnesses. He included me in the beginning because he knew I was a pilot. The only weak thing about Adams was a fear of flying he kept hidden from the Company. He could never bring himself to learn to fly. For a time, he needed me more than I needed him, but I realized that would last only until we got to our destination. I grabbed Chet's pack with the million dollars and another half million in diamonds and ran for my life.

I got to the plane before he did and took off. He's been looking for me ever since, and I knew he would kill me if he ever located me.

Now I have a bad heart. Probably not long to live. Cowardly to wait until now? Yeah. But there it is. There are tapes and journals in the box as well as five hundred thousand in diamonds and Chet's money belt. I hope it will clear your name.

Del Cox

Jake silently passed the letter and diamonds to Ben Taylor, who skimmed over it, then handed it to Kirke, who read it.

"Will that be enough?" Jake asked.

"With the stuff he says is in the box, I would think so," Taylor said. "In the meantime, though, I have to take you in."

Kirke put her hand on Jake's back. He was finally vindicated after all these years. She could only imagine what he must be feeling.

She started to turn and say something to Robin, but a sudden glint caught her eye, and she saw a figure outside.

*Adams!*

His hand held an automatic. He lifted it and pointed it directly at Jake. She couldn't think. She could only react, and she stepped in front of Jake as the pistol fired.

Robin and Ben accompanied Kirke when she visited Jake in the hospital. He was in the detention area, his wrist handcuffed to the hospital bed. Ben Taylor had assured her, though, that it was a temporary thing.

The agent had shot Adams almost at the same moment the rogue agent had fired. Adams—his real name, she and Jake had learned, was Ames Williamson—died on the way to the hospital. It solved any number of problems for both the government and Ben. No long trial for Williamson. No embarrassment for the government, unless Jake made the affair public. That put him in a great bargaining position.

Jake looked pale. He'd been shot in the chest when he'd pushed her out of the way and fell on her. She remembered the weight of him, the blood that flowed.

A lung was hit. She was able to pack the wound and help him breathe until they got to the hospital, then waited for hours during surgery.

He gave her a faint smile. "I hear I'm lucky that I had a paramedic with me."

She grinned at him. "Good thing to have around," she said.

His smile turned into a frown. "I thought . . . I might lose you when you did still another damn fool thing. You need a keeper, lady."

Her hand reached for his. "Any offers?"

He looked to Ben.

"I've talked to JAG," the FBI agent said. "They've already reopened your case. Williamson is dead. Now that we know who the hit-and-run victim is, we can compare his DNA with the contents of the storage area. It's only a matter of time before you're cleared."

"My thanks to both of you," Jake said to the Taylors.

"Thank Robin," Ben Taylor replied, glancing fondly at his wife. "She's like a bull terrier with a bone. She wouldn't let it go." He put an arm around his wife.

After they left, Kirke sat next to Jake and took his hand. Her fingers played with it, wanting to reassure herself they were, indeed, warm. He was alive. And soon he would have his life back.

His fingers caught hers, and he brought them to his lips.

"I always thought I didn't need anyone," he said. "My father taught me that. You take care of your own problems. You keep your troubles to yourself." He shifted in the bed. "Thank you for not letting me do that. I've been thinking of all the people who helped me along the way, sometimes because of you, sometimes because they thought it was the right thing to do."

"And sometimes because of you," she said.

He looked pleased at the observation.

"What are you going to do when you're cleared? Go back to the military?"

"No," he said flatly. "I should have a hell of a lot back pay due. I'm going to talk to Mac and Cole about going into business with them. Some kind of investigative agency."

"That sounds good," she said, a lump forming in her throat. So that was that. He hadn't meant anything when he'd teased her about needing a keeper.

"I think we'll need a manager," he said. "Someone who can think of university libraries and solve puzzles and sew up people if they ever get in trouble."

Her hand trembled in his.

"There will be another duty, if she's interested," he said.

"What?"

"Taking on a cynical old warrior."

Her heart started to beat hard.

"That a requirement?" she asked.

The light left his eyes. "No."

"I accept," she said. "But only with the last duty guaranteed."

"I can't kiss you," he said, his hand tightening around hers.

"I can," she replied. She leaned over. "I love you."

He closed his eyes for a moment, then opened them and smiled. Really, really smiled.

"Ditto," said the man of few words. But when her lips touched his, his expression could have filled a dictionary.

# EPILOGUE

Kirke straightened Jake's collar.

He pushed back a curl, leaning down to kiss her neck as he did.

"Mrs. Kelly," he said, "you look beautiful."

"Beautiful," agreed Merlin from the corner.

"You look . . . delectable," she replied.

"Help!" squawked Merlin.

"The only one who is going to need help is a parrot," Jake said in mock threat.

Merlin cackled.

Kirke looked at his watch. She didn't like watches when she wasn't on duty, and she wouldn't be, after tonight. Watches shouldn't control one's life, she believed.

But now they really should go.

She gave him one more look.

He was wearing navy blue slacks, a light blue shirt, and a navy sports coat. No tie. She didn't argue about that. She liked the way his shirt opened at the neck.

She wore blue, as well. A simple dress with a flared skirt.

She and Robin had shopped together, and both fell in love with it immediately.

"Time to go," she said.

"I would rather do something else."

When his eyes looked at her like they were at this moment, she would, too. Their time would come, though. In just a few hours. Heat flooded her at the thought.

But this was their wedding reception, and guests were waiting.

The wedding had been held in a small chapel in Richmond. Their only attendants were Robin and Ben, but now they wanted to share their happiness and appreciation with everyone.

Sam had returned to Atlanta, and he'd arranged to use the nightclub where he once again was playing the saxophone. It was the night when the club was usually closed, so they had it all to themselves. His band had volunteered to provide music.

Cole and Mac had flown in, as well as Cole's father, who'd helped so much when Jake had been released. Dallas, her husband, and her brother had agreed to come as well. Jake was paying their expenses.

There were others: fellow paramedics, including Hal and young Ben Wright, who had fully recuperated; some old friends from the newspaper. The invitation list kept growing.

Kirke couldn't take her eyes off Jake. His hair was longer now, and he looked tan and fit, and he was, indeed, utterly delectable. He smiled more now. Not as much as she would like but certainly a vast improvement. He was more open as well. It had even been his idea to have the party. She'd been stunned. And delighted. In the past months he'd learned that everyone needed someone. Many someones. Friends were to be valued.

Tonight was to be a celebration of many things: Jake's exoneration, the subsequent wedding in Virginia, the coming together of friends who'd made it possible.

The investigation that had followed Cox's confession and the death of Ames Williamson had lasted four months. Jake had been in custody two of those months, and Kirke had taken a leave of absence to be at his side.

Williamson's cell phone had led authorities to the CIA official who had been assisting him for eight years, first in helping set up the mission, then in protecting him. He'd been the one who'd helped intercept phone calls between Robin and her husband. Williamson was easily able to get inside the storage facility; the security system posed few problems for someone trained in burglary techniques.

The government had finally learned, too, that it had been Williamson who'd been leaking CIA secrets during the past six years, a leak now effectively plugged.

And, as Ben had indicated, Jake had been in a great bargaining position. In an agreement with the government, his rank had been restored, and he was given an honorable discharge. He'd also been given all his back pay as well as an additional settlement. No official apology, but then Jake had never expected one.

They were moving to Denver next week. Jake and Cole and Mac were pooling their resources and talents to start a personal protection agency. They would provide protection for businessmen and public figures throughout the world. A fitting business for men like these. But she'd decided not to join the business. There was a demand for paramedics, and she realized in the past weeks how much she'd missed it, how much satisfaction it gave her.

She looked around the duplex. She would be leaving it forever this weekend. She'd sold it to Sam. He would rent out her side and use the income to repay her. He'd already found a tenant: the singer with the throaty voice. She wondered whether Sam and the singer would soon join the two sides. Part of her would miss it. It had been her refuge for many years.

But now she had another one.

As if he knew what she was thinking, he put his arms around her. "We'll come back often."

A knock on the door. They parted, and she went to the door.

Robin stood there with a smug look on her face. "Cut it

out, you two. You have tonight and the rest of your lives. And believe me, it only gets better."

"I'm not sure how it could get better," Jake said with a leer.

"Ummmm," Robin said. "You two are dangerous."

Jake put an arm around Kirke's shoulder. "Come on, laggard, we have friends waiting."

She looked at him. For a loner, it was a miraculous statement.

He winked at her.

It was annoying how he read her mind. Beautifully annoying.

Merlin saw her pick up her purse. "Bye-bye Merlin?"

"Oh no," she said. "Merlin's going, too. Everyone wants to meet such a wonderful guard bird."

Jake chuckled. It was a very fine sound.

He took her hand and brought it to his mouth and nuzzled it. "If anyone had told me a year ago I would be taking a parrot to my wedding reception, I would say they were nuts. Or something worse."

"But you make such a good stepfather," she said, standing on her toes to kiss him. His dry humor was showing now, and she loved it. In fact, she was filled with such joy that she wanted to dance around the room. She would have to wait a few more moments for that.

"Stepfather to a parrot," he muttered.

And, she hoped, soon to be a father. But that had to wait, too. He still had scars that had to heal.

He lifted Merlin's cage with one hand and took her hand with the other. "Let's go celebrate our miracle," he said.

"Or two or three of them."

"You always have to get the last word."

"Oh yes," she agreed, her hand tightening around his.

Forever.

In 1988, **Patricia Potter** won the Maggie Award and a Reviewer's Choice Award from *Romantic Times* for her first novel. She has been named Storyteller of the Year by *Romantic Times* and has received the magazine's Career Achievement Award for Western Historical Romance along with numerous Reviewer's Choice nominations and awards.

She has won three Maggie awards, is a six-time RITA finalist, and has been on the *USA Today* bestseller list. Her books have been alternate choices for the Doubleday Book Club.

Prior to writing fiction, she was a newspaper reporter with the *Atlanta Journal* and president of a public relations firm in Atlanta. She has served as president of Georgia Romance Writers and River City Romance Writers, and is past president of Romance Writers of America.

**Don't miss the page-turning suspense, intriguing characters, and unstoppable action that keep readers coming back for more from these bestselling authors...**

Tom Clancy
Robin Cook
Patricia Cornwell
Clive Cussler
Dean Koontz
J.D. Robb
John Sandford

**Your favorite thrillers and suspense novels come from Berkley.**

penguin.com

# *Discover Romance*

**berkleyjoveauthors.com**
See what's coming
up next from your
favorite romance
authors and
explore all
the latest
Berkley,
Jove, and
Sensation
selections.

*Fall in love*

- See what's new
- Find author appearances
- Win fantastic prizes
- Get reading recommendations
- Chat with authors and other fans
- Read interviews with authors you love

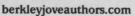

berkleyjoveauthors.com